W9-AEG-263

Rory
Great to
re-connect with
you! Hope you enjoy
my story.

Rich M...

YARDSTICK

A Life Measured

Copyright@2014 by Rick McGee

All rights reserved. No part of this book may be reproduced in any form or by any electronic or mechanical means, including information storage and retrieval systems, without permission in writing from the publisher, except by a reviewer who may quote brief passages in this review.

Eastside Gent Press
Austin, TX

This is a work of fiction. All names, characters, places, and incidents are the products of the author's imagination or are used factiously. Any resemblance to current or local events or to living persons is entirely coincidental.

Quotes: The price of greatness is responsibility, Winston Churchill, Quebec Conference, 1943; Attitude is a little thing that makes a big difference, Winston Churchill, *The Finest Hour*, 1940. Talent is God given. Be humble. Fame is man-given. Be grateful. Conceit is self-given. Be careful. John Wooden, Winning with Principle (Life Wisdom), 2013; Perfection is not attainable, but if we chase it we will achieve excellence, Vince Lombardi, "On football," *New York Times* (10 Dec 1967); The object of war is not to die for your country, but to make the other bastard die for his, General George S. Patton, *War as I Knew It*, 1975; We must learn to live together as brothers, or perish together as fools, Dr. Martin Luther King, Jr. "I Have a Dream Speech," 1964.

Cover Design by Douglas Brown

Library of Congress Cataloging in Publication Data
P S 3 5 6 3 M 4
ISBN: 978-0-9915630-0-5

Printed in The United States of America
at Lightning Source

*This book is dedicated to my wife Kim,
our daughters Kati and Sara,
the only team that matters.*

And to Bob Uecker, a good buddy.

YARDSTICK

A Life Measured

A novel by
Rick McGee

Eastside Gent Press

Foreword

I became a football coach for the usual reasons, at least that's what I wanted people to think. The love of a game where you could hit someone just for fun; the camaraderie of teammates who were more like brothers than your real siblings; the pure joy of taking the field in front of a capacity crowd. I wanted my buddies and my family to believe in my devotion that football was more than a job for me; it was a way of life and the only way for me to be truly happy. I wanted them to know football was a calling, akin to the priesthood. The football gods had chosen me from among the masses to join the fraternal order of coaching. My destiny was clear, my path straight, there was no choice in the matter. At parties and bars around town, I wanted them all to say to each other, "Of course Bob became a coach, and he will be one of the greats!"

It was all bullshit. I became a football coach because there was nothing else I could do. That's the real reason. Sure I loved the game and its trappings: the smell of a freshly mowed, natural grass field with painted white lines ready for an autumn Saturday. The stadium filled with the school colors adorned by rabid fans; a mix of idealistic youth and aged wisdom, sitting side by side. Nothing can beat that, not for me anyway. However, my motivation to become a coach was more banal; I needed a job: one that put food on the table. Hunger and fear drove me back to football; no other incentives were needed.

Being a coach was an excuse, an escape, some way to

explain to myself and my buddies that I could never stack up to them, never quite compare to their inevitable successes. Being a coach absolved me from the money I would not make, the house I could not afford, the vacations I could not take. After all, I was chasing my dream, which was noble. I could hold my head high and walk into any bar in town and receive respect. I imagined folks thinking, *there's coach, let's buy him a round. No matter he can't afford it, he did have a winning record last year.*

And then I got lucky. The game I loved, and needed, became a business, a very big business, awash in money so great that college coaches on lots of campuses became the highest paid employees on the payroll, by a very wide margin. The economics got out of whack but no one cared. College football money paid for things, a lot of things. It paid for larger staff, new stadiums, campus dorms, and merchandise. Colleges became brands, their names stitched, sewn, and painted anywhere the consumer wanted. Football weekends meant full hotels and restaurants. Winning records led to even more fans, which put more money in the till. Football sprayed its money to other sports, helping them overcome a lack of interest. Football was king of the hill, no other sport, event, or activity came close, not even graduation day…that holiest of days on college campuses.

The college money filtered down the food chain quickly. High schools built shrines to watch their sons play and their daughters kick and cheer on Friday nights. Weight rooms were expanded, practice facilities updated, and rivals argued about the size of scoreboards more than their manhood. Athletes gave up secondary sports as football monopolized their time year round. In football states there were only two seasons: Football Season and Pre-Football Training. Winning the state championship and college signing day were spectacles for towns large and small, one last chance to celebrate the gifted who would soon move up the golden ladder.

And much to my amazement, with all the money and attention it brought, the game got better. The money helped football and hurt everything else in equal proportions. Kids had safer environments to test their skills, better training from larger staff, better equipment donated by boosters, and coaches who had more money in the bank from ever increasing paychecks. But other sports suffered, some were cancelled, many learned to make do with less, and many went cup in hand to the only coach who really mattered. The smart coaches obliged, spreading the treasure trove without asking anything in return. Better to fund lights for the tennis courts than risk the ire of kids who brought those rackets to school.

The high school football coach set the tone for the team, and by extension the school, and more often than not, the town. The coaching role expanded way beyond the field of play; new skills were needed to handle the press, the community, the boosters, and the college recruiters. Football staff not only grew in size, specialized roles were created for weight training, nutrition, and of course QB coaches who focused on a single position. High School coaches aspired to be like college coaches who were increasingly becoming CEOs of small and midsized businesses.

I went into coaching to survive, thinking I would

scrape and claw each day, expecting to love my work and hate my life. As players became gladiators, the casual fans were drawn to the game and watched the battles alongside their avid husbands, brothers, fathers, and uncles. In hindsight I now realize it was the violence of football that was the primary draw. The female fans helped put TV ratings into overdrive, compelling advertisers to succumb to the numbers as they always do. Numbers mean eyeballs and eyeballs mean money when crazed fans are the target market.

Football became the rainmaker and it poured and poured, spilling enough drops so that even I had a chance to make a success of myself and to measure up to my buddies by spending my life around a game.

I often wondered if I would have stayed if the money didn't materialize. It's a shame I would even contemplate it because I am a good coach. I did not realize at the outset how much I cared about the players, helping them along their journey, in or out of the game. I had no idea I could motivate others, leading men into battle, helping them attain more than they could imagine. I even adapted well to general management and the pushing and pulling of all the hangers on. Being a football coach just came naturally for me, there's no clearer way to say it. Luckily, I was able to have it all, so to speak, getting paid unreasonable amounts of money to hang around a game I first played in grade school.

Being a football coach allowed me to learn about life, the pain of losing, the glory of winning, the nature of people when they are under pressure, and how they handle adversity on and off the field. I learned how to help engineer a meaningful outcome in someone's life by creating a path forward beyond the game. I learned more from my players than they ever took from me. It was humbling and exhausting; yet more rewarding than any other career I can imagine. And my imagination is first rate; mostly due to my buddies and the comparisons we've made with each other's lives over the past 25 years.

It really is a great game.

Table of Contents

Chapter 1

Championship Bowl Game (circa 2007)

"Time out! Ref, time out! Ok, gentlemen huddle up. This is exactly where we want to be. 10 yards to a championship."

Damn that was close. Two more seconds and the announcers in the booth would have my head. The alumni would go right for my balls, no fooling around by these yahoos. My wife and daughter would still be on my side, I think.

10 Yards. 30 Feet. Many say the ten-yard line is the hardest place on the field to score from. The defense only needs to cover 20 yards, including the end zone. No need to stretch out over a longer field of play.

I love the ten-yard line; it's well suited for our style, our speed. We practiced all week, scoring from this distance. We know the defensive gaps to exploit. We know their tendencies. The defensive ends are slow to the sidelines in the fourth quarter. We should be ready.

But is anyone really ready to call the final play of the

season? Am I ready?

Hoping I sound confident, I pull our small group together while trying to think of a play, "the" play. I've been calling plays for the past 20+ years, leading up to this moment.

"Ok, V what are you seeing out there on the field? What will work?"

Vince, or "V" as we call him, is our quarterback. He is the best athlete I have ever coached, or seen. He has all the tools. He can run, pass, and is a leader of men. The guys on the team and even on the coaching staff would follow him anywhere. I am fairly certain the cheer squad would follow him anywhere as well. If I am to believe just a portion of the locker room talk, more than half already have.

"I don't know Coach, what are you thinking?"

Crap, is V losing his grip? He always has a strong opinion on plays that will work. Why is he buckling now...at this moment? No way, this can't be happening. And then I see it. That grin! Working his way up to a full smile. With two seconds remaining in the biggest game of his life...our lives, V is toying with me. I'll get him later, "when" we win.

"Roll right, tight end curl under the wide out at the post. I'll hit the open guy or run it in. It's been open all game, Coach. The D is exhausted."

He's back. And with the exact right play, the same I was thinking. But, I can't agree with him, at least not right away. We have another 30 seconds remaining in the time-out.

"I don't think so V. You've lost a step this game. You can't outrun the opposing D. You're too slow and soft. You already have one interception, now you want to throw another? Or worse, fumble at the goal line?"

For a moment, a very quick moment, V loses that grin. Either he thinks I've lost it, or I pulled one on him.

"And by the way, you're falling hard, down to the fifth round in the draft, maybe lower. I don't know what you plan to do with that Fine Arts degree, but you just might need it sooner than you realize."

I keep my face tight, my look serious. I pretend to use the headphones, discussing plays with the coaches upstairs. I doubt V is buying into my shtick. He could very well be the top pick in the draft, especially if we pull out this nail biter. But, I gotta' keep things loose right now.

"Let's run it up the middle behind Zach. He's been burying the nose tackle all game long!"

I love Zach, can't help it. He's the son that every mother wanted. Zach is our center, the hardest worker on the team, not the most skilled, not pro caliber. This will be his last game, his last football play. Zach banged on my office door fours years ago, escaping the death claw of my assistant Alice, who was ½ step behind him.

++++

"Coach, sir, can I have one minute of your time, sir?"

Two sirs in one sentence, either this kid is ultra-polite or he had some good parenting as a teen, I'm thinking.

"Ok kid, I'll give you a minute. Alice it's ok, go ahead and put the call through and I'll be right there."

"Coach, sir, I mean Coach ... "

Zach hangs his head and pauses to collect himself. He's

3

nervous, yet he seems determined. He's in terrific shape I notice, and think he must have played ball; he's got some moves to get past Alice.

"Kid, what's your name?"

"It's Zach, sir."

"Ok, Zach, what's on your mind, son?"

"Coach, I want to play ball. For you and the U. I will work my butt off for you and the team, sir. If you give me a chance, one chance to make the team."

"Zach, we already had tryouts for walk-ons a week ago. Did you sign up for that?"

"No sir. I hung up my cleats after high school. I passed on a Division II scholarships to come to the U and get my degree. I promised my mom...but...but...I miss football coach. I miss the work, the discipline, the guys, and being on a team."

This kid had his priorities straight. I'm sizing him up as he talks. He wants to work, values being on a team, he's respectful. He looks in good shape.

Zach raised his head and looked at me dead on, not saying a word. The silence must have been killing him; it was starting to make me a little tense. There was something about this kid, I could not put my finger on it, but I liked him. It was against the rules, my rules, and besides, the odds were against this kid making the cut. My head yelled 'move on coach', my heart and gut ganged up, a 2-1 winning vote for Zach. I knew he would be ready to go at practice tomorrow morning. Little did I know then that he would keep showing up the next four years!

V is waiting, and his grin back! He knows we won't run up the middle. It did not take him long to see I was keeping everything loose, just like him. Well, honestly I'd love to be half as loose as V.

"Split left; roll right, 45Z Under, Red. We need 10 yards, not 9 ½, so if you choose to run, get it all the way there. You ready V?"

"You got it Coach."

V was born ready. He was meant to be on this stage, conducting the offense on the gaming winning drive, the ball his baton. The Cook County DA had a different view; he must have been an SEC grad. A few short years ago, he offered Vince a single room with three squares a day, no expiration.

I want to say something more. Like, I trust you V, we've been through a lot together. But there are no words that could convey my feelings about our journey, and I did not want to screw up the moment. Instead, I just looked at Vince. Our eyes connected, our heads nodded in unison, like we had done many times before. He knew I trusted him and words were not necessary. This was one of those times when less is more. Besides, my mouth was completely dry.

"Water! Get Vince and me some water."

Vince laughs and passes on the water. I gulp. The ref prods us along and we know it's time. We take one last moment, soaking it all in. The grin returns and then fades, replaced by stone. When V gets in the zone, his face becomes rigid, his eyes narrow, and nothing can break his concentration. Vince wore a lot of stone during his teen years on the streets, a defensive maneuver to protect him from the bad. He found his grin when he came to the U and lived amongst a family that cared.

V turns and trots back onto the field.

I feel Mac standing next to me and turn to face him. Mac is our defensive coordinator, an elder statesman of the game, and my longtime mentor. I shrug and start to say something, perhaps an apology for not asking his opinion of the game winning play. Before I can get a word out, Mac says,

"Coach, you and V have just called your last play together. Better work."

Damn, Mac. He never pulls any punches, always hits 'em right in the gut where it counts most.

What a sight. V makes his way to the huddle, with 100,000 fans in the stadium, and millions more watching on TV. An eerie silence meets V as he kneels down to call the play. Most of the guys watching wish they were V, or have pretended to be V in their dreams.

Including me.

♦♦♦♦

I used to be a QB. They called me "blur" for my speed, though the nickname was a better fit for my life, my career, and the initial years after college. I played the High School hero, winning state and getting the girl. A respectable college career followed, but that was it for me. No future in the pros. I was too small, too short, and even too slow for the fast NFL game. The "blur" was too slow, what a letdown.

After college, I had no direction, limited skills, and lost

confidence in myself. I could not find a job and had no idea what to do next. I was an above average athlete with no career in sports. There was no time remaining on the clock to hit the books, four years had flown by. Sure, I had a great time at school, and performed well on the field, if not the classroom. The team, the coaches, and the whole town respected me. All the bars gave me free drinks. That counts for something, though I had a hard time putting it on my resume.

I never had to work that hard outside of football, relying on athletic skills and good looks to get by. Well, maybe just better than average looks anyway. Lucky for me, there was Amy. Standing beside me since high school, and now sitting on the 50-yard line.

Amy has never been one for private boxes. As usual, she passed on invitations to sit with the "in crowd." Instead, she is sitting with the other moms, dads, and students who have made their way west to the championship game. She is also sitting with my buddies. I loved her for that. She has kept me grounded, sane, and happier than I deserve. She is the one who helped me survive the chasm after my playing days were over.

◆◆◆◆

TWEET! TWEET! The ref's whistle brings me back to the game.

Ok, Vince let's see what you got! V brings the team to the ball, scans the defensive scheme and readies to call the play.

"Time out Ref!"

The defense calls a time out and V trots back toward me. *What the heck am I going to say now?*

"Coach, we got this."

V doesn't wait for me, or Mac, lurking in the background. He instills confidence in both of us. Vince has his stone face on. I can tell he needs to stay focused, not play loose and cool like the last time out.

"All right V, but let's go to the left. They are expecting us to go right, so let's shake 'em up."

Vince does not say anything for a few seconds. He's visualizing the play in his mind, rewinding all the tapes we watched to prep for this game. For this play.

V stares at me. Once again our eyes connect. We nod simultaneously. As he turns to run back on the field, I see a small grin forming on that stone face. But I can't be sure. It relaxes and worries me at the same time.

Mac nods. That means he agrees going left. Although he ran the defense, Mac always had a strong opinion on my plays. Hell, he has a strong opinion on everything and I listen to his every word.

Ok, V let's do this again.

Just before the play, I look into the stands and see Amy.

My closest friends surround her. There's Mike Harding, prosecutor turned criminal defense attorney. Known as "Swish" to his friends, he never misses from the baseline. Mike gives me the best leads on recruits for the team. Down and out kids, in and out of trouble, in sore need of a father figure and loaded with talent. Scott Larsen, stockbroker and perhaps the richest man in the stadium. Known as "Sticks", Scott loves to bang on the drums; he also hires kids I send him, often helping them to great careers. Kevin Long, private equity executive, known as "Strings", his hidden talent is playing guitar, and writing songs. Kevin helps with the alumni, giving generously and keeping most of the yahoos away. And Harry, known as "Skirt", not because he chased girls, they chased him. Harry had a knack for showing up to the dance with one date and leaving with another, or two. Skirt is a recovering alcoholic, starting a new career as a mortgage broker. Putting Harry into rehab was an evening I will never forget.

I would do anything for these guys and they for me.

Our other friend is up in the box suites working the "in crowd". Seth Wright also known as "Slick" is a corporate exec with a big computer firm. There's a rumor about insider trading and his name is right in the middle of it. Sadly I am not surprised, Seth was always fond of shortcuts.

Vince shouts out a formation change at the scrimmage line. The defense is jumpy, moving all around, trying to throw off Vince. They should know by now, he can't be ruffled. Might as well save some energy.

Everything slows down. I smell the grass from the field, the sweat from the players. The noise from the crowd is deafening, but I can't hear a thing. The wide-out goes in motion, V shouts the cadence.

I look down the sidelines and see Tony kneeling to watch the play. Tony was a star defensive end who played for me in high school. There was none better than Tony. He glances over his shoulder and sees me looking his way. He gives a quick wink and smile, knowing I welcomed both.

"Blue, Oklahoma. Blue, Oklahoma."

Oh no, Vince is calling an audible at the line. Crap, the play we agreed to run was perfect. *Why is he calling an audible?* My mind is racing, a tennis match playing in my head: *Call a time-out, or trust Vince?*

Timeout or trust in V?

Is V wearing stone or shining a grin? If I could only see his face then I would know what to do.

Timeout or trust in V?

It took me a very long time to learn how to trust another, and I'm still not very good at it. It's an acquired skill that needs a lot of practice. I'm much better at the controlling part, doing things my way, deciding when to take a risk or fold my cards.

Timeout or trust in V?

It's funny where your mind wanders at times like this. Mine went back to college graduation, for just a split second.

Chapter 2

Job Offer

It was Amy's idea.

"Give Coach Mac a call. Maybe he needs an old QB to help with the team."

Amy had put a lot of emphasis on 'old', as she giggled.

Old at 22? I wondered. But I had to admit I was a washed up jock with zero chance of landing a job, well a real job. For the past four years, while on scholarship, I had been provided with everything. Becoming a man would have to wait, right now I just needed some money since there were no more free meals at the U. "I don't know Ames, going back to high school seems like a step backwards. Besides, what are the guys going to think?"

"Bob, you're a silly man sometimes. You and I both know a lot of people who are taking jobs just for the money. You just watch and see how miserable some of your buddies will be in the future. You have a wonderful opportunity to do something with your life...something that you love and are

11

really good at."

"What opportunity?"

"Here comes Daddy, get ready."

"I brushed my teeth this morning Ames, I'm ready."

Amy scowled at me.

I still did not know what opportunity she was talking about. How would she know if Coach Mac had an opening, an opportunity with my name on it?

Amy's father came over and gave his daughter a hug. As I watched their embrace a question haunted me: *What are college athletes supposed to do when the last bell rings at school?*

He came over, shook my hand, and looked at me a second or two longer than I thought necessary. I could not tell if it was out of sympathy, or desperation. Amy and he had always been very close. "So, Bob, what's next for you?"

Look him in the eyes, I told myself. *Dead square in the eyes, not the chin, head, or cheeks.* I knew the eyes were where the truth lay.

Before I could speak, Amy jumped in, "Daddy, Bob is going into coaching."

"Coaching, huh. Is there any money in that?"

Amy's dad always got right to the heart of things. Money. It was always about money. And it wasn't just Amy's dad. Money had become life's scorecard.

I wanted to say, *why do we measure our success by money? There has to be something more—right?* But instead I replied, "I don't know, sir. Can I take a rain check and get back on that?"

He grunted and turned back to face his daughter.

"Daddy, let's go celebrate," Amy implored.

She always called him Daddy in a singsong voice. Never Dad or Father. It made me sick, or jealous, or something I could not quite explain to myself. There was a bond between them stronger than steel. I understood they were a close family, but they were more than that. There was something deeper. I teased Amy about it, but in truth I envied her family and their closeness. I wanted to be part of it, but I had to earn it. Amy's daddy had made that fact very clear.

"Bob, you are welcome to join us," he said. It seemed like a genuine invite, but I wasn't sure. Daddy stared at me without blinking or moving. He was testing me again; he seldom eased back on the throttle.

"Thank you, sir, I have a thing with the coaches and players. Maybe I'll catch up with you at Graham's after."

Graham's was the best bar on campus and I was their best client. I got more free drinks there than anyone else. We parted and I was off to meet with the guys. *Is there money in coaching?* I wondered. *Hell, is there a job in coaching? Is there a future?* Amy had pegged my next step for me, yet there were so many unanswered questions. At least I thought there were.

Before I went to Graham's I stopped to call Coach Mac, my high school coach. He answered on the first ring, as if he were expecting my call. "Hey Blur, congrats. A college graduate."

I did not mind the nickname; I'd had it since my freshman year in high school. Coach Mac had given me the moniker, and he was gonna' keep using it, forever. "Thanks Coach. I was wondering if you might be free to meet this week?"

"Bob, I was hoping you would call."

What a coincidence. It seemed that Amy did know a thing or two. Coach only called me Bob when it was time to get serious. I wondered if he and Amy had cooked something up. *Had a decision about my future already been made for me? Is that a bad thing? Should I be angry?* My mind was racing. *Doesn't a real man make his own way in the world?*

"Bob, I need some help on the team. We've got some good kids coming up from Junior Varsity, and a QB who could break some of your records. But he needs a lot of help. His footwork is terrible and his attitude is worse. Reminds me of someone I used to coach a few years back."

There it is. Coach needs me. Someone actually needs me, I thought. This was a real job offer, but I wondered if Amy's dad would give me credit for landing it or hold is against me and make me try to keep earning his respect.

I turned my attention back to Coach. I thought about what I wanted to say to the man who had been more than a coach to me. He rescued me, shaped me, and helped me land a college *scholarship.* Had he been preparing me for this next step the past four years? I wondered. *Did it matter?* "You can count on me Coach." It was an automatic response seared deep in my bones. What Coach wants, Coach gets. No hesitation, ever. It was a sir; yes, sir relationship, much like the army. But that didn't stop me from asking, "Is there any money in coaching?" *Crap. Why am I channeling Amy's daddy?*

"Blur, let's talk when you get back. This is an entry-level coaching position. You will work with the quarterbacks, reporting to Corby, the offensive coordinator. It's a great place to start, let's see where it goes. It's hard work. I'd love to have you back on the team!"

I wasn't certain if calling me Blur was a good sign or a bad sign, but I was in no position to press my luck. So I responded, "Sure Coach; sounds like a plan. I'll look you up in a few days.... And Coach, thanks for the opportunity. It means a lot."

"Don't worry Blur, you'll earn it."

"There we go again with the earning it thing," I muttered to myself. "First Daddy and then Coach. How will I know when I have earned it?" I didn't try to answer that question but knew it would come back again and again.

Job Offer

Chapter 3

Last Night on Campus

I went for a long walk, or what I thought was long. Ten minutes later my feet shuffled into Graham's. "I swear there is a long wire connecting my feet and this bar," I often remarked. The owner attached me to the tap freshman year, hoping to draw other kids to his place of business. It proved to be a good plan. The bar, as usual, was full and the line wrapped around the corner. As my custom, I went to the door and waved to those standing in line. I was careful to avoid gloating, although no one expected me to wait in line. I did not want to be the kind of QB who expected special treatment. A cut in line and a free beer or two was good enough.

The bouncers saw me walking up, shook my hand, and pushed me into the bar. They were under strict rules from the owner, "When you see the QB, grab him quick and get him inside. Do not let him move on down the street to another bar, bringing the team and their hangers on with him."

As I entered, I nodded to one of the co-owners in the corner. He was counting cash from the cover he had collected from the kids. Pete was a beast of a man; he kept the prices low and the fights outdoors. The two-buck charge was a reasonable demand whenever Pork and the Havana Ducks played on a Friday night. Few would argue with Pete, he could still get low and take you down with one of many moves he had learned on the mats.

"Blur! Hey man, the usual?" Willy, the bartender, called out. He was an institution on campus, known as Big Willy, but not for his size. Well not his total physique, just a small portion.

"Hey Willy, sure fire one up. The grad ceremony gave me a thirst; let's start putting it out. Might take more than a few tonight!"

"You got it Blur. Where are you heading now that school is over? Got any plans?"

"Yeah, I got plans Willy. Big plans!"

"Ok Blur, you can share later after the beers hit ya. But be warned, your buddies are in some kinda mood tonight."

I was not ready for my buddies, not yet anyway; besides, it was always fun hanging with Big Willy at the bar.

"What about you Willy? You got some plans?"

Willy leaned forward and sipped his water. He never drank while tending bar. "I just signed up for three more years, Law School is next for me."

"That's great Willy, well done! What kind of law do you see for yourself?"

"Family law to start, my dad has a practice that I can

learn from. Then I'll probably work for a large corporation or two, getting ready for my real gig."

"Your real gig?" My curiosity was peaked, "What's the real gig?"

"Hold the laughter until you walk away, don't laugh in my face or I'll cut off your free beers and you know how much that will hurt!"

"Willy, it's my last night on campus, I can handle the pain. But, I'd prefer a few more rounds on the house. So, what's the secret gig you got planned?"

Willy looked around, making sure no ears were prying. "After working for 20-25 years, I want to come back to the U and be the AD. I can't imagine a more fun role than Athletic Director back where we went to school." Willy was dead serious. He had his life all planned out and it was a great plan. I had to give him props, not grief.

"Willy, I love it! I can just see you coming into Graham's in 25 years, taking my bar seat and sipping on a cold one, hanging with the kids, rapping about the players and coaches under your thumb."

Willy winked at me and smiled. Then he was off to the other side of the bar to pour a couple of beers for two young ladies. I laughed to myself, thinking Willy already had a great gig going.

I saw my buddies at a round table, not far from the band. I wanted to stay at the bar a bit longer near the protective aura of Big Willy, not wanting to start our last night together, at least not yet. I figured if I could delay it just a bit, it might last longer. *Maybe I'm not ready to face any more ques-*

tions about my future. My career. How much money I'll earn! I
decided.

I hated being jealous of my buddies. It seemed that
each of them had a plan. I was amazed at how large their starting salaries were and wondered if money would change them. I
wondered if I would measure up. I didn't even know my starting pay or if I was getting a salary or an hourly wage. *How stupid am I to accept a job from Coach without knowing that small
detail?* I chastised myself. Although I was a QB, I didn't feel
like much of a leader any more. I took a deep breath, *OK, Blur
quit crying in your beer and get on with the evening.*

It was our last night together at school, although we
had plans, none of us could know what the future held. After
three beers, my own plan felt rock solid and sounded better by
the sip, in my head. I hadn't told anyone yet and rehearsed "the
plan" for the onslaught of questions that I knew would come
when I did announce it.

Seth came over when the music stopped. Seth was like
a bad fart that clears the room and takes the good air with it. I
learned long ago to avoid Seth when possible, or take him in
small doses and never alone. He lived across the hall from me
sophomore year, in a cubbyhole of a space that never smelled
right. Somehow he got a girl in there one Friday night and she
stayed for a few hours. We thought about throwing her a gas
mask for protection, but no one wanted to put his own life at
risk since the door had been closed for a while. About 2:00 a.m.
Seth and the girl made their exit, sneaking out the fire escape,
hoping to avoid nosy neighbors. The boys hammered Seth up-
on his return from walking the girl home, pushing him for de-

tails of the night's events. Seth just smiled and summed up his entire character with a single quip, "Boys I walked her home half way 'cause that's as far as she went with me tonight."

The boys laughed until they figured out what Seth had done, he stranded the girl in the middle of campus, all alone on a cold, dark night. He did not kiss her nor even say good night. He reached the halfway point then spun on his heel and ran his sorry ass back to the fraternity while the girl fought dark shadows the rest of her way.

While the band took a break and headed outdoors for some fresh air, Harry came over with a drink in each hand, preventing Slick from stealing the spotlight.

Great move Skirt! I thought.

"A toast. My good buddies, I drink to your health, your wealth, and your future! "And Blur, I drink to your lady. That's one fine piece of..."

"Watch it Skirt, down boy." I cut Harry off before he embarrassed himself. We all took a careful sip, knowing once Harry got going; it would not stop for several rounds.

Then Harry surprised us. He turned serious, leaned forward in his chair, urging each of us to do the same. "Gents, I want to issue a challenge to each of us. Rather than this being our last night together, I challenge each of us to meet every five years. We will rotate ownership, one of us will have hosting duty and select where we shall meet, anywhere in the world. We are all honor bound by friendship to attend, no excuses. We will use each other as benchmarks to assess our progress in life. We will drink to old times, celebrate our successes, and lament our failures. What say you gentlemen? Can I count on you to accept this challenge, and maintain our friendships over time?"

I could not explain what had just happened. Harry had pivoted from college to the real world in a few short sentences. He was ready for the next chapter of his life.

I had no idea what to say. I hesitated and looked around the table, fearing I might be the only coward in the room. The silence without the music was deafening.

Not many college grads would formalize a revolving five-year rendezvous for a group of guys. Most of us thought we would remain friends, hang out on a regular basis, and drink a lot more beer now that we had paychecks. (Well, most of us had paychecks.) I think Harry was able to look into the future better than the rest of us, knowing our lives would no longer be easy to manage and not ours to control alone. We would be chained to our careers, and our future mates. He showed a lot of foresight that night, challenging us not only to reunite, but more importantly and interestingly, to share what was going on in our lives with our buddies. Guys don't share, they hang, they drink, and they go to sporting events.

Harry had a touch of brilliance with his idea, clearly going against the grain, challenging the norms that guys follow. But the silence dragged on and I wondered if Harry felt any embarrassment as no one took up his offer. I put the odds at less than 50% that anyone would respond, much less agree with Harry's plan. As the seconds moved by the odds went even lower. I was about to order a round of drinks to break the ice when Kevin stepped up and took the bait.

"Count me in Skirt. I'll take hosting duties for round one."

Strings had never lacked confidence. Although he would be starting with a big consulting firm in a week, I was sure he had not forgiven me for nearly causing both of us to fail out of school our last semester.

++++

After football season, I was nervous about the future and wanted to catch up on some class work, so I signed us up for an advanced financial class. It was complicated, and could have scarred us for life. The professor could sense fear and one morning he mentioned it was the last day to drop or add a class, suggesting ever so kindly we pull the trigger. He was taking out the trash, and I felt the garbage bag tightening around my neck. Kevin felt the same.

Dropping his class was the easy part, finding a new one proved much harder. We banged on doors all afternoon, begging professors to take us in. Around 4:00 p.m. we knocked on the last door of the day and a small professor with a beard down to his waist opened the door and we pleaded our case.

"You are most welcome to join Russian History 201, on one condition. We have an exam today that counts for one third of the final grade, and you must take it now."

The blank answer sheet stared back at me, daring a response of any kind. I looked to my left and saw Kevin scribbling away. *How the hell did he know anything about Russian History?* I wondered. The only things Kevin ever excelled at were guitar and girls. Often, one led to the other.

We got back our grades the next week and Kevin

scored an A-. He was rewarded for being bold and witty by answering each question with an analogy from American History, saying it reminded him of something that occurred in our country. Kevin was well on his way toward being a true consultant. So it was no surprise that Strings was the first to accept Harry's proposal.

✦✦✦✦

We had always been competitive with one another and each of us pounced on Kevin's acceptance of Harry's challenge with our own. At the time, it was easy to agree, though I was a bit concerned about the "to benchmark our progress in lives" part.

I looked over my shoulder and saw Amy and Daddy sitting at the bar chatting up Big Willy. I was conflicted: *Walk over or stay with the guys? Walk over or stay?*

Amy gave me a wink, which made my decision easy. As I approached the bar, the trap was sprung and I ended up sitting next to Daddy as Amy and Willy headed to the other end of the bar. I understood Amy's intentions, somewhat, but Willy was my guy. I felt abandoned, but I couldn't blame him for succumbing to Amy's spell, I had been happily in her trance for years.

"Hello Bob."

"Hi sir, welcome to Graham's."

"What will you have Bob? I'm buying."

"Sir, I haven't paid nor had anyone else pay my bar tab in four years, no need to start now." I signaled Willy to pour a couple cold ones and he obliged then moved along, still leaving me alone with Daddy.

"Bob, you said something about coaching this afternoon, tell me more about your plans."

I thought for a moment how to play this one out but could not determine an angle so just spoke from the heart. The irony is I had not debated the coaching decision with myself yet, it happened so quickly. As I spoke, I was hearing my feelings on the subject for the first time. Besides, Daddy's eyes were unusually relaxed and signaled he welcomed a dialogue.

"Coaching is a good starting point for me, I can use the skills and knowledge gained these past four years and apply myself in a teaching role. I can help some young kids gain a real appreciation for the game."

"I didn't play sports in school so I don't have the same appreciation you do, Bob. But I've been wondering something since I saw you this afternoon. Do you see football as a game or a career?"

Damn good question, I thought. *Leave it to Daddy to get to the heart of the matter, again. I guess when your daughter is involved, it's much easier to have extreme clarity.* "Well, I haven't thought of it that way. It's not an either or to me, I really hope it can be both. Honestly, I really don't know yet."

"Bob, I don't have a lot of great advice for you, especially about football. But I can tell you the same thing I told Amy. As you start working for a living, don't let the work define you. It's a good thing to apply yourself to your craft, especially one you enjoy. But also find something beyond your job, beyond your career that gives you satisfaction, something with real meaning, whatever that is."

I did not have a reply. His surprising statement required some time to digest. I took a few sips and tapped my foot to the tunes coming from the band. Daddy downed his beer and I could tell it was time for him to go. Amy must have seen the signs as she arrived just in time. "Hi Daddy, you ready?"

My gut was screaming at me; *don't let them go, not yet. Don't leave that last bit from Daddy hanging out in the open, about to float away in the air. Grab it and make it your own.*

"Sir, thank you for the talk. I have something in mind beyond the job, but I need to try it out, see if it works, before I know if it's real. I hope that makes enough sense, for now."

We shook hands, the two men in Amy's life, and for the first time I finally felt accepted, well just a little. Daddy wore a welcoming smile and held onto my hand a tad longer than necessary. I still had a long ways to go to earn it, but now I at least knew the rules of the game.

Amy and Daddy headed for the front door. She never kissed me in front of Daddy; she thought it made him uncomfortable. I think this time she sensed we finally connected on a deeper level than we had before. She spun away from Daddy's arm, looked into my eyes, and planted a perfect, sweet kiss on my lips. I was more surprised than Daddy, he just laughed and moved toward the exit with his daughter.

Willy had a cold one standing ready. He shrugged his shoulders, both of us knowing this was Amy's play, we were just actors doing our bit parts. Daddy had the lead role for this scene and played it well. He imparted wisdom to me that night, in Graham's of all places. Now the ball was firmly in my grasp, I just had to figure out what to do with it.

Chapter 4

High School Football Practice

"Come on ladies! Get a move on! Up. Down. Up. Down. You pussies, what have you been doing all summer? Gotta quit drinking beer and get in shape! Up. Down. Up. Down. It's a long season ladies! Get your asses moving or I will hang 'em up to dry! Up. Down. Up. Down."

Coach Mac never minced words; it would have been hard with such a limited vocabulary. He was well known for clearly communicating to the team what he felt. And we all loved him for it. He molded more men out of field turf and mud than anyone I know. He molded me.

"Up. Down. Up. Down. Up. Down. You big babies! Does it hurt? There's no such thing as pain ladies! There's only you and me and your teammates! And I got all night!

Coach was a throw back. He broke kids down, sometimes more than they could take. Yet, he found a way to build them back up. He certainly believed in the no pain part.

Up. Down. Up. Down.

Tweet! Tweet! Tweet! "Ok, gather round men, take a knee."

That was the signal that practice was nearly over. When he referred to the ladies as men, it meant it was nearly time to hit the showers. I could see the relief in the kids' faces. *Man, they look young,* I thought. *Was I this young four years ago?* Our first practice went well. Actually it was just ok, especially for me. I was lost. Totally lost. Which surprised me greatly. I was back on the high school football field. My field! This is where I won games, awards, and conference championships. I earned my nickname here, on this field. Everyone gets a nickname; it's a rite of passage. Some stick for life.

I was lost because my role had changed. No longer could I rely on my quick release, or speed around the corner. My athletic skills were only useful as teaching tools now. I had to transition from player to assistant coach, or rather, assistant to the assistant coach. It was humbling.

Yet, I was ready. Something felt right about returning to the place I was meant to be. Tossing footballs with the QBs and Ends was a skill I excelled at. It was the teaching part I had to learn, and fast.

As Coach talked to the players, raising their spirits after a long and tiresome first practice, I realized I had a front row seat to a true artist. He delivered his sermon with passion and spit, usually the two went hand in hand with coach.

"Men, we have a short few weeks before our first game against Lyons and we are nowhere near ready. I'm gonna drill your asses into this ground time and again until you spit up all the weeds in this field.

"You will be in the best shape of your lives when we are done with two a days! At the end of it, we will come together as a team. The players, coaches, ball boys, all of us! Men, you are all winners otherwise you would not be here sacrificing your bodies. You chose to work for your team and your school. You could be out at the pool lounging with the other sissies in town. Instead, you chose to be here with me, spitting up weeds!"

It was getting dark by the time Coach made it to the uplifting part. He would be wrapping it up soon so the kids could catch the buses home.

"Men, you made the right choice to be here. I feel it in my bones; we have a good team, maybe a great team. You have the skills; perhaps better skills than any team I have coached. But you gotta' put in the work. You gotta' sweat! You gotta' beat on each other to make the team better! Men, are you prepared to make the commitment necessary to win? Are you committed to each other? Are you committed to the team?

"Let me hear you; are you ready to make this season your absolute best?"

The kids roared back at Coach, staring with wide, bulging eyes. They could sense it was shower time; the water would soothe the bumps and bruises from day one. *Man they look young!*

"Ok men, off to the showers. Put some ice on tonight and come back tomorrow ready for tackling drills! Let's go!!!"

Like most high school coaches, Mac believed that ice was a miracle drug. "Put some ice on it you big baby and quit your whining," was a phrase I knew we would hear all season.

Mac trotted along with me, we always ran off the field, it was tradition. "Only pussies walked after practice," was another Mac-ism. "How'd it go today Blur?"

"It was solid Coach. Enjoyed your send-off to the team. Never heard that speech while standing upright before."

Coach Mac stopped running and signaled I should do the same.

"Bob, take a look around you. I want you to create a new image for yourself than the one you had here as a player. Back then you saw the whole field, and I'll say this one time and one time only. You saw the field better than any QB I ever had. You won more games with your head than your arm or legs, and that's why I wanted you back here at this school, on this field. The other players looked up to you not because you were the QB and star of the team. They knew you could figure things out, you had smarts and they trusted you. It's those traits that will help you be a good coach."

Coach let the silence work its magic, allowing his message to sink in just enough before he told me what he really wanted to say. He had a father's eyes that showed a mixture of care and concern.

"Now, as a coach, rather than seeing the field, I want you to look beyond it, beyond the field. Take it all in, the stands, the cheer squad, the moms and dads, the referees, the teachers, the coaches, the players, the entire stadium and school. Breathe it all in and paint a new image in your head about all the facets of the high school football experience and how it impacts the kids on the team.

"Then I want you to think, really think, how you as a coach will impact the lives of these kids after football is over. Most of these kids will play their last game on a high school field; a few lucky ones like you will get a taste of college ball. And then what are they supposed to do?

Coach eyed me closely and placed a hand on my shoulder. "I want you to answer one question, not to me, only to yourself: How will you help set these kids on the right path, whether it includes more playing time or not?"

I had no reply for Coach, and that was the right answer. I was to answer that question for myself, not now, not tomorrow, in time. So instead I nodded to coach as he turned and started running to the lockers.

He looked back over his shoulder, breaking my trance. "Get our QB ready Blur, we're gonna win district this year." Then he was off, sprinting ahead of me to the locker room.

Coach was a man's man, not one to dawdle on conversation. As I trotted off the field, I made a life decision that day. I wanted to be just like Coach, but with a twist: a coach with a little more passion, and a little less spit.

Chapter 5

Coach's Meeting

My first coaches' meeting was a real teaching moment, with me playing the naïve student. As a player, I had often wondered what the coaches did behind closed doors. *What do they talk about? How do they choose starters? Do they really know what the players do on Saturday nights?* I was now in position to find out the truth about coaches and the tricks and schemes they invented behind closed doors. I sat forward in my chair, awaiting the unveiling of the coaching secrets.

Coach Mac entered the room. It was an unwritten and unspoken rule that the assistant coaches were to be seated and ready to go when Coach walked into the room. I sat next to Corby, my boss and the offensive coordinator. Corby played ball in college and still had the look of a right guard who could lead a sweep around end. He was big and strong, with a smile that would not quit. He was the gentle giant type who cared deeply about the kids on the team, a necessary skill to survive on Mac's team.

Coach Mac hit his chair with a thud; the cushion cried a whimper, knowing a new season would soon begin. I pitied the chair, especially the cushion, it looked worn and then some. "Ok men, you know the drill. Let's go around the room, and hear from each coach how their units are shaping up. Defense first."

The coaches on defense took turns discussing the players under their command. The details they knew about the kids' lives was stunning. They knew about their grades, teacher reviews, parents' names, and girl friends' names. They knew a lot more than I thought possible. Each player's name was on a folder, many filled with papers a half inch thick, which the coaches referred to as they spoke. When we got to the offensive side of the ball, Coach Mac gave me a pass... one pass. It was expected that by next week I would be able to recite the same level of detail on the QBs under my command.

Next we went through the depth chart, one position at a time. The depth chart lists the starter, followed by second string, third string, etc. The coaches covered the strengths and weaknesses of each player and the critical improvement areas they would focus on during the upcoming week.

We discussed team leadership, determining the players most likely to influence their peers. We needed a few players who could persuade others how to behave on and off the field, willing to go against the popular grain as needed. We talked about locker room decorum, our sanctuary on game days. We discussed values and team goals for the season.

I began to realize the amount of work coaches put in

between practices and games, especially on team personnel. The job was so much more than reviewing tape and inventing new offensive plays and defensive schemes. Coach Mac was just as intense in the meeting room as he was on the field, though his tools changed from fear and intimidation to analysis and research.

I learned about outcomes from Coach those first few seasons. Results mattered, and team achievement mattered most. Football is filled with individual statistics: touchdowns, yardage, sacks, catches; the numbers are endless. The coaching staff tracked and analyzed all these numbers and more. But to Coach, there was really only one outcome that mattered at the end of a game. It was a team measurement, displayed for all to see on the scoreboard. A scoreboard result might be analogous to a stock quote. At the end of the day, the public has a visual image, one number to judge your performance. To me a scoreboard was more personal than a stock quote; it was large and bright and in your face the entire game, visible to the fans in the stadium and those watching on TV.

Coach drilled us on team-based performance. The kids could compete during each week for starting roles, but once decided, every player was held accountable to help improve the team. No excuses, zero tolerance, everyone in for the team or go home. It was that simple with Coach and he made it work.

There was one more outcome that mattered to Coach, one not seen by the public, not shown on the scoreboard. The outcome that mattered most was helping the "ladies" become men, with a path forward after high school. The paths varied widely, none more important than the other. What mattered to him was helping each player establish a plan. The assistant coaches were held accountable for reporting on the plans at the end of each season, quietly going around the meeting room, one "lady" at a time.

I learned the coaching secrets from one of the true greats that day. High School football was not merely a game to Coach. When the kids went home the coaches continued on and not only behind closed doors. Coach knew that kids were easily influenced at this life stage; their hardened exteriors could be torn down, their edges softened by an authority figure who cared as much about the souls in his hands as the win-loss record as season's end. I had no idea if Coach Mac was the norm for a football coach; his rough treatment of the kids on the field was balanced by a deep concern for each "lady" in the back room. His was the style I wanted to copy, the approach I wanted to take, and the model I wanted to aspire to.

That's when I knew Coach Mac had a plan for me all along.

Chapter 6
Ronnie

The five-year mark was coming up soon and I had not heard anything from Strings. I was secretly hoping they would forget, and keep their busy lives to themselves. I thought *what a terrible friend I turned out to be, avoiding my good buddies because I'm afraid to face them.* I was proud of the last four and a half years with Coach and the team. We won three district championships, went to state twice, winning last year. I was still living at home in my high school room, saving the few bucks I could. Dates with Amy did not have many dramatic conclusions, which only heightened my desire for her.

Living at home near Chicago had its benefits, mom cooked and cleaned and sewed and did everything else. She was an all star to me, and I was delighted to be on her team. Mom was a ferocious supporter of all things related to her son, using a wide variety of tricks through the years. It had been mom and me ever since the divorce when Dad picked the harlot over us two. Harlot, that's what mom called her anyway, I never did get a first name.

Mom played dual roles, mother and father, and I played the kid, a role, which I excelled at. We lived in the same house my folks purchased when they first got married situated between the big city and the rich suburbs. Our town and neighborhood had the burden of balancing the "street kids" to our east and the "spoiled kids" to our west. The high school drew talent from town and occasionally from the two fringes, making the teachers and coaches feel like anthropologists in an ongoing social experiment.

After I moved back home, it took me a good six months to figure out my mother's latest treachery, though I never said a word to her. You see, it was mom who contacted Coach Mac, or it could have been the other way around. They paired up and concocted a plan that included Amy as the third leg of the stool. My call to Coach Mac was a set-up, well played by this gang of three. I never stood a chance, against their conspiracy. After ten seconds of rage, I was overcome by gratefulness and pride that these three people cared so much to pull a fast one on yours truly. I will repay this debt … someday.

It turns out Coach did not actually have budget for my position, the assistant to the assistant coach. He made as much room for me as he could, and I settled in for a long ride at the high school level.

I was slowly learning how to teach the kids, and once in a while impact their lives. They looked up to me, especially when I threw the ball around. I still had a quick release, a tight spiral and could throw further than in college. Amazing what you can accomplish when your job includes daily workouts!

I also enjoyed helping the kids outside of football, which was surprising to me. I was good with people, listened more than spoke, and related better to the high school group than did the older coaches. I became the "safe coach" to talk with when a kid got into trouble and had nowhere else to turn. Some of their stories blew me away; I had no idea how hard some of the poorer kids had it. Many came from broken homes, had no father figure, and were pressured by gangs.

It was probably for the best that I slept alone most nights, since the phone would often ring without warning. Besides, Amy's daddy was monitoring my progress; making it clear I was still earning his approval. On the occasions when Amy and I were together, I learned to silence the damn phone, only to hear from one of the kids, Ronnie, one Monday morning how he could not reach me. "Coach, where were you Saturday night, man? I needed you and now I got trouble, big trouble."

"Slow it down Ronnie, tell me what happened."

"Coach, it's too late."

"Ronnie, let's go sit outside and talk this through. Tell me everything, one step at a time."

The bell rang for first period, but we ignored it and headed outside to a bench under the trees. It was a perfect spring day, but Ronnie was shivering as if it were the dead of winter.

"Ok Ronnie, I'm here for you now."

"Coach, the Kings got me. They grabbed me, covered my head with a bag, and threw me in a van. They beat on me for an hour and made me join up. Initiation is Friday night!"

The Kings were the Latin Kings, a long running gang that wrecked havoc wherever they went. Terror and coercion were their weapons of choice, control their ultimate goal. The

Kings were expanding their turf, heading westward in our direction, one street and one block at a time.

"What's the initiation Ronnie?"

"I gotta rob Hank's on Friday night."

Hank's was the liquor store a few miles east of school. Hank was a tough man, brutal to kids who stole from his store. He led with the bat and finished with a .22-gage shotgun. He was not a man to fool with, especially on a Friday night when all too often he was playing defense and itching for a fight.

Hank put two Kings in the hospital last month crying out self-defense as the EMTs sped away. Hank's VCR conveniently stopped taping as he put a beat down on the kids, their blood dripping from his Louisville Slugger.

"Damn Ronnie, you can't mess with Hank."

"Coach, I can't mess with the Kings."

Ronnie was our second string QB, a capable substitute who often finished games that were out of reach for our opponents. His football skills were ok, he did not make many mistakes, but he would not win us any games. Ronnie was a straight "A" student, his intellect was off the charts, way above my pay grade. It was all due to Ronnie's mom, Armanda, his only parent. She worked two jobs caring for Ronnie and his sisters, and still made it to every game. She sat in the first row, yelling for the team, especially at the end when Ronnie came off the bench.

I admired her and how she raised Ronnie, a strong arm when needed, more often a library book or two for him to read. She worked part-time at the public library branch, shelving books on evenings and weekends. She got me started on easy reads at first, over time she upped my game, challenging me to read some of the classics, current fiction, and even a non-fiction now and then. I resisted at first, believing my way of life was under attack from this onslaught of unwanted knowledge. With each book, my jock pride melted a little, and I learned about the world. History books and mysteries were my favorites, and she loaded me up. Armanda gave me a path to an unexplored world I never knew existed. I learned more from Armanda's books than I ever did at school. Now it was my turn to help her son.

"Ronnie, I have an idea, give me a little time to work it out. Can we get back together tomorrow afternoon?"

"Sure Coach. I'm scared and haven't told my mom yet. She will freak out! You know she will."

"I know Ronnie, I know. We gotta' tell her soon, she will be part of the plan. Now get off to class."

✦✦✦✦

Amy's place was my escape and I took full advantage of that fact that evening. She listened to Ronnie's story, reflected for a short moment, and then pounced. "Bob, the Kings don't re-cruit high school seniors, they start in sixth grade or earlier. Something is not right."

Bang, she nailed it as usual. With that insight, I could craft a play to help Ronnie run past the Kings.

After school the next day, I made my way to Hank's.

"Hi Coach, drinking on a Tuesday?" he asked when he saw me. "Is the team going to be that bad this coming year?"

I was a Hank regular, usually buying a twelve pack of beer on sale. My forte was the quantity of alcohol not the quality of spirits. Hank loved to talk football; he always had a pointer or two for the young coach. He reminded me of Big Willy and we had become good friends.

"Hi Hank. No beer tonight, I'm a man on a mission and need a sidekick. You got a few minutes for me to bend your ear?"

"Sure Coach; let's go in the back where it's quiet. You got my attention with this mission thing."

I laid out the situation with Hank and proposed a daring plan. I was getting good at calling plays on the field, now we had to call a real-life play to save Ronnie. Hank did not hesitate, accepting my proposal before I finished. I saw a book on the table and it surprised me that Hank would be reading historical fiction.

I looked at Hank, then back to the book. Before I could speak, Hank chimed in. "Armanda got me started on books. I pretended to read 'em at first, but she kept after me. This one here is about Ireland, the potato famine, the Irish Republican Army, the story of a family through generations. 'It's a gripping read,' as Armanda would say."

Hank went silent for a few seconds, both of us lost in our thoughts. Hank, the liquor store dude was reading a very large book about Irish history. If I had not seen it I never would have believed it. We nodded at each other, the silence capturing our agreement to help Ronnie and Armanda.

Armanda was next on my list. I held my breath at the front porch, rehearsing my speech as the door opened.

Armanda listened intently as I talked about Ronnie's predicament regarding the Kings and Hank's. She dissected the play I wanted to run and Hank's involvement, agreeing to the gamble with one twist. Armanda would ride shotgun with me in the car down the street from Hank's. I knew better than to challenge her, she would be in charge when it counted most.

Friday came quickly, especially for Ronnie. As Hank began closing up shop we set our play in motion. Our gambit required some acting from Hank and Ronnie, and we were betting on Amy's instincts that the Kings were not really adding a new recruit to their team. What they probably wanted was payback from Hank and his red soaked bat. The Kings wanted a win at Hanks, having gone 0 for 9 the last three years. Ronnie's initiation was to stop the streak before it got to double digits. Our plan was for him to succeed.

Armanda, Hank, and I split the cost of the $300 till. Armanda wanted to pay in full, but Hank and I stood up to her, maybe for the first time. She was that tough, but acceded to our wishes as the game clock wound down. Ronnie entered the store, an unloaded gun in hand. Hank took a big whack with the bat, slipped and hit his head. As Hank lay on the floor, Ronnie stuffed the $300 in his pants and ran through the doors.

We watched Ronnie run down the street and into the alley. The entire time I was praying he would not look our way, not wave or stop and say hello. *Please Ronnie, I know you got the loot and you want your mama to be proud, but don't stop now, just keep going.* Ronnie was not accustomed to carrying the ball so I only thought the worst.

43

Ronnie met his group in the alley, unsure if they would give him high five's or take him down to the ground. The Kings did not fool around, not when there was free money to be had. They took the money and let Ronnie go. No pain, no torture, and no threats. They just took the money, gave Ronnie a slap on the head, and told him to roll on out of their turf.

It would not surprise me if the Kings had figured out the ruse. We were betting that their roster was full with no room on the bench for Ronnie and only wanted to settle the score with Hank. Even so, we celebrated as if we scored the winning touchdown on the final play of the game with Ronnie our QB and Armanda the head coach.

Some might say we took a big gamble at Hank's that night, we bet the whole wad: rolled the dice, pick your favorite saying. In reality we took a risk, a measured risk. We made our assessment, built a plan, had a back up in case of failure, and then dove in, hoping and even expecting a good outcome.

Yep, that's it. *Measured risk.* It sounded a bit strange to say it out loud. *Measured risk.* Made me feel and sound like a corporate wonk of some kind, a consultant who gets paid to spit out gibberish.

Measured risk.

What crap. The truth is we got damn lucky.

Chapter 7

Travelling to Five-Year Meet-up

The phone rang on my government issued, grey metal desk. "Blur, how you doing?" the caller asked.

"Hey Sticks."

I have a client meet so I can't talk long. Strings asked me to call you. He's picked a place for our five-year meet-up this summer. It's in Kohler, Wisconsin. Get ready for Brats and Beer, or more likely some fine wines. Strings is quite the connoisseur these days!"

"Count me in Sticks. Hope we have some light beer to go along with those fine wines. I still have jock tastes." I wanted to say fine wine wasn't in my budget.

"Second weekend in July, get your golf game ready."

"See 'ya then Sticks."

"Holy crap!" I said when I hung up. I had hoped the five-year meet-up thing was forgotten long ago. My stomach tightened as I remembered Harry's speech, the part about sharing our successes and failures. I worried about the stories I would tell and how my buddies would measure my life. *Damn Harry, where the hell did you come up with this sharing thing? I wondered.*

++++

Sticks and I had been friends since high school. We worked summers together, drank beer, and chased girls. Most of the time we watched as the girls chased Harry.

After college, Sticks worked at a jewelry store, selling trinkets to old ladies in a ritzy part of town. The old ladies loved him, and bought more jewelry that first summer than the last two combined. Sticks was biding his time, looking for the next opportunity. The key thing he learned at the store was how to sell product to a generation or two older than him. That proved to be a fertile training ground as he moved on two years later as a trainee stockbroker.

Sticks held investment classes at libraries around town, inviting the old ladies and their husbands. He taught them how to invest, diversify their portfolios, and plan their retirements. He was smart, funny, and respectful of his audience. They responded by setting up new accounts, entrusting Sticks' with their hard earned savings. Most of them tested Sticks for a year or two, and then followed with the rest of their dough. Sticks had called a play, and ran it beautifully for years to come.

++++

In July, Sticks and I began the drive up to Kohler to the meet-up with the guys.

"Blur, how's the coaching gig working out?"

"Sticks, its great. I love being around football, learning from Coach, and working with the kids. It feels right to me, but Amy's Daddy keeps reminding me I have not earned it yet. The money is paltry, as you know."

"Yeah, I thought as much. We're hiring stockbrokers if you're interested. It's hard work and you need to be good with numbers."

"Thanks Sticks; I appreciate the offer. I want to keep with the coaching thing a bit longer and see how it plays out. My biggest fear is measuring up to all the guys this weekend, including you."

"Nah, don't worry about me, Blur. I'd be more concerned about Amy's Daddy if I were you."

Sticks was right. Measuring up to the guys was one thing; gaining trust from Amy's family was on a completely different level. But, the weekend was ahead of us and I had to find some way to measure up to my best friends.

We were to pick up Mike along the way, another buddy from high school; we played on the basketball team together. Swish had the smoothest stroke on the court, dialing 'em in from the corner. At times he was unstoppable. I chuckled to myself, *that's what his girlfriend always told me, unstoppable.*

✦✦✦✦

We played pick-up games next door to Swish during our teen years, a place we called Squire Ball, named after the owners.

There were no rules at Squire Ball. Black eyes, sprained ankles, and wounded pride were served up with slurs and insults on Friday and Saturday nights. It was our Garden of Eden! Swish honed his game on Squire's court, parlaying into a starting role on the high school team. He walked-on at college, making the squad through brute force and a strong will.

One evening after Squire ball, Mike was asked to pick-up his father; he'd been conducting "business deals" at the pub in town. It was a short ride, but a long walk especially after all day negotiations. We arrived around 6:00 p.m. as the sun set on the horizon. Mike's dad was a wheeler-dealer real estate exec, who commanded our respect and affection. We helped him out of the bar, into the blinding sunlight. Mike's Dad turned around immediately, saying to Mike," I never walk out of a bar while there is still sunlight! Bartender, pour us three beers!"

That was my first beer in a bar, but not my last. Mike's dad called a play, and I was ready to execute it!

After college, Mike went to Law School and then became a prosecutor in the DA's office. He threw the book at criminals, sharpening his legal arm like it was shooting baskets, and notching an impressive win-loss record. Mike learned about the criminal mind and saw an opportunity. He learned the soft spots in the legal system, and the gaps in the processes. Years later, Mike changed teams, defending criminals, exploiting those gaps and soft spots, yet staying well within legal bounds. He was well liked by both sides and often got leads from prosecutors on clients he defended. Mike set up his play over a decade before changing teams, then ran with the ball for many years to come. Mike was saving lives, one jailbreak at a time. Mike saved Vince from a long jail sentence, and delivered him to me.

++++

We rode north out of Chicago, into Wisconsin and were talked out after an hour, listening to tunes, lost in our own thoughts. I found myself thinking about the upcoming basketball season.

++++

To make ends meet with Coach and the hole in his budget, I was also the girls' Junior Varsity Basketball coach. At first, coaching the girl's team made me uneasy. I grew up holding doors, saying yes ma'am, and chasing pom-poms. Managing a team of girls, ladies, women, whatever the right term, was not a task I was prepared to handle. One evening after practice, I learned a hard lesson about locker room civility; I made the mistake of entering the girls' locker room. I simply forgot it was a team of females and charged in with something important to say to the team. Wet towels never hurt so much. It was a girl's team after all!

In my third season we had a good team, a very good team. The first team thrashed the second team each day in practice; we needed a tougher challenge to test our most skilled players. I toyed with the idea of playing against the high school boys, but quickly dismissed it. There would be too much grabbing, too many fouls and way too much pride on the line if the girls played them close. So I asked Mike to get a few guys together for a scrimmage, and downplayed the quality of the girls' team.

"Mike, the ladies would love learning from someone like you and the boys at the gym. Besides, when was the last time you ran up and down the full court?"

Mike was looking a little soft; the DA's office burned out the young ones fast. Anyone still standing at closing time was usually found at the nearest pub, dousing out the courtroom beatings with a couple of pints. Even though Mike showed some waistline bulge, I still feared his baseline shot and wondered how that was holding up.

"Bob, I can get a team together, what's our motivation?"

"If you guys play it straight up, and watch the fouls, I'll buy the beer."

"That will do the trick, see you tomorrow at five."

The girls were psyched up and out at the same time. Playing a group of older guys sounded like a good idea, but in reality it was a bit scary. Mike showed up with four friends who played pick-up games on weekends at the park where we met them. There was no way I could have arranged this scrimmage at the high school gym. I was already on the fringe of a firing offense. I tried to hide my smile or was it a smirk, knowing our girls would run them into the ground since the guys had no subs and our girls were in great shape.

The boys had good energy at the start but their shooting needed work, a lot of work. They scored a couple easy buckets on rebounds, towering over our girls by three or four inches. We moved the ball quickly up and down the court, daring Mike and team to keep up. The game was to 21 baskets, win by two, call your own foul, and no free throws. I volunteered to ref, but Mike wisely rejected the idea, never challenging my fairness but not trusting it either.

The longer we played the better our odds as Mike and the boys tired while the girls kept going. Our best chance was to force the boys to hoist shots from the outside and do our best to box them out. We trailed 12-6 as we broke for a short recess, the shorter the better in my mind. Mike was sweating up a storm, the prior evening pints had found their exit and his friends were not doing much better.

Cindy, our best player hit me with some tough questions during the break. "Coach, we're getting killed out there, what should we do different?"

"Cindy, you girls need to realize we are not playing in the school gym. There are no rules out here, no ref with a whistle."

"Ok Coach, got that, but what do we do about it?"

I gathered the girls in close; it was time for some street ball coaching. "This game is call your own foul, right? Have the boys called any fouls on themselves yet? No, they have not and they won't. It's an unwritten rule, don't call fouls unless there is blood."

"You want us to foul the guys coach?"

"Damn straight. Play them close, make them work for it, and take some risk out there, more than you would back at the gym. Play tougher defense and run the boys up and down the court, tire them out. That's our plan."

I put the girls back on the court after a quick five, and then glared at Mike, yelling time. The boys managed to get up off the floor, groaning and moaning their way to the court. We closed the gap with some hot shooting, a full court press, and some tight defense but still trailed 16-13 when Mike called time. The boys needed their rest and more fluids. After a short lapse, we tied the score at 19 and the game was on. We see-sawed back and forth and felt the momentum on our side at 25 all, a longer game as we had hoped. Another time-out by the boys and I let them know it was their last; the boys had called three and the girls none. After the timeout, Mike bumped me on his way to the court then looked back.

"Time to end this one Bob."

Mike had his game face on, just like back in high school on a Squire ball night. He was playing to win, girls be damned. It took two more trips down the floor, the boys dominated the boards and Mike nailed two from the corner, nothing but net on both. The boys had lain back most of the game, enjoying the scrimmage but had no intention of tossing one to the girls. When they needed the spark, Mike lit 'em up, just like old times.

I was expecting to console the losers, they had played hard and held their own and was surprised there was no remorse, no sad faces. They enjoyed the match, it had been a while since they played someone better, at least it took some real men to take the girls down and that was solace enough.

I bought the beers for Mike and the boys as promised. "You boys looked ok out there for some old fat men."

"Bob, we are happy to drink the beer you buy any time."

We left it at that. Mike and I both knew it could have easily been a blow out if the guys had played rough. They were gents and helped teach the girls a thing or two, though they would never admit how out of shape they had become. They were glad to be sitting on a bar stool back on comfortable ground.

I did not schedule any more scrimmages with Mike and the boys, figuring I was ahead of the game. No one ratted me out and the girls appreciated the challenge, if not the outcome. I did notice our team taking a lot more long shots from the baseline, hoping for the magical swoosh sound of the net blowing in the wind.

✦✦✦✦

Coach assigned me one additional role to close the budget gap. During the summer, I taught the kids how to drive a car. Some of the students began calling me Driver Bob rather than Driver Ed, and like many names in school, this one stuck. I could not imagine sharing this experience with the guys, we used to make fun of the Driver Ed instructors back in the day, and now I was one of them.

Each night I drove home hoping and praying the same small thought. Please God; I hope no one knows I am Driver Bob.

Chapter 8

Five-Year Meet-up

The weekend in Kohler started like most guy weekends. We drank a lot, ate a lot, and hit the white ball around the links. We laughed with each other and at each other; no mercy was shown when a short putt was missed. On the last day, Harry and Mike were riding in a cart on the back nine, chugging their beers, not paying attention, as is often the case. Harry took a bad angle down a steep embankment and the cart rolled over once, then twice, before coming to a halt upside down.

The rest of us held our breaths, not knowing if we should laugh, call 911, or run for cover. Mike made it out of the cart first, clutching his right shoulder. He grabbed an iron with his left hand and made his way over to Harry. That was our signal to roar with laughter and sprint to Harry's defense before Mike ripped into him.

Harry was unhurt, but both Mike's shoulder and my face were in great pain. I had not laughed that hard since college, and my cheek muscles paid the price. I called a timeout to gain some composure, as Scott and Kevin helped Harry roll the cart back onto its wheels.

We elected to skip a few holes and moved on to the 19th, taking our seats at the bar where we had quickly become regulars. Our bets for the match were hard to tally since we missed five holes, so we made Harry buy the beers. He obliged, keeping a safe distance from Mike who was still rubbing his right shoulder. I was betting a few free beers would do the trick and Mike would recover just fine. Thankfully, the right shoulder would not affect his baseline shot, but I dare not bring that up. After a couple cold ones were down, and war stories from school had been retold, we were ready for a shower and a nap to gear up for our last evening. I stopped counting beers after the cart crash, and was glad none of us were getting in a car. Kevin was smart to arrange hotel, golf, and dinner all within walking distance.

My fears for this weekend had been misplaced; I had one more meal to get through and then I could escape back to the football field and my clandestine identity as Driver Bob.

And then it began:

"Hey Harry, maybe you need some lessons from Driver Bob. He can show you how to use the brake!"

"What the hell Slick, you bless us with your presence at the 12th hour, shank balls out on the course all day, and hit your best shot in the bar. I should expect no less from you."

Crap. I thought. *You could always count on Seth to take a cheap shot for his personal pleasure.* Seth flew in late the night before from New York, carping about some bigwig corporate meeting in the "Big Apple."

Kevin could see me clenching my fists and stepped in to keep the peace. I was clearly overwrought, or just too intense for the revealing of Driver Bob, the best student education instructor in the Midwest. It was easy for me to misplace my frustrations on the shortcomings of my career against one of my buddies and Seth obliged as the first bag to punch.

"Gents, we can measure our dicks at dinner this evening. Which by the way begins at 8:00 p.m. with steaks, fine wines, followed by cognac and cigars! I will see you all there in a couple hours."

While I enjoyed the fine meal, I could not keep from wondering the cost. The wines were from California, heavy Cabernet; mostly I stuck with Bud Light, my go to drink after a long practice. I did not understand the whole wine thing at the time, five years removed from quarter beer nights at Graham's. The cheap suds at college provided the sustenance needed to get a degree. I would not learn much about wine until later in life, first observing then mimicking others who went into the deep end of the pool as I waded in the shallow waters.

We moved onto the porch and the outside air. I skipped the smokes. I never liked the taste, though my nostrils welcomed the aroma. *Just a couple hours longer and I can put this weekend in the rearview mirror,* I thought.

Harry stood and commanded our attention. "Gentleman, it's been a fine weekend, cheers to Strings for making the arrangements!"

We all saluted Kevin, fearing our turn would be next.

"Before we put this initial five-year meet-up to bed, we

have two items on the docket. Item #1, we need a host for our ten-year meet up. Can I see a hand to accept the honor?"

Scott took this one, a calculated move to avoid being first for Item #2 on the docket.

A cheer went up for Sticks with many saying, "Well done."

"For our second item, the benchmark discussions shall commence! The rules are straightforward. We will take turns, sharing one success and one failure over these past five years. Your buddies will help you celebrate the former and lament the latter. As a reminder, our purpose is to compare our progress with each other, as trusted friends, so we can keep learning from each other, much like we did back in school."

Everyone nodded.

"Gentlemen, may we have a volunteer?"

Harry was masterful in his orchestration of the festivities. It just came natural for him, and I was sure helped in his high tech sales job. *No wonder the girls chased him at school*, I mused.

Slick grabbed the pretend microphone and dove into his "kick-ass" bigwig meeting in New York, the reason for his lateness. He landed the big tuna (a large computer sale to a big account) and was expecting a stock bonus from his Fortune 500 firm. I noticed Seth never used words such as team or we, it was always me or I. At the end of his story there was great clarity on what mattered, individual achievement and reward. I got the big sale, I get the bucks; it was a direct correlation, an expectation. I could tell it had been etched into his brain.

Slick had already established his career pattern, every

story an autobiography, the spotlight highlighting his image, his lone voice bellowing to an adoring crowd. I wondered how long his followers would stick around, perhaps only as long as Seth's wallet remained full and open. Nonetheless, our buddies congratulated Slick, and I faked an air high five.

Not too surprisingly, his failure was some lame story about a married girl who went back to hubby after a weekend at Slick's. Sadly, this too was in character, a repeating chorus that would not end.

I was tempted to comment about Seth raiding another man's lair but the evening was still early. Kevin was sitting next to me moving back and forth in his chair his hands gliding along the tops of his thighs. He and Seth had been pals since grade school but Kevin was ready to pounce.

"Seth, let me get this straight, your big failure is a married woman spent the weekend at your place then went back home. Is that right?"

"Yeah, she was a great lay, a real shame her guilt got the better of her."

I could see a gleam in Kevin's eye. He had baited the trap and Seth was dangling in it, hanging by his feet, his head a foot off the ground. He just didn't realize it yet. "Seth, did you think there could be another reason?"

"What do you mean Kevin?"

"Well, maybe she concluded you were not worth it, maybe you're just a bad lay and she fast tracked herself out the door as soon as it opened."

Everyone smirked and tried to hold it back, but the laughter roared out from all in the room, except one. Seth always led with his chin and his buddies would do their best to give it a whack now and then. Seth wisely waived this one off and I wondered if he would have the guts to do the same in future meet-ups.

Harry took the mantle next, I was eager to see how well he transitioned from the Campus Adonis to corporate life. Harry had an Elvis persona; attracting females into his web did not take any effort, just a smile or nod of the head. He seldom woke alone on a weekend morn and he was not a big fan of reruns. His conquest list filled volumes, but I never heard Harry utter a bragging word. He was a true gentleman, well practiced at his craft.

Watching Harry on a Friday night at college was pure entertainment from my reserved bar seat at Graham's. Big Willy provided the suds and corn, while Harry starred in the live show. Willy and I often placed bets, wagering a sawbuck on the lucky gal who would take Harry home.

++++

I remembered one evening Harry attracted the attention of two sorority girls, one a blonde and the other a redhead. The girls called their play then separated, each walking around the bar toward Harry. The blonde headed clockwise and red took the counter route. Willy and I could see the pattern emerge, Harry trapped in dual sights. I put ten down on red and Willy backed the blonde. The girls arrived on target at precisely the same time. Harry never knew what hit him and probably did not care. I sat back in my seat to enjoy the show, and Willy let the tap flow.

Ten bucks back in college was not chump change, so the tension rose as the competition raged. Red or Blonde, which would Harry choose? Blondie resorted to a cheap trick, dropping her purse so she could bend down to retrieve it, but Red took advantage and snuck in to steal a kiss. These girls were good, Harry stood no chance, but that was the plan. He had no intention of working for it. Harry simply had to be himself.

The game clock wound down and winners would soon be separated from losers. Harry whispered something to Red, and then did the same to Blondie. Both girls eyed each other; Willy and I were ready for the claws to strike. Instead, they giggled in that shy girlish way. Harry put out both arms; Red took the left and Blondie the right. The three of them headed for the door, Harry would soon exit stage left, with two girls in tow. As Willy and I gawked, Harry pivoted and walked back to the bar, then reached out and grabbed our sawbucks. Willy and I did not budge; we were too in awe to make a move.

"Boys, you both lose your bets tonight." Harry winked at us and then he was gone with Blondie and Red. Willy and I did not speak for a minute or two, marveling at our friend.

"Willy, I got a thirst and need to douse some flames."

Willy opened the tap and poured two beers. Even Willy needed a drink and he offered the toast, "To Harry, may his good fortune spread to friends in need."

"To Harry, indeed."

✦✦✦✦

We went around the horn, sharing and benchmarking. I was emotionally torn as my buddies discussed some terrific successes, validating my pride in their accomplishments. As expected, each one measured his success in monetary terms. There were bonuses, promotions, raises, and more stock options or grants; I didn't know the proper terms for the awards. It saddened me to see their successes wrapped in greenbacks, as if that were the only measuring stick that mattered. I only half listened, as I planned my own speech in my head.

The guys had to dig deep for their failures, clearly not experiencing many problems over the past five years. Most were made-up vignettes similar to Seth's weak attempt.

My turn came last. For my success, I discussed the promotion to Offensive Coordinator, reporting directly to Coach and calling offensive plays. I capped it off with our victory at State and the offensive explosion to run away with the game. I forgot to mention my salary increase, going from an hourly wage to full salary. I figured most of these guys made my annual salary in a few short months.

Before passing the fake mic I downed my drink, then took a risk and shared the success of Ronnie's escape from the Kings; overcoming fears my buddies would laugh and poke fun. Helping Ronnie and Armanda did not place much weight on the money scale being used to measure our career progress. It was more important to me than that, and I needed to see how my friends would react to the kind of coach I hoped to become. I was damn scared they would hoot and holler, wondering why they kept me in their circle.

A few seconds of silence can seem like a lifetime when

you feel naked in front of guys more accustomed to ripping each other than sharing emotion.

Finally, Harry took the mantle. "Bob, that's one hell of a story, and I'm proud to have you as my friend."

Harry had not called me Bob in years. He walked over, gave me a bear hug, and the guys drank a toast in my honor.

I gulped hard and held back a few tears. No way would I let my emotions go that far, the guys would have no mercy. Gaining this approval from my buddies was a key milestone in my personal development. It shaped the arc of my coaching career for the years ahead.

My failure had been a constant thorn going further back than five years. I had yet to persuade Amy's Daddy that I had "earned it." But I had a plan, one I dared not share with my good buddies, not until I crossed the goal line. My plan had an element of risk and I needed Amy's help. However, the biggest risk she had ever taken was eating yogurt two days past the expiration date.

The sharing thing had not been as hard as expected. I saw smiles around the room, everyone having a good time. Then I saw his face and that shitty smirk he wore with disdain. And then Seth took his shot. "Why are you going backwards Bob? Back to high school, back to the football field, back to playing with teenage boys. Why are you so afraid to get out in the world and earn a real living? I don't get it."

Boom. Seth leveled me with a slam that rocked my core. Normally I would have brushed it off and would have given back more than I got, but not this time. I needed a moment, hell I needed a life preserver, maybe an ambulance. Seth scored a real hit because what he said had been wrapped in truth and it exposed my innermost fears. I was not earning it out there in the real world because I was hiding on the football field with a bunch of teenage boys. That comment scarred me. I felt as if my skin had been peeled away and my insides were hanging out in the open. I started getting warm, beads of sweat formed on my head, neck, and chest.

Harry moved in for the save, "Let's move it along boys, time to put a bow on this first meet-up and call it an evening."

I took one last deep breath and looked at Harry, thankful to have a friend who would take a bullet. The courage came to me at last. "No Harry. This is exactly what you intended by sharing our successes and failures, opening our lives to criticism from our buddies. Let's play this one out some more, the game is not over, not by a long stretch."

Everyone got real quiet; we had reached the climax for tonight's show. My mind raced, *Ok Seth, you son of a bitch. You will be my foil for these damn meet-ups. I will measure my life's path against yours and I'm gonna beat your ass.* I calmed myself a bit and replied, "Seth, your comments hit the mark, hit me right in the gut. My biggest fears are just what you said, that I am not earning it out in the real world like you and these other guys. And those first couple years were hard. I didn't make any money and still don't. And I was afraid of measuring up to you guys, and still am. But I am finding my way with these young kids, those 'teenage boys' as you call them. And I know how to make a difference in their lives and it's important to me."

Seth wanted to have a different discussion and kept his

foot on the gas: "Those that can do and those that can't teach."

"It's early Seth, we got a lot of years ahead and a lot more meet-ups. You'll be eating my dust before it's all done."

The challenge I issued to Seth was not planned, not smart, and not a good idea. My ego was bruised, pride was on the line, and I needed to act. It just came out of my mouth and I couldn't put it back in.

Seth was not phased, not one bit. The asshole welcomed the challenge, one he was confident of winning. He just grinned and drank more wine.

As I sat down, Harry started a chant and my good buddies joined in. "We want Driver Bob. We want Driver Bob." Harry knew how to end on a high note.

They were not going to let me off the hook easy. With my fists relaxed this time, I took the ribbing better, and launched into one, and only one, Driver Bob story.

"Ok boys, one Driver Bob story. I had two kids in the car, one in back and one behind the wheel. The girl in back started feeling sick a few minutes after we pulled away from the curb. She groaned and whimpered, then suddenly lost her cookies all over the back seat. The car reeked and we needed some air. The kid behind the wheel panicked and jammed the window buttons. It was getting muggy and reeked in that car. The driver could not take much more and pulled to a stop, opened his door, and dove out of the car. Unfortunately, he did not put the gear all the way into park, and the car moved forward when he took his foot off the brake. I grabbed the wheel, but we ran over the kid's leg. I could not get my foot on the brake and the car picked up speed. I started feeling sick to my stomach, and threw up on the front seat. The girl in back was screaming, the former driver was yelling about his leg, and I let go of the wheel. We veered into oncoming traffic and I looked up to see a cop car crash into our front bumper.

The guys were rolling on the floor, begging me to stop. I paused for a few seconds so they could collect themselves.

Harry got his breath and said, "Blur, come on man, this story can't be true."

I looked around the room, and smiled from ear to ear. "Nah, not true boys, just payback for all your sniping about Driver Bob!"

✦✦✦✦

It had been a memorable weekend, with fewer glitches than expected. Telling the Ronnie story and even the Driver Bob story was more important than I expected. It helped me learn about humility and the benefit of putting everything out there in the open. Poking fun at my failures allowed me to deal with them better than a knot inside my stomach.

As we made the drive home, I sensed my path in life, at least the way I measured it, was much different than my buddies. The challenged issued to Seth worried me some... actually it worried me a lot. It would come back to bite one of us hard.

I went to sleep dreaming about the upcoming season and tallied the benchmark results in my head:

Primary Yardstick: Money

Scott: Pass

Kevin: Pass

Mike: Pass

Harry: Pass

Seth: Pass

Me: Fail

Secondary Yardsticks:
Me: Saving kids

Scott: None

Kevin: None

Mike: None

Harry: None

Seth: None

Chapter 9

Greg

Zip. The spiral launched from my right shoulder toward its target 30 yards downfield. I had not seen many tight spirals in my playing days; the throws had improved as I coached. Over the past nine years I kept practicing my craft on the field. The physical response from a ball well thrown gave me enormous satisfaction and an ego boost I kept hidden from the kids, or so I thought. Staying fit helped me teach proper technique, and kept my waistline under control. I could not imagine a desk job with a phone stuck to my ear, my pant buttons popping from fancy client dinners.

Amy and I bought a small house not far from school a few years ago. Daddy saw he was losing control of the situation and finally gave me the thumbs up, saying I had been earning it all along. Three state championships and promotion to head coach must have shown him I had a good, if not great career ahead, though the money remained a challenge.

Fortunately, Amy was a super star real estate agent. Her hours were 24/7 and clients loved her, returning time and again, and sending more referrals than she could handle alone. Our combined earnings made us respectable, and we were happy. Amy managed our books and I measured success on and off the field, as I always had.

Hut. Hut. Seven strides back, look right, look downfield, throw left to the wide out on the sidelines. Zip. Another tight one, on the button. *Man, this feels good.*

Coach Mac moved on to college ball as a defensive co-ordinator. He was much more into hitting people while I looked at the field as a chess board with many moves to make. The players on the field were always moving, not waiting for a master to tell them where to go. For me this made football much more interesting than a board game with stationary men. While Mac spent his energy on tackling drills, I was more suited for offense and calling plays. And as head coach, I allowed myself the pleasure of working with the QBs.

Zip

"Ok Greg, you're up. Remember your steps, count them as you go back, looking, always looking downfield for the open man."

Thwack.

Greg threw a poor ball, a full yard behind his man, a lazy toss that would get intercepted in a real game. Greg was competing for the open QB spot for the upcoming season. We were replacing a State winner who went onto a full ride to Tech. Greg had talent, but his downfall was that he lacked a work ethic. He was one of those rich kids accustomed to handouts and compliments. He probably got trophies while growing up for losing, as had become the practice over the past few years. I would often ask Amy, "What happened to the winner take all mentality in this country!" Sadly, Greg represented the new normal; comfortable kids who spent more time watching TV, than outdoors climbing trees, playing ball.

My coaching style is very personal. You might say up close and personal, in your face, challenging your manhood. I never lost the fire and loved to stoke the flames, pushing these kids to improve their game. Helping them become men. Kids like Greg didn't have a chance with me unless they grew a spine.

Dud.

Greg tossed a floater on the ground, two yards short of his target. It was a weak ball with no zip, no spiral, and no heart behind it.

I was also a very cynical coach, using my wit and bad humor to deride the players, making them angry, anything to test their will. "Damn, Greg. You might disturb the gophers if you keep tossing balls into the ground. Hell, we can pretend its basketball out here on the field and teach our ends to catch bounce passes. We can track a new statistic for your game—bounce passes caught."

Greg had no reaction. He took a ball from center and turned to drop back for another pass. His feet got tangled, followed by a full-face plant into the mud. Greg sat on his butt waiting for someone to help him up.

"Jesus H Christ! What the hell are you doing? Where's your energy? Where's your focus?"

Our bench for starting QB was not very deep. It was

Greg, Jerrod, a junior, and two underclassmen.

"Greg, step aside. Jerrod, get in here. You know the drill, let's see what you got."

Greg tossed his helmet in frustration and swore at me under his breath.

I thought, *If he is the new norm, we need to expand the school district.* I yelled, "That's it Greg, hit the showers and see me after practice. You're all done here."

Jerrod stepped in behind the center and took seven good, strong steps back in the pocket.

Zip. Crash.

Jerrod had game, but no aim. His first ball sailed over the receiver's head into the Gatorade tanks, splashing a green river onto the table.

"That's ok Jerrod, we can work on your aim. Count your steps; look downfield for the open man. Let's go, do it again."

Zip. Crack.

He took out a row of helmets on the bench, another tight spiral with some speed on the ball. Good technique on his steps, and not a bad release, just a little high.

"Again Jerrod. Again."

After practice, Greg was in my office; wet hair dripping on the floor, shirttail out, and no sign of respect as I entered the room.

"Sit down Greg. What was that out on the field today? You disrespected your uniform, your teammates, and the coaches. Your attitude is lousy."

"Coach, you're always getting in my face. Making me

look bad. I just got angry is all and threw my helmet. No big deal."

"Greg, it is a big deal. You are a leader on this team. You set the example for others to follow, especially the younger kids. What's wrong with you?"

Greg just sat there, wasting his time and mine, looking out the window.

I did a ten count, not wanting to let an emotional moment cause poor judgment. After hitting ten, I waited another count for Greg to say something, anything. *Show me some emotion kid!* I thought. "You're off the team, Greg! Go get your stuff and clean out of here. Now!"

"Yeah-right Coach, good luck without me."

Greg's snarly response proved I was right to throw him off the team, at least temporarily. He needed more than a kick in the ass, but I just didn't know what at that point.

The next day after practice, Greg's father was in my office. He was a big man in town and owned a lot of real estate, including many of the retail stores.

"Hi Coach."

"Hello Mr. Adams. What can I do for you?"

"Please call me Bud. It's my son Greg; he says you kicked him off the team for no reason. I suspect there's a lot more to the story and wanted to hear it directly from you."

I took Bud through practice from the day before and reiterated that this was not the first episode. I explained that Greg's poor behavior had become commonplace and his attitude was affecting the team. I braced for Bud's reaction. Dealing with players' parents, I had learned from Coach, was an art form that required patience and backbone.

"Coach, I envy you. Sometimes I want to kick my son off our family. I don't know how to get through to him any longer."

I didn't expect that from Bud, but I was not surprised. Kids like Greg meander through life putting in the minimum effort. Their fancy toys and thick wallets eventually run out of juice. "That's pretty sad, Bud."

"Coach, Greg does not deserve it, but I'm asking if you will take him back on the team. He needs the discipline, needs to learn how to work. Hell, he needs to be roughed up a little, get his nose bloodied. Know what I mean?"

Bud was clearly a committed father; at least Greg had that going for him

"Bud, I have an idea. Let me work on it, and then you and I can talk again in a week. Tell Greg I want to see him before the first bell tomorrow."

The next day Greg and I took a long walk around campus. He made a weak attempt at an apology and I waived him off.

"Greg, I don't want to discuss football with you. It's just not that important. High School is a testing ground on how you will handle the ups and downs of life. How will you react when someone hits you in the nose? Are you able to defend yourself and hit back within the rules? Can you be a good teammate, placing team goals above personal ones? Can you learn how to work hard, every day, to accomplish a goal? "

"I know this all sounds like a cliché to someone like you, perhaps it is. You want my observation Greg? Your silver spoon is sticking way out of your mouth, and someone will steal it some day and you won't be able to get it back. Then you will be lost. Maybe you'll keep that spoon for the next ten years, until your boss fires you for being lazy, or your co-workers ostracize you for being a jerk. Or your customers stop buying from you because of your lousy attitude toward them. That's the path I see for you."

Greg hung his head and shuffled his feet, not daring to say a word.

"Greg, you know how to take. You don't know how to give. That means you will never know what it's like to love someone and have her love you back with all her heart. You don't know what it feels like to earn it. Greg, you are failing in life and it's just going to get harder."

Greg stopped shuffling; he looked at me, and his eyes started to water.

"Here's the deal Greg. I am willing to take a risk on you and give you another shot on the team. You will not be the QB; you will work your way back up the ladder one rung at a time. We need a third tight end who can make the cross block, handle the defensive end and the blitzing linebacker. A tight end who can catch the tough balls down the middle and not fumble when you get nailed by the safety. It's not a starting position, but can become one if you put in the work, keep your mouth shut, and show me you are willing to earn it. You can reroute your path in life Greg, starting now."

He looked at me with uncertainty.

"You see Greg, I have been where you are now, lost and unable to find my way. Someone took a risk on me, stuck by me, and helped me find my path in life. I was lucky to have a mentor who cared that much about me. It's your call. Be at practice today ready to work and if you show up and keep showing up and earning it every day, I will be right there beside you."

With that I turned and headed back to school unsure if I reached Greg, hoping I did for his sake, for his dad's sake, and for my own.

Chapter 10

District Championship

"**G**ather round men."

It was time for the big speech, time for me to light the emotional flame, get these kids ready to take the field for the district championship. We had a good season, a slow start, followed by seven straight wins. Jerrod had stepped up after throwing away the first two games, and the team gelled once we began counting Ws. Team morale is directly correlated with winning, and ours was peaking at the right time.

"A wise man once said: 'The price of greatness is responsibility.' Think about that, greatness from responsibility, one enables the other. Winston Churchill, the British Prime Minister during World War II bore a tremendous responsibility. He, more than most, had the burden of defending the free world. For him, greatness meant survival, and to achieve it, he instilled in a nation, and its allies, the will to fight. Their responsibility was to defend a way of life.

"Now, let's not confuse war with football. However, we can learn from Mr. Churchill. If each of us tonight handles our responsibilities, to block, tackle, kick, run, catch, or pass then we have a chance for greatness. Not greatness as individuals, greatness as a team. If each of us executes our assignments just as we have done the last seven games, we will beat our opponent."

The kids look dialed in, listening intently, and eager for the game to start. I knew to keep these speeches short; I did not want to risk boring the team before a big game. "We are playing a very good football team tonight. Oak Park is tough, they are big, and as we all know, undefeated. They expect to win tonight, and we respect them. But men, we are not going to spend an iota of our time worrying about Oak Park. It does not matter whom we are up against tonight. If you stay focused on your assignment, on your role, on your responsibility, and help your teammate when he is down, then together, we will win this game! It's not very complicated men. Do your job, handle your responsibility, support your teammate, and we are District Champs!

"Men, are you ready?"

The kids let out a roar. Damn, they sure seemed ready.

"Let's take the field!"

I gave myself a seven out of ten as we headed out of the locker room, wondering if Teddy Roosevelt and the Rough Riders would have provided a better lesson. History stories and sayings had become my crutch for inspiration. Armanda got me started down this path, and I accelerated as the years went by.

We trailed by six at halftime, making a long field goal as the clock wound down. Our defense held Oak Park to 16 points, with only two mistakes, each resulting in long TDs. Our offense needed to pick up the slack and get more points on the board.

The team had overcome an awkward start to the season as Greg's demotion startled many of the seniors. Jerrod needed space and time to win over the offensive line, since most of them were older. During our winning streak, Jerrod connected on a regular basis with his prime target, our new starting tight end. It took three games for Greg to win the starting role. After being picked on, spat on, and dumped on his rear end, he got tired of the bloody noses and started fighting back. His dad came to all the games and many of the practices, supporting his son's transition.

Late in the game, we closed the gap to three by holding Oak Park to a field goal, and scoring on a long punt return. We were running out of time and had one last drive with the game on the line. Jerrod scrambled all game from a fierce defensive rush, so we kept Greg back to buy some time. On the final play, Greg crushed a blitzing linebacker, both men hitting the ground hard, enabling Jerrod to hit the receiver for what turned out to be the winning score. For some reason, my eyes stayed focused on Greg, rather than watching the winning throw. I saw him look up from a prone position, blood dripping from his nose, and a smile forming on his face as the announcer yelled, "Touchdown!"

I looked over my shoulder at Bud, he too had watched Greg's winning block. We nodded and grinned at each other, both knowing we had witnessed Greg's ascension toward manhood.

We lost the next game, a high scoring romp, with Jerrod connecting for three touchdowns and running in another. Our defense was beat-up from the Oak Park game and it showed in the score, a 15-point loss.

The boys were dispirited after the game, casting blame around the locker room wherever it could stick. I quieted the team down and brought them into a large circle.

"Men, we put up a good fight, and we lost to a better team today. The Oak Park game took a lot out of us, we all know that. It's easy to cast aspersion on the person to your left or right, shielding yourself from blame. That would be a very natural human reaction after a tough loss. But, that's not who we are. We are better than that."

I let the silence hang for a few moments, wondering how to make an impact on these kids, my kids. I could not afford to let them unravel now, not after the comeback season we just completed. It did not matter that we lost the regionals, what mattered was setting these kids on the right path forward.

"There is an adage I have lived by, that might be useful for us today. 'It's easy to critique and hard to create.' That means you can take the low road and criticize your teammate, talk behind his back, and blame someone other than yourself for tonight's loss. That's not very hard to do. Or, you can take the high road and reflect on the full season we completed together as a team. The work we put into winning eight games in a row, including district, is an accomplishment we created together. The higher road is to take pride in the outcome we achieved as a team."

The players remained quiet, slowly removing their mud stained uniforms.

"Let me put this a simpler way. Teddy Roosevelt once said: 'If you could kick the person in the pants responsible for most of your trouble, you wouldn't sit for a month.'"

The players chuckled at that one. I hoped my speech was sticking; sometimes it's hard to tell with high school teens. We pulled closer together, said a prayer, and began the slow recovery process from losing the last game of the season.

That evening, Coach Mac called me at home. "Hey Blur, you had a great season, congrats on winning district, tough loss at regionals."

"Hi Coach, we gave it a good run, but did not have enough left in the tank after district. Jerrod sure showed he has a bright future at the college level."

"Blur, I'm calling to let you know about an opportunity. There is an opening for a QB coach at the U next season. I just finished telling the head coach a few lies about you, be expecting to hear from him in the next few days."

I hung up with Coach. I was too tired to contemplate my future and fell asleep on the couch. The next morning Amy seemed a bit antsy, pumping me full of coffee and pancakes. Finally, she dove in, "Bob, we will need a larger house when we move to the U."

As usual, Amy already knew more about me than I did about myself. She knew I wanted to take the QB job at the U. It was my dream job and it was now more important than ever that I be able to take care of my family. Amy was pregnant. She held this jewel of a surprise until the season ended.

Chapter 11

10-Year Meet-Up

I felt somewhat better about my career prospects during the lead-up to our ten-year reunion. Over the past decade, the money in college sports had risen dramatically, spilling beyond the head coach. Coordinators made a very good living, and assistant coaches did not starve for a meal.

As Amy and I prepared for the move and the loss of her income, we were more than hopeful about our trajectory, and looked forward to life back on a college campus. While Amy made our new house into a home, I hit the road to recruit a QB, and along the way saw my buddies for our ten-year meet-up.

Scott picked our hometown for the get together, starting with a ball game at Wrigley followed by dinner at Lawry's. It's hard to go wrong at Wrigley Field, unless you are betting on the home team to win a game. Wins mattered less than a steady stream of cold beer and an easy breeze rustling the ivy walls. Chicago is a professional sports town with no peer in my biased mind. The blue-collar work force mixes with corporate types, high fiving the guy in the next seat regardless of attire. During the Jordan run with the Bulls, even the criminals paused for a few hours. When games ended, the violence spiked and we watched on TV how Chicago earned its reputation as a murder capital.

The streets are mean, the streets are bad, and the streets are a place to avoid. That's what we all knew, stay away from the south side streets and be safe. I could not imagine living on those Chicago streets, defending my turf, looking over my shoulder, and playing defense all the time. Maybe that's why I focused on the offensive side of the ball. The rest of the city was forced to care more about defense; someone had to balance the scales.

Harry brought us back, banging his glass for attention. "Ok, gentlemen, entertainment hour will soon begin. First, let us thank our host for the weekend, Scott job well done! As expected, our Cubbies lost another close one, but all at Wrigley had a fine day. Now let us move on to our next matter. I kindly request a volunteer to host our 15-year meet-up. Gents, may I see a hand?"

I was not fast with the draw and Mike beat me to the punch.

"Thank you, Mike! We look forward to another meet-up in five years, with Mike as our host! Now gents, let us retire to the private room arranged by Scott for our benchmark discussion."

We had a small room near the bar with a U-shaped table, making it easy for everyone to face their accuser, I mean buddy.

As host, Scott picked the batting order and chose to be our leadoff man. I was up second this time around, rather than bringing up the rear, which had been the case at our five-year meet-up.

Scott talked about his rise at the brokerage firm and the new accounts he reeled in. He spoke with confidence and pride, his communication skills were always good, but now he sounded more polished. His was not a rag to riches story, he had more than rags to start, yet it was becoming clear riches would wash over him. Scott's pattern was sewn early in life, his parents were his teachers, showing him how to work hard and relate to people. It took me a while to figure it out, after many conversations with Scott it finally dawned on me that he asked a lot more questions than anyone else. As he spoke, the thing that struck me was how he talked about his clients. He had heart-warming stories about helping clients establish credible paths to retirement they never thought possible. He knew his clients well and understood their fears and goals. It woke me up that at least one of my buddies, while extremely successful financially, also measured success beyond his wallet.

Years later, I learned all my buddies invested their money with Scott, just as I eventually did. We all knew a smart decision when we saw one.

Next, I took the boys through the district championship, and Greg's heroic block to win the game. Helping Greg rebound and establish a positive path was another milestone for me and again I feared the reaction from my buddies. I was clearly sending signals to them that developing boys into men was my critical measurement for a successful career. I never talked about money, since there was so little to toss around. My buddies did not waver; they applauded my strong stance with Greg, easier now in hindsight than at the time.

After Greg's story, I felt the time was right to mention the QB job at the U, which had not been announced to the public. Stupid me, I got stuck buying a round of drinks as we sang the school song.

Seth spoke next, my back braced against the wall. He had moved to a brand-marketing role to "round out his skills" and the annual review with the division vice-president was on the calendar. Seth struggled with the presentation and lacked innovative ideas to grow his part of the business. He fretted over the review and feared he would not compare well to his competition, the other brand team. Somehow he found a copy of their pitch and knew just what to do.

On game day, Seth was brilliant. His charts screamed out novel strategies backed with facts and figures and detailed execution plans. The division vice-president praised Seth and suggested the other brand team should mirror Seth's approach. The competing brand followed Seth and did not fare as well. Their thoughts and ideas seemed like an old record that had already been played. The division vice-president was polite yet quiet, and even yawned a time or two much to Seth's delight.

"Boys, that's called a two for one at the office. I scored the winning run and beat the crap out of the competition at the same time." Seth stood there beaming with pride, like a poodle expecting his bone.

Scott reacted first, "Come on Seth, you want us to feel happy for you and the games you play? Give it a rest, why is it so important to deceive your colleagues anyway?"

"You just work with old ladies and retirees Scott, you don't understand corporate politics and the games we play. If I let the other guy get ahead or embarrass me, I'd lose everyone's respect at the office."

I could not let this one go and offered an idea, "Seth, have you thought about turning your supposed enemy into a friend, or a colleague? You could be the larger man and reach out, apologize if necessary, but don't let the bad blood simmer."

Seth responded quickly, "You guys are all such rookies. I would be seen as the weaker man in that equation. There are unwritten rules at the office, it's kill or be killed. We don't rely on referees with whistles and yellow flags to keep a clean game."

Harry shook his head and said, "Seth the bold action is to make amends. Why do you view the other brand as the competition anyway?"

Kevin jumped in to defend Seth, "That's just how a lot of large firms work these days. Seth has to differentiate himself from his peers, get some separation from the pack so he can move ahead."

Harry was not buying it. "Kevin, come on. Are you saying it's ok to steal someone else's work and make it your own? Isn't that what Seth did? And he got rewarded for it."

During the back and forth I noticed Mike was quiet, absent from the dialogue. Something was brewing and it wasn't the beer.

Before Kevin could respond Scott called a truce. It was

time to move on. "Next batter, Kevin you're up."

Kevin was moving up the corporate ladder quickly, knocking down six figures, leading large project teams, and collecting more promotions than I had trophies from Pop Warner. He was comfortable in a suit and the boardroom, more than acting the part of a future exec. He also played corporate politics like a game of checkers, jumping across the board, bypassing his peers, and winning the attention of people who mattered. It was easy to see Kevin deserved the accolades and earnings he attained, though many of his successes often left a trail of unfortunate victims who were elbowed off the board. Kevin did not dwell on this; it was more matter of fact, an expected result of the game he had to play.

Harry kidded Kevin, "Hey Strings, maybe it's time for a new nickname. I'm thinking Elbows may be apropos, with all the body checking you got going on at the office. Man, you are putting a real hurt on people who get in your way."

"You can call me Strings or Elbows, but know this; I play to win. The corporate office is full of blowhards, sand baggers, and lazy people. If a sharp elbow or two gets them out of my way so be it."

I thought Kevin and Seth were headed down the same path and said so. "Strings or Elbows, both seem to fit your style of play Kevin. You and Seth are on the same page; office politics dictate your behavior, and the type of people you want to be."

"The rules were written long ago, I'm just playing by them. Sure, I'll bend the rules, but not break them," Kevin said.

Seth could not hold back and one-upped Kevin, or so he thought. "Hell. I don't mind breaking a rule now and then;

penalties only apply to those who get caught."

We settled a bit further into our chairs, each buddy sipping on his drink, thinking hard about this last conversation. I wondered if Kevin and Seth were always this ruthless or had learned and adapted to office norms. I tried to apply their work environment to the football field, but it was a forced fit. Sure we had competition on the field and in the locker room, the "young ladies" taking swipes at each other to get ahead. The competition for starting roles was fierce, and it played out through the season. But we mostly left the bad blood on the practice field, coming together as a team on game days. Perhaps we benefited from the physicality of the game, beating on each other alleviated tensions. Our decisions on starters was transparent, the winners clearly defined by their performance during the week, and witnessed by the players and coaches. We had good clarity on which players to play, unclouded by backroom mischief.

Scott took over, "Ok, let's keep things moving. Mike, you ready?"

Mike shared a heartbreaking failure story that quieted the room. He had become one of the lead criminal prosecutors for the county and wanted to settle a case with the public defender, avoiding a trial, but the DA would not allow it. The District Attorney wanted to use this particular case to set an example for the county teens who were running rampant over town.

Tommy Piccolo got caught up with the wrong crowd. Once a star athlete, toughest kid on the team, he got hooked on drugs and stole money from neighbors' houses to settle his accounts and feed his habit. Tommy never emptied a wallet or purse, taking just enough for the next fix. After winning big at the track, he replaced some of the loot he took, risking a reputation hit on the streets. At his core, Tommy was a good Catholic kid, adhering to guilt, respecting his priest. He had a gentler side, but did not want anyone to know.

Tommy was on borrowed time when he walked into the courtroom for the third time in twelve short months. The public defender assigned to Tommy was a bit green and lacked the nerve to challenge the judge. He was more than content to go through the motions, doing just enough to appear in the game, never taking a real shot to save his client.

Mike knew the score, and also knew Tommy Piccolo, better known as "Pic" around town. Pic was no more trouble than other kids, just unlucky. Mike fought the DA harder than the public defender, but could not sway his boss to shift his sights away from Pic. Mike felt he had no choice but to throw the game, going out of his way to set-up the PD for the win. But Pic's poor luck was a strong force. The Judge owed the DA a favor, and Pic was the prize. In the end, the public defender fumbled his way to a pre-determined loss and Pic slept on a hard bed.

Mike intimated he was done with the District Attorney's office and I knew one of his future clients would be a lucky kid named Pic.

Political games were no longer foreign to us after ten years in the work force, but none of us had seen the game played out with prison time on the line. In my mind the DA was callous and lacked human decency, he only cared about the scorecard. Putting kids away was a win, helping them get out of the system was deemed a loss. It all seemed backward to me, although the DA's behavior was directly in line with his measurements. Putting more kids in the slammer and thus more wins on the board allowed the DA to keep his large, cozy office and build toward his real goal of someday being mayor. Funny how that model works in all professions, from the corporate office to the gridiron to the courtroom. The things we measure dictate our behaviors so we can attain more money or more power or both. I could tell Mike was fed up and done with the game.

What a sad story, I thought. "How many cases like Pic's is out there Mike? Is this the exception or the rule?" I asked.

"Election time is near so this kind of case spikes around now, then calms down until the next cycle. It's all too predictable." Mike shook his head and downed his beer, the signal for us to move on and not press him with more questions.

Harry wrapped up the evening with tales of scoring big in his high tech sales job, closing large deals usually with female clients. His wallet and waist had grown, and he raised a toast more than most. I could feel trouble brewing for Harry down the road and I was worried for him. But it was too early, much too early to intercede, or so I thought.

The benchmark discussions were becoming more meaningful than I predicted at the round table in Graham's bar ten years ago. The yardstick that counted most was still money, in its various forms. My new salary at the U put me on the map; I no longer bowed my head when we compared W2s. I still trailed the field by a number of lengths, but I was in the race. My slow start out of the blocks was no longer an embarrassment as I had closed some of the gap.

More interesting to me were the unspoken measures some of my buddies had developed to gauge life's progress. Harry was still counting notches on the bedpost; he never tired of the chase. The ledger in Scott's head tracked retirees that he saved from financial collapse. I could tell he would spend a lot of time seeking and helping this type of client. It was easy to foresee Mike tracking the jailhouse saves he would soon make as a criminal defense attorney. Losing the Tommy Piccolo case was a game changer for him.

◆◆◆◆

Here's how I scored the benchmark results at the end of our ten-year meet-up:

Primary Yardstick: Money

Scott: Pass

Kevin: Pass

Mike: Pass

Harry: Pass

Seth: Pass

Me: TBD

Secondary Yardsticks:

Me: Kids Saved

Scott: Retirees Saved

Mike: Jailhouse Sentences Saved

Kevin: None

Harry: None

Seth: None

I had entered the money race after ten long years, though my passion was helping "ladies" become men.

Chapter 12

College Recruiting

My first assignment as QB Coach was to hit the road and find a quarterback who would be our starter in two years. Someone we could rely on to lead the offense on the field and the full team in the locker room. *No pressure!* I thought.

My boss, the offensive coordinator, had given me a list of high school prospects throughout the Midwest. I scanned the 12 names and saw Jerrod's on top. Then the panic attack hit. *Did they really want me as QB coach, or were they only interested in Jerrod, and expecting me to deliver him.* The more I thought it over, the more I stewed, the madder I got.

I called the person who mattered most. "Amy, can you believe this, they just wanted me as QB coach to get to Jerrod. I should have known this job was too good to be true. Amy what are we going to do?"

I kept going for a while. Amy let me get it all out, she knew from lots of practice to let the storm pass before picking up the pieces. "Amy, are you there?"

I felt Amy take one last five count before responding. "Bob, what would you have thought of the coaching staff at the U if they did NOT have Jerrod's name on the list, and at the very top?"

My mouth was open, yet nothing came out. *Damn, Amy, you nailed it. Brain to mouth, repeat those words, this time out loud.* "Damn, Amy, you nailed it."

"Bob, you are a great coach and they are lucky to have you. Now, go get Jerrod on board. They won't give you points for Jerrod; they are definitely expecting you to reel him in." With that, she hung up the phone.

I was not a natural recruiter at first, no gimmick to elicit a laugh from packed living rooms. My reputation as a winning high school coach helped me get in the door. There was a lack of trust in the recruiting process, the volume of calls, stacks of mailers, and the infamous campus trips, all were booby traps and landmines to navigate. Parents were especially leery of front door knocks from grinning assistant coaches.

I had heard stories about tricks and gimmicks from famous coaches intent on closing the deal. One head coach purchased a Nerf Gun, suggesting the family oblige him with a shot to the head for every lie told. Another coach wore a T-shirt under his coat and tie, with the school logo, which read, "Come to State." He would rip open his dress shirt, revealing his plea at the end of his pitch. Another coach entertained recruits with card tricks and a smile. Everyone had a gimmick or some approach to set the parents at ease while enticing the player at the same time.

I had no such tricks up my sleeve as I rang the bell on Jerrod's front porch. There were plenty of open seats in the living room, only four of us in attendance, Jerrod, his parents, and me. Jerrod's father sold insurance after playing college ball, his mom was a high school English teacher.

There was no time for me to invent a trick, not that it mattered. To me a gimmick would not have been genuine; I was not well suited to playing the humor game. Jerrod's living room couch was virgin territory; I fumbled around for a while then recovered to score.

We reminisced about the district game last season, lamenting our failure in regionals. Jerrod was disappointed about my departure, yet looking forward to his last year of high school ball. Jerrod's father Rod was the quiet, strong type, interested but not engaged. His mother was clearly the heart and soul of the family, beauty and grace mixed with smarts and wit. No one was getting close to Jerrod until they got through or around Janelle.

"Coach, we know you well, of course. We respect how you worked with the boys on the team...always have."

"Thank you, Janelle."

"We are moving into new territory, and want to be thorough to ensure Jerrod goes to a good school that values his education as much or more than his football skills."

"Certainly, I understand your concern, and fully agree with it."

"Coach tell us why is the U a better choice for Jerrod than Michigan, Notre Dame, or Wisconsin?"

I was not surprised that Janelle quickly got right to

what mattered most. She was clearly focused on Jerrod's education.

"Janelle, Rod, I am sure you are hearing wonderful pitches from all those schools. I could tell you just as many good stories about the U. Here's the thing, your son is very fortunate that some terrific universities are recruiting him. All of the schools you mentioned are top notch, on and off the field. Honestly, I don't believe you can make a mistake; any of the schools on your list would be a good decision for Jerrod."

Janelle, Rod, and Jerrod took in my assessment, looking somewhat surprised at my honesty. However, I knew more tough questions were headed my way.

Then Rod spoke up, "All the other schools had better records than the U last year coach. Why will Jerrod be in a better situation at the U?"

"Here's the thing. At the U, Jerrod will have one big advantage over the other schools. He will have me there as his QB coach. As you said earlier, you know me well, and you know how I work with the players on the field, in the locker room, and after the game is played.

"Coach, how do we know you will still be there a year from now? You left us in the lurk at the high school. Jerrod's senior year will be with a different coach than he had the first three years."

"Honestly Janelle, I don't know for sure, but I can tell you my plan is to be at the U for a while. The U feels like home to me, I hope to stay there."

I never knew a living room could be so quiet. My last answer did not wow anyone. The seconds passed and my collar tightened. My next statement needed to be something that truly impressed. "And, I have a bit of news to share. My wife Amy and I are expecting our first child, just in time for the season." *When in doubt, use the family as leverage to win an emotional point,* I mused.

Janelle cracked a small smile and everyone gave me warm congratulations. I felt the tide turning in my favor, just a bit.

As we talked, my brief case spilled over, revealing my current reads. Janelle picked up the heavier book, seemingly surprised a football coach would lug around pounds of literature.

"Coach, what are you reading?"

"I just finished that book about Ireland, a generational struggle against the potato famine and British rule. It's a gripping read (as Hank and Armanda told me) about one family and their will to survive suppression."

"Did you read a lot of books in college, Coach?"

I hesitated for a moment, trying to think of the right way to respond. "No Ma'am. Honestly, I spent my time on the field and in the bar at school. I was ill prepared for life after football." *Way to go Blur really wowed them with that. I guess the truth hurts sometimes.*

"Jerrod was always telling me about your half-time speeches, the historical facts and quotes you use to inspire the team. What prompted you to cite history?"

"I've been lucky to have two great teachers in my life. Coach Mac showed me how to coach ball and challenge boys to become men. Armanda Rodriguez started me on books ten years ago; she's partly to blame for my dry speeches and historical quotations."

Jerrod opened the novel and flipped through the pages. I could tell he was on familiar turf, as mom watched on with a smile.

"Jerrod, I just finished that one. Why don't you hang onto it, maybe take it for a spin if it looks interesting. You can return it when you come down to the U for a visit."

Jerrod smiled. "Down to the U for a visit, huh?"

Janelle made up her mind. "That's right son, we will go for a visit and see why Coach feels the U is like home. And you will have time to read some of that book on the way."

I developed a few rules over the years to guide my book giving/lending approach:

Rule #1: Each book should be tailored to the prospect.

Rule #2: There should be a lesson or moral in each story.

Rule #3: I had to read any book I gave away.

Rule #4: Always hard cover, never paperback.

Rule #5: Always give the book to the prospect in front of the parents.

They began calling me Coach Book on the recruiting circuit, but I didn't mind. For me it was a significant improvement over Driver Bob.

Chapter 13

Tony

Since I was back in town, I stopped by Tony's to see how he was getting by. Tony was our All-State defensive end, highly regarded and heavily recruited by college scouts. Tony missed Regionals; Oak Park would be the last game of his career. His knee was crushed on a blind-sided chop block. The flag was thrown, we got our fifteen yards, and Tony got a new life. He had a meal ticket punched with a Pac 10 School on the West Coast, the sand and surf would have been his beat, instead of the Chicago streets.

Tony had earned his way out, combining skill and smarts to terrorize opposing linemen who struggled to defend their QB. Tony was unpredictable on the field, running through, around, under, and sometimes over the offensive tackles who dared to block his path. Double teams did not deter him; he took pride beating a pair on his way to a sack.

Tony set a fine example for his teammates, showing

more than talking, teaching more than taking, helping others improve their skills. He forbade drugs in his presence, preferring the weight room and a great work out as his natural high. Everyone knew Tony was destined for greatness, he just had to bide his time through high school.

I heard a story about Tony one time, although never had it confirmed.

It was not necessary to ask a lot of questions, you just knew it had to be true:

✦✦✦✦

He was at a party late on a Friday night, our game in the rear view. The right side of our offensive line was in the house, snorting lines with underage girls who should have been at home. A scream from upstairs stopped Tony in his tracks, the four-letter word painted a vivid horror in his mind. A second scream was unnecessary as Tony bounded the stairs three at a time, coming to a closed door where the rape was underway. Tony busted through the locked door and grabbed hold of the two offenders. They were hurled down the stairs; face plants both, and out for the night. Tony helped the poor girl get dressed and drove her home to the ritzy part of town, a place Tony had seldom seen. It did not matter that she was white and Tony black. A true hero wears no color; he rescues the girl and moves on. That was Tony.

It took a few days for the police to gather the facts and arrest the accused the next Tuesday. That left one day of practice on Monday, a bruising display of ferocity and payback that

I have never seen in all my years of coaching. Tony was usually our right defensive end in good position to attack the blind side of the QB. On Monday, he switched to the left side and squared up against the accused rapists. He did not speak, did not ask permission, he just lined up as the left defensive end.

Tony did not chase a quarterback that day, nor did he make a single tackle of a ball carrier. He did not even try. He spent every play punishing the right guard and tackle, driving them into the dirt, time and again. Nothing could protect the accused, not their helmets, or their pads, and hardly the coaches whistle. Tony ignored all of it and dished out pain on each play until he decided he was done.

The other coaches looked to me for guidance as Tony whipped some butt. I only offered my silence in return, trusting in the enforcer, our defensive leader. He was on a mission and I wanted him to see it through to the bloody end.

◆◆◆◆

I tried to fathom Tony's mindset as he hobbled to the door. "Hi coach, what brings you to town?"

"Hey Tony, good to see you. How's the knee doing?"

"It's fine Coach, the doc says I can start working at the auto shop in a few weeks."

"That's good Tony, real good."

There was a pregnant pause in our conversation, we both knew the knee was shot and it would be difficult for Tony to handle manual labor. I did not want to tell Tony about my recruiting trip to see Jerrod and a few other QB prospects in the area. I decided to make my move. "Tony, I wanted to continue our conversation about putting a plan together. You know I always said that you should have a plan, and we did not finish yours. You ready to get to work?"

We had not spent much time on Tony's plan, he was all set with that Pac 10 school, with a good shot at the pros to follow. Tony stayed quiet, taking it all in. I could feel the flashbacks running through his mind of the Oak Park game, and the chop block that kept him out of the California sun. But I dared not speak, not until Tony gave me some kind of reaction. My head was shouting, *Give me something Tony, something, anything we can work with!*

"Coach, I don't need...I mean, I have a plan...at the auto shop..." Tony trailed off, not finishing his thought. The knocks on Tony's front door had stopped when the season ended and scouts learned he could no longer make the grade on the field. Mine was the first knock in months.

"Tony, a good plan has some options, a few alternatives to choose from. If you want, we can kick around a few ideas I have been thinking about for you. What do you say?"

I had done some research at the U, looking into scholarships at the engineering school. I knew Tony was good with his hands, molding, welding, and building things. He liked to make drawings of the things he built, then bring them to life. To me, an engineering degree would be a great fit for Tony, if we could get him into school. "How about it Tony, we can do this together."

Two hours later we had crafted a plan. Tony's high school grades were not bad, but not great. However, his SAT score was quite high, which gave us the leverage we needed. His parents could not take the financial hit of college, even the in-state costs at the U. We needed a scholarship or two, and maybe an income for Tony.

Tony's father walked me to the door after our work was complete. He had a warm smile and an appreciative look on his face as we shook hands then embraced.

"Mr. De Luca, I wanted to ask you one last thing. To close the financial gap, Tony may need to get a job at school. I was wondering if you thought it would be too hard on him to be around football. That is, if I could get him a job on the team, would it be good for Tony or bad?"

He did not hesitate, letting me know football would always be a good thing for his son. Tony and his parents did most of the hard work, filling out financial aid forms, applying to the engineering school. I worked behind the scenes, making sure we knew all the angles to play.

I drove down to the U that night with a smile on my face, knowing another "lady" was on her way to becoming a man.

Tony

Chapter 14

College QB Coach

Size and Speed. If I had two words to describe the difference between high school and college football it was these two words. The players were bigger, much bigger. Their hands, feet, legs, shoulders, and their egos were all big. The stadiums, locker rooms, showers, work out facilities, the campus were all much bigger. The only thing that seemed the same size was the football field, it still measured 100 yards plus two ten-yard end zones, but it was dwarfed by stadium capacity, which of course was big, damn big.

Over the past ten years the game had become more and more about speed. Which team had the players to run downfield for the deep throws, or to the sidelines to get around the defense, or even up the middle, exploding through the holes that might only be open for a split second? Which team could get off the ball quicker, get around their man, sack the QB or avoid the rush? This was more often based on speed rather than size and strength. Speed trumped size, although size still mattered and was evident all around.

Perhaps the biggest change was happening at quarterback, my position. The power running game had given way to the long ball, the short ball, and any kind of ball thrown in the air to the open man. QBs with strong arms, and the quickness to avoid the rush or turn a busted play into a long run, escaping tacklers with fast feet, were prized recruits. One obstacle loomed large for a new college QB, the playbook. No longer aptly named, the playbook had become more of a work encyclopedia. The voluminous plays and formations demanded hours of study and rehearsal, making it difficult for a freshman to take the field.

The transition ahead for me was also multi-faceted. I was moving up and down at the same time…up to college ball, which was becoming more of a business and less of a game. There were many more people and activities vying for attention all around the game, too many of them distractions, which did not add much value to our preparations. It was no wonder that the coaching staffs and administration offices had large budgets and payrolls. After all, someone had to deal with the alumni, students, press, parents, and everyone who mattered, or thought they mattered. I was also moving down, from head coach to a position coach. Once again I no longer carried the whistle or was the voice that directed human traffic on the field. I was not the one who inspired souls in the sanctuary before games. I had a lot to learn about college ball and leading young men, yet I yearned to be the lead dog on the sled with a clear path ahead, not back in the pack eating dust. I wanted to be head coach again, and knew full well that lack of patience was a character flaw I had inherited long ago.

Ego has a funny way of sneaking up on you, inserting itself into your bloodstream, flowing through your body and becoming a defining part of your character. I was a close friend with my ego during my playing days at the U. The status and attention hoisted on the starting QB was a prescription I readily filled. The drugs ran out in a short four years and it seemed as if my good friend had moved on to a younger carrier with more time on the game clock.

My ego was on hiatus, but returned to set up roots when I became the high school's head coach. This time sated by the maturation of young men as they obeyed, listened, and took to heart my sermons and sayings. I thoroughly enjoyed leadership, the burden of responsibility, and the desire to guide a group of young boys. As the college season approached, I missed my friend and the adrenalin he provided. I wanted him back in my life and built a plan to get it back. The initial step was to turn the U into "Quarterback University," and Jerrod was my first real weapon. He possessed the necessary tools, both the size and speed to make an impact, even to excel.

Zip

"Nice throw Jake. Let's run it again."

Zip

"That's good. Watch your footwork, keep good spacing, set-up a bit faster."

Jake was our starting quarterback, returning for his last year, one more chance to get noticed by the pro scouts. He was very good, maybe good enough to be a back up in the pros, but not a starter. He would not command a premium draft pick, or a big contract. Jake had a strong arm, but he could not escape a fast lineman bearing down for a sack. He was a leader on the team, but could have been the slowest man on the field. His slow feet would keep him contained in the pocket more so than the opposing defense.

Zip

"Ok, let's switch it up. Jerrod, take a few snaps."

Zip

"That's good, again, let's run it again."

Jerrod's freshman year was uneventful for the initial five games. He improved each week in practice, demonstrating his skills for an eager audience. Our plan was to red-shirt Jerrod, letting him improve his technique, learn the college game, and be better prepared to compete for the starting job as a sophomore. In our sixth game, that plan was thrown away in just two plays. We had three wins against two losses with a shot at the conference title and a solid bowl at year-end. First, Jake went down and then out with a game ending hip injury. He tried to stretch a scramble into a longer run, his slow feet betraying him, allowing three defenders to converge, with Jake's hip taking the brunt of the hit. On the next play the second string QB was sacked hard by a blitzing cornerback, hitting the turf headfirst. He was dazed and confused, and headed for the defensive huddle rather than his own.

We were down two QBs in just two plays. That's when the head coach stared me down. "Is Jerrod ready? Can he take us home?"

The honest answer was, *No, not ready.* He needed

more time to get a grasp of the playbook and a feel for the game. He could not read the defensive schemes, unable to predict a blitz or coverage change. The only answer the coach wanted and what he expected to hear from me was, *Yes, he's ready, Coach.* The thing that mattered most was getting another win, keeping the alumni and fans at bay and maybe playing for the conference title. Titles and bowl wins were college football currency, they paid for everything and the coach was hungry.

Jerrod circled nearby, helmet in hand ready to get on the college field. I mouthed to him 'you ready Jerrod,' looking for validation, reducing the risk of making this decision on my own. He strapped it on and gave me the go ahead.

Time to vote. My gut and head said no, but my heart and ego said yes. I did not realize my friend ego, was eligible to vote, he had not been around for some time. It's never a tie vote when ego is involved. It was time to get going with Quarterback University and my ego had signaled the play, throw Jerrod to the wolves and let's see what happens.

"Yes Coach, Jerrod is ready to go!"

What Coach wants, Coach gets, I rationalized. Besides, our opponents had not prepared for Jerrod and his quick feet, fast legs, and strong arm. They had not seen any tape since none existed. Jerrod was a racecar on the football grid; he could change the tempo of a game, and did so every week at practice much to the chagrin of our starting defensive team. And of course, the coach noticed, he even drooled a bit, his mouth agape watching Jerrod shift into high gear, escaping his pursuers.

Jerrod and I were not ready, but it was time. We

walked toward Coach, excited to be contributing to the team and hopefully a comeback win. That's when it hit me. As a lowly position coach, I was not needed to help conduct the game; Coach and his offensive coordinator would take the reins, calling the plays, directing Jerrod and the offense. They would even pat him on the butt when he did well. *That was my butt to pat, no one else's,* strangely entered my mind.

I became a slave to jealousy for the rest of the game, equally proud and frustrated every time Jerrod engineered a touchdown. I was not very good at letting go of my creation, the pangs of envy hitting me in waves as Coach lauded praise over the QB and the offense, each time they scored.

They say college ball players have a lot of growing up to do when they hit campus, enticed by new thrills, many of them not so cheap. I faced a similar gap in my maturation and realized I had to hide my emotions and take satisfaction in the plan. When I took a moment, I realized the plan to turn the U into Quarterback University was working. Jerrod was a star after one game, at least a star in the making, and I was the QB coach who recruited him to the U and taught him his trade. Sure he brought the skills, but I brought the craft and gladly molded Jerrod as I had been taught to do. The credit was mine to take, or at least to share, if I could bottle up the red devil on my shoulder that was crying foul every time Coach patted Jerrod's butt.

After the game, Jerrod proved the bigger man, pushing through his many new admirers and even the press that hounded him for a quote. He pushed past Coach, passed his teammates, and skipped handshakes from the opposing team.

Jerrod took straight aim and ran me down on the way to the locker room. He would not let me escape, forcing me to share the spotlight, our embrace captured on the sports pages the next day. That picture became the enduring symbol of QBU, our calling card for living room recruitment pitches. You never forget your first, Jerrod got me started and he never thought about it twice. He was pure, maybe born that way, certainly raised that way.

The student taught the teacher how to behave as a man, and thankfully I was ok with that.

Chapter 15

Jerrod

Jerrod was in familiar territory, taking over a seasoned team loyal to the senior QB. If he was nervous or hesitant, Jerrod did not show it. He came to practice Monday after winning the game on Saturday, ready to be the starter, not expecting it and not feeling entitled to it. He knew it was just one win and as the former third string QB he got lucky to be in the game. Two freak plays in a row gave him a shot and he took full advantage. Jerrod was ready for a repeat performance and could play his part coming off the bench or starting behind center. Either way, he was good to go and everyone sensed it.

Jerrod had a confidence about him, it was not voiced and certainly not bragged about. His confidence seemed to arrive a step or two ahead of his feet, letting others know the starting QB was in the house.

Now it was the head coach's turn; he had the ball and had to make a call. We were out on the practice field; the offense huddled up, waiting for a play and play caller. It was really down to two choices, Jake or Jerrod; either option could easily be defended to the press, alums, and most importantly, the players. Jake was the safer bet, a two-year starter who oozed leadership in and out of the locker room. He was definitely the low risk play and I fully expected to hear his name called. Jerrod was still a crapshoot, a much higher risk than Coach would normally go for.

As Coach hesitated, making it clear to me he had not yet decided, I wondered what would Coach Bob do. So, I asked myself, *Bob what is your call?* I was surprised at my answer, without any hesitation my lips mouthed a single name: *Jake.* Just like that, I went with Jake, the proven leader of the team, the safe choice. It was instinctual; I had posed a question to my conscience and gotten a quick response. It made great sense for the team, for Jake, and for Jerrod who needed more time.

As I mouthed Jake's name, I looked at Coach looking at me. He read my lips then nodded and smiled. *Ok,* I thought, *Coach and I are on the same page.* I did not let my bias toward Jerrod affect my decision on the starting QB, and it looked as if Coach felt the same. Then he yelled, "Jerrod, get in the huddle, let's see more of what you showed on Saturday!"

I was a bit quick out of the blocks and stammered. "Let's go Jake ... er, Jerrod."

I jumped the gun and Jake let me have it, staring me down with more firmness than I had seen in him before. He was hurting on the inside, pride sapping his energy and his spirit. Jake rubbed his hip; giving every indication the injury was the reason for Coach's slight. I felt bad for Jake, and scared shitless for Jerrod and the rest of us.

Coach threw the dice on our season and Jake's career, putting all his chips down on a college freshman. The players on the field took the change in stride, unsure if Coach was making a permanent move or challenging Jake, pushing him to up his game. Sadly, no matter how much Coach pushed, Jake could not find that next gear, the one that allowed him to escape a blitzing D.

It was Jerrod's team now, so long as he got us to the end zone on a regular basis. His ability to remain at quarterback was directly proportional to our win-loss record. A lot of freshman would be hesitant, or so pumped up their throws would drift over the heads of receivers. Not Jerrod, he knew the leash was tight and that Coach would reverse course back to Jake if warranted. Jerrod simply walked up to the huddle and barked out a play. His voice did not waiver nor show any sign of nerves.

Jerrod's first throw in practice that day went for 30 plus yards, a solid spiral down the right sideline to a small window of space between two defenders, into the receiver's outstretched hands. *Boom!* On the next play the defense put on an all out rush bringing two linebackers and a corner. Jerrod escaped one, two, then three would-be tacklers, dancing around thrusts and dives. He scooted around end and ran out of bounds for a 15-yard gain. *Boom!*

Jerrod had announced his presence without saying a single word. While others gaped, Jerrod went about his business, shouting encouragement to the O-line for the next play. Coach tried not to show it, but he preened like a proud new papa. It was only two plays on the practice field, zero impact to our record. Coach understood that more than anyone, but he also knew Jerrod won the team over that day, buckling into the pilot's seat, ready for the battles ahead. I just shook my head, biting my tongue, not allowing the, "I told you so" to enter airspace. It seemed a wiser move to hold on tight and go along for the ride.

After practice Jerrod and I sat in the bleachers, enjoying the calm after the dust settled from the players exit. "Were you surprised, Jerrod, that Coach named you the starter?"

"I didn't think of it that way. I would have been happy coming off the bench again like last time, biding my time until next year. Did you know? You sure didn't give off any signal that it was coming my way."

"Nah, I thought Coach would go with Jake, the safe bet. You're still a young colt with long odds to payoff."

Jerrod laughed and sat back against the bench, letting the fading sun wash over him, seeming at peace, not at all disturbed with his new burden to lead the team. I sat there ready to dissect the practice just completed and run through plays for the upcoming game. Then Jerrod went in a completely different direction. "Coach, what do you dream about? I mean, how do you get away from football, where do you go and how do you get there?"

"I don't know Jerrod; there isn't much escape, certainly not during the season. The practices are long, the preparation even longer. It's hard to get away if that's what you're asking."

"Come on Coach, that's a standard answer if I ever heard one."

"What about you Jerrod, what are your dreams?"

"Ok, I'll go first. There are two places I go in my mind when I need to escape from the daily grind of practice and school. First, I want to travel across Africa and Asia, see the countries where my ancestors are from and visit exotic places that you only read about in books."

"I can just picture you on safari, rifle in hand, taking dead aim on a charging rhino!"

"No, not a safari. I want to visit real villages, see how the people live, and understand how to help those in need. Then I'll recharge the batteries on some island near Thailand and head back to Africa."

"Sounds like a life's journey, not just a vacation. Where's the second place you go Jerrod?"

"I imagine myself as a small town mayor who knows everyone in the community. Our crime rate is low, the homes are in good shape, and people care about their neighbors. There are good schools, parks for the kids, and the local high school has a football team with a great coach. His name is Bob."

"Well, thanks for including me in your dreams, better than making a guest appearance in a nightmare. So, is that your plan after ball, to be mayor where every house has a white picket fence?"

"It's a step, an important step. The town is a comeback story that goes against the normal patterns. The town has been a dump for years, more stores are boarded up than open, and people who live there are scared. They stay at home; avoid eye contact when they go out, afraid of what might be around the next turn. It takes a while, but the mayor and the city pull back the layers of muck and crime and turn the city around. People learn how to be proud again, they greet each other with smiles, they pat each other on the back, unafraid to reach out and touch another human."

"That's a great story Jerrod, I hope for you it happens someday. So tell me, how will you accomplish the town turn around play? What's your secret?"

Jerrod looked out onto the field with sharpness in his eyes, rigidness to his frame. "Coach, I don't have it all thought through yet. My plan is to work hard 'cause that's the only way I know. And then I hope to get lucky. If I am fortunate enough to make it to the pros and hang around for ten years, I'll make good money from the game and a few sponsors. Each of my sponsors will be required to invest with me after football in a town of my choosing. That money will bring jobs, which will enable people to earn respect. When people have jobs, a little money, and self respect there is nothing they can't do. I will sponsor community projects, and roll up my sleeves to get things done. I will also lean on my athlete buddies to help out, and put that town on my back. Hopefully I will earn their vote and learn how a town wants to be governed."

"Be careful, sounds like you are buying their votes, not earning it."

"Yeah, that's the part I have not figured out yet."

"Earlier you said it was a step, what did you mean by that?"

"Coach, after I prove myself in a small town, I want to plot a path to a higher public office. If I can make a difference in a town, why not do the same for a big city or even a state?

That's my dream coach, to make a real impact in as many lives as I can."

I looked at Jerrod and saw nothing but sincerity and believed he would have a chance, a very good chance to achieve his dreams.

"Coach, I may need your help to put this plan together, you in?"

"Yeah, I am definitely in Jerrod. I would love to see you as town mayor, especially on parade day."

"Coach, if you are in then you'll be sitting right beside me in the fire truck, waving to the citizens and tossing candy to the kids. What a sight, Coach Bob in the town parade."

The sun had set and the lights had been turned out. We began a ritual that day and followed it the rest of the season, and the three after that. We sat in the bleachers and talked. We discussed the practice just held and we discussed the upcoming game. Mostly we talked about life, it was our time to relax, to get away from football, if only for a few brief moments each day. We talked about the books we had recently read, the trips we wanted to take, the places we wanted to see. We talked about our families, and the influences on our lives. We spent a lot of time talking about girls, and the many admirers Jerrod had around campus. He was flooded with attention and opportunity. We discussed our dreams and started putting a real plan in place for Mayor Jerrod.

We became close friends during those conversations; the gap in our ages faded away as we shared our dreams and our fears. Next to Amy and my mom, this was the closest I'd ever felt to another person. With Jerrod it was just easy. We did not have to force conversation and we allowed ourselves to enjoy the silence, though it came too rarely. Jerrod was so full of life; I was mostly in awe of him and tried to hide it. Guys who were friends were supposed to meet each other on the same level; I did my best to keep up.

All these years later I still have trouble believing it happened:

✦✦✦✦

Jerrod made one mistake in college, one error in judgment over four full years and it cost him dearly. It cost him a diploma. It cost him a college degree. It cost him a first round draft pick in the NFL. It cost a small town its mayor. It cost Jerrod a life.

"Hey Jerrod, I know it's been a while since I came to see you"

The tombstone stared back at me, offering nothing as the wind whistled through the trees.

"Looks like I am doing all the talking again. I miss our conversations, the back-and-forth, the sharing. I bet you miss it too."

More silence from Jerrod's tombstone.

"I'm back at the U again, they made me head coach! How does that one grab you? Yeah, I can hear you rolling around. Give it a rest and let's chat for a while."

The clouds covered the sun and everything seemed a bit greyer like the stone.

"I have a new QB to break in, he reminds me of you in some ways. He's not as smart as you were, does not read books or think about trips to Asia and Africa like you did. He's not a dreamer outside of football, at least not yet. But he's got a great arm and faster legs than you ever had. His name is Vince, and we call him V. I think his best attribute is leadership, he's some kind of pied piper, and people follow him wherever he goes."

The wind hurled some leaves against the stone making a flapping sound.

"I need some help to guide Vince, get him on the right track. He's had a tough life, in and out of juvie jail and no mother or father to help him grow. But I can tell he's a special kid, and not just on the field. He can really be something, lead a great life and impact so many people in a positive way. I know it in my heart, and my gut, much like I knew with you. He needs a map, a set of paths he can choose from. He needs someone like me to show him what's possible."

The leaves fell to the ground as the wind moved on.

"Jerrod, I don't know if I can do this again. Part of me wants to dive in with V and invest everything I got in him. But, I'm afraid. There, I said it. We were always honest with each other Jerrod, no need stopping now."

The sun broke through the clouds and shined on the stone.

I needed more time to think, so I shared some silence with Jerrod and reflected back on his last day. I had not thought about it in a long time and I could not prevent the memory from bubbling up.

It was spring after Jerrod's fourth and final season. He opted to stay his senior year, knowing we were not in position to win a major bowl, too many starters had moved on after our top twenty ranking the year before. I never had to ask Jerrod why he stayed, it was always part of his plan to finish school with a degree and not let football define him. He would use football not the other way around. Jerrod had bigger things in mind; he wanted to be governor of his home state and knew an NFL career would give him name recognition when he needed it.

We had planned to drive up to Chicago and stay at Jerrod's home to watch draft day with his parents and hometown friends. Jerrod stopped by my office late in the afternoon, the day before our drive.

"Coach, how goes it? You getting out tonight or hanging with the family?"

"Hi Jerrod, it's a home night for me; we got a long couple of days ahead and this old guy needs his rest."

"No surprise there old man, you get some rest and I'll sleep on the drive home tomorrow."

"What are you boys up to tonight?"

"Coach, I can't turn my boys in, not even to you. I'll see you at nine a.m. tomorrow; tell Amy and Taylor good night for me."

Jerrod turned and headed for the door, he looked back and stared at me with a wide smile and spoke the last words I heard from him. "Coach, I will sure miss those bleacher talks. Thanks for hanging with me these past four years; I'll never forget it."

Then he was gone.

Jerrod did not drink much at school and never took drugs. A cold beer or two only during the off-season was his usual self-imposed limit. The man had class and discipline.

The police report tallied a blood alcohol level of .18, far exceeding the legal limit, and even further beyond Jerrod's norm. He rode shotgun that evening, the death seat as many call it. It seems he was making up for four years of calm with a single evening of rebellion. The driver did not make it either, seat belts were optional that night. Only the two players in the back seat survived if you can call it that, one lost a limb and the other was paralyzed for life.

The silence got louder as if Jerrod could understand my thoughts, the memory haunting us both.

"Jerrod, you would have been a great mayor and maybe, just maybe, you would have gotten my vote. You had some work ahead of you to earn it."

My weak attempt at humor was not helping me cope with my loss and it was not helping me figure out what to do with V.

"What do you think Jerrod? Should I give it a go with Vince? Would you mind if I gave everything to him like we did with each other? Are you ok if I use some of our stories as lessons?"

The tombstone remained quiet.

The silence I longed for was not helping me get to an answer. "I didn't expect you to make this easy. Yeah, I know, you want me to figure it out on my own. It's instinct, isn't that what you used to say?"

The sun shone for just a second, highlighting Jerrod's name on the stone.

"Ok Jerrod, I'll go with my gut on this one. It's gonna hurt some, and I'll be back to share with you how things are going and I'll be expecting you to contribute. Got that?"

I wiped a tear, still not accustomed to crying, not since Jerrod's last night. I figured all the tears my body was allotted for in a lifetime left me that evening. It almost felt good to cry again, if it hadn't felt so bad to relive the memory of my friend.

◆◆◆◆

Jerrod left a legacy at school; with a little help from me we recruited two terrific QBs, each of them ready to take the helm once Jerrod moved to the pro game. It seemed we were just starting out on our plan to turn the U into Quarterback University when Jerrod left us for good. I needed to get out, get away from the U otherwise I would suffocate and bring Amy and Taylor down with me. Luckily, I received a call from Coach Mac about an Offensive Coordinator position at a state school in Michigan.

There is so much I learned from my good friend, I am constantly reminded of something he said or the way he approached his life. If I had to narrow it down to one thing, Jerrod taught me how to chase your dream. He was not afraid to dream big dreams, to set lofty goals, and to go after them. Not enough people apply themselves the way Jerrod did, it was one of my own personal shortcomings. Sure, I had dreams, but I kept them in a bottle, fearing how others might react if they knew my inner most thoughts. Jerrod taught me to put everything on the line, out in the open in the light of day. Only then did my dreams have a chance of coming true.

Chapter 16

15-Year Meet-Up

Harry took us for a ride for our 15-year meet-up; luckily no golf carts were involved. He was a year late in scheduling our gathering but made up for it in great style by winning a lottery for Masters' tickets. We were off to witness Tiger win his first major at one of golf's temples. Harry scored tickets for the Wednesday practice round, not the real event, no matter, we were thrilled to walk around those majestic grounds if only for a day. Try as I might, I could not find a single weed among the 18 holes and grounds.

The players were loose and carefree with the fans, stretching their limbs and playing one last round before the Thursday start. Mark Calcavecchia came to the first tee as we arrived on the scene, his belly shaking, his cheeks jawing, everyone enjoying his presence. He unleashed a powerful drive that must have gone 300 yards down the middle of the fairway. As he walked off the tee he looked back at the fans and said,

"Tell Tiger where I hit that one." He laughed at his own joke, and then ambled away toward his ball. Even the players knew it was Tiger's time to begin his assault on golf records.

I sprung for lunch, my penalty for the promotion to Offensive Coordinator; I had been in the new role for almost a year. The laugh was on my buddies as the bill was less than $20; Augusta had the best lunch deal in town. I guess they figured fans had to work hard enough to get to the event, why not give them a break on the eats while there. The Masters was a class act all the way around.

We made our way to Charleston for the weekend, playing a few rounds on the drive up. Harry arranged a private room for our last evening and none of us could have predicted the emotions of that night and the buddy that would walk away, his pride wounded from multiple body blows, the truth landing harder punches than Harry's fists.

The boys knew I was hurting, unwilling to share Jerrod's ending from a year ago. They gave me a pass for the night, although they hoped I would find some way to let them know I was ok.

Seth loved starting things off and began by telling a success story that sounded like a failure, a very bad failure. Seth recruited a talented employee to join his team from a different part of the company because Tim had the best skills for a particular project. Tim advanced the ball further and faster than anyone had anticipated. As Tim excelled, the engineers in Seth's group who had been there for many years resented him. They filed formal complaints about Tim, making up stories about his behavior, lack of teamwork, and his approach to the project. Tim was quickly surrounded and outnumbered; he fought back by doubling down on the project and lashing out at his accusers.

The long time engineering team realized that Tim was accomplishing more than they ever could, but refused to acknowledge it. After two years, Seth and his engineering team figured they had drained Tim of his knowledge, and with the project near completion they wanted to steal the credit. They conspired to have Tim fired, ganging up with the help of Human Resources.

Seth told this story as a political success, throwing one person off a sinking lifeboat so the greater good could survive. It did not matter that Tim built the lifeboat and plucked Seth and his engineers from the drink so they would not drown.

Harry reacted first, "Seth how the hell is this a success story, sounds like a terrible failure to me, especially for Tim's sake."

"I plotted Tim's demise for more than a year, carefully crafting a story for HR to believe with the help of the engineering team. Tim was an outsider who did not fit the established culture. I displayed amazing patience; setting up Tim over a long time. It took a lot of back room work to get it done."

"What happened to Tim?" I asked.

"We had him on the ropes, halfway out the door and a Senior Executive in a different part of the company gave him a job. Tim actually excelled there doing similar work. It made me look bad that he did well outside of my grasp."

Seth felt the bad vibe in the room and knew he was losing trust from his buddies. He tried to recover, but only made things worse. "I even offered Tim a promotion at one point but he turned me down."

Harry was not buying it. "Why was that Slick?"

"Tim wanted to bail on the project and head back to another group in the company. I took back the promo offer since he was a traitor and had to be punished."

Harry stared at Seth and just shook his head.

I needed to escape this madness and thought of Jerrod, welcoming the intrusion and the chance to reunite with my old friend. I began calling him "The Mayor," honoring his dream. The Mayor would sneak up without warning, taking me away for a brief respite or challenging me in some way. After hearing Seth's story about trying to destroy Tim, I wondered what The Mayor would have done if he were in Seth's shoes. It was not a fair comparison, and not meant to be. The Mayor improved everything and everyone around him, seldom taking credit alone, while helping others better themselves. Seth on the other hand took great delight in sending a person spiraling downward, then stepping on his neck while seeking applause.

I wondered if Seth was a product of his environment, perhaps molded by corporate management expectations. Seth was not strong enough to be the better man, to resist monetary temptation, to put a team on his back as The Mayor dreamed to do with his town. It was a sad realization that one of my buddies was simply not a good guy. I don't remember Seth as a bad guy in college, maybe he kept it hidden, or maybe corporate politics teased out the real Seth.

I could not get something out of my head; I kept repeating it over and over again. *What would The Mayor do?*

What would The Mayor do? And then I let it slip out without realizing my lips were moving, "What would the Mayor do?" *Shit.*

Harry had heard me. "What's that Bob? The Mayor?"

"I was just thinking to myself."

Harry would not let it go. "Come on, spill those beans. Who is the Mayor and what would he do?"

My buddies were waiting on an answer. I felt trapped, wanting to blurt out Jerrod's name, to hear it spoken out loud again. I wanted to say he was The Mayor who saved a town and taught me how a man should behave. I was not afraid of telling my buddies that I learned more about life from a college kid than he ever learned from me. I wanted to feel the relief in finally talking about my friend after a year of silence.

At the same time I was not ready and felt I would never really be ready. I would leave Jerrod buried; keep him to myself, and the annual tombstone chat. I mulled that plan over and could only think how selfish and childish that seemed. I closed my eyes and heard a whisper. I may have asked for a whisper, I'm not sure, but the message I heard, or thought I heard, had great clarity. *It's ok Coach.*

It sounded like something Jerrod would say. Three words, barely a breath needed to spit it out. A simple message, yet with direction on the action I needed to take.

"The Mayor was Jerrod." I said his name, finally. Then I cried, somehow finding a new reservoir of tears. I wept in front of my buddies but I didn't care. I tried to make it a manly cry, but did not know what the hell that was. So I just let it out and did not worry how it may have looked. My buddies surrounded me, offering drinks, towels, anything that was nearby.

Kevin spoke quietly, "You've been holding on to that for a long time, Bob. It's good to see you let some of that pressure out."

Scott knew it would help if I talked about it and encouraged me on, "Tell us about the Mayor."

I took another heavy sigh and asked for a cold one; it was time for a swig or two if I wanted to be a good storyteller. "Jerrod had a lot of dreams and one of them was to be a small town mayor."

I told my buddies about the bleacher talks with Jerrod and some of the dreams we shared. I explained the plan we had worked on for nearly four years, about the small town turn around play, led by Mayor Jerrod and backed by sponsors and friends. I even told them about the parade. They were silent, taking it all in as I rambled for twenty minutes. I finally paused and took a long breath, not knowing how much of a story I wove; the words just came, and came some more.

Harry took a deep breath then spoke first, "Bob, that is some success story. And don't be fooled for a moment, even though The Mayor is no longer with us, the relationship the two of you shared and the plans you made are inspirational to me, and I bet could be to others as well."

Leave it to Harry to say the perfect thing. I thought, then said, "I called Jerrod The Mayor as a nickname and lately whenever I run into a tough situation, I ask, 'What would The Mayor do?' Jerrod had this knack for seizing the moment, bringing his teammates along for the ride, making everyone better. Of course, I adapted the saying from the Christians with

WWJD, but it works for me."

"So you asked what would The Mayor do about Seth's story?" Mike asked.

I locked on Seth, and then dove in the deep end of the pool. It was time for Seth to hear some truth and I figured it might as well happen here and now. "Yeah, I thought Seth took the coward's way out with Tim, buckling to peer pressure from his engineering team. It was a total lack of leadership, in my opinion. So, I asked what would The Mayor do?"

Seth was not happy. "You don't have a clue what I was dealing with," he said.

"It doesn't matter Seth. Your tell was showing, and besides, it sounds like Tim excelled when he moved away from your team. I don't know why this Tim guy hung around you for so long."

"My tell?"

"You've become a different person Seth, or I did not know you very well back in school. Though someone sure nailed your nickname, Slick is a mighty good fit."

"My tell?"

Kevin could not resist any longer, "Seth, the right side of your face twitches when you tell a lie. We've all known it for years."

"You guys, my buddies, have been lying to me all these years? Why didn't you tell me?"

Scott took a swing, "Seth, you got it backwards. You are the one who has trouble with the truth; bending it to fit the angle you want to play. It's going to bite you in the ass one of these days."

"What about the rest of you guys. Don't give me grief and pretend you are perfect. Kevin, you don't seem to mind knocking people over at the office."

"There's a difference Seth. Sure I compete hard at work, and my elbows are sharp, no denying that. But I don't take pleasure in destroying someone, that's not who I am. Unfortunately, it is who you have become that concerns us."

Scott jumped in again, "We all compete in life, especially at the office. And I'll admit a lot of the motivation is financial. But Seth, you take things way too far. You seem to enjoy power more than anything else. Why does your firm let you get away with all the games you play anyway?"

Seth deserved and needed this baptism in front of his buddies, guys who would not take any BS from him. I guess this truth discussion came out because of my memories of Jerrod, but it had been building for some time.

Seth was steaming, pacing back and forth, unsure how to respond to the attacks from his friends. It's not easy being the monkey stuck in the middle, being pushed to exhaustion by truths you thought were hidden, now exposed, and fed down your throat by your supposed buddies.

He tried to defend himself. "At least I'm not getting paid to coach a game or defend criminals or sell bonds to old ladies like some of you jerks. You guys aren't in the big leagues like me or Kevin or even Harry."

That was the tipping point for Harry. "Seth, you really don't get it do you? Have you been paying attention at all to the stories these guys have been sharing with us? What do you think motivates Scott? Do you have any clue?"

"He's a Wall Street guy living in the Midwest. He's in it for the money like everyone else. He just said so himself."

"And what about Mike, what is his motivation?" Harry asked.

"I really don't know, I thought he wanted to be District Attorney some day and throw the book at criminals, but he gave that up to defend bums."

"And what about Coach Bob? What drives him?"

"Hell, he wants to be head coach at some big school and pull down a few million per year. He wants a hundred kids to call him sir while they are running stairs and eating turf."

"Seth, what are you getting out of these meet-ups? It's pretty clear you aren't tuned in, not even trying to learn a damn thing from guys who care about you."

Seth sat down and chugged a beer, hoping the conversation would just go away. Harry was on a roll and building toward a knockout punch, no way would he let this end without a moral.

"Seth, let me tell you what I have learned at these meet-ups. Scott is making a lot of coin, no doubt. But that's a byproduct of where and how he spends his time. He's saving people from themselves, helping them diversify their investments and creating a real retirement plan for old age. It's a win-win scenario."

Harry paused to let that settle in. "And Mike here, he gave up the DA office just like you said, but not to defend bums. He's saving kids' lives, keeping them out of jail, helping them get on a better path. And he's good at it. I know a few kids who went to see Mike when they got in trouble. He saved them."

Harry let that one sink in. Seth slumped a little further in his chair, staring down at the bottle in his hands.

"And Bob, sure he wants to be a head coach, and I hope he attains that. But more important to me is the stories he told us about kids who were heading in a wrong direction and he helped them craft a life plan to get back on track. He doesn't care about having power over his kids; he wants them to succeed after football."

Seth got up out of his chair and walked toward Harry, who rose to meet him head on. "It's all for shit Harry, these guys got you fooled and you don't even realize it. I never knew you were so stupid."

Harry unleashed a quick left jab to Seth's chin and an undercut to his belly, taking all the air out of Seth and the room. Seth hit the floor then slowly sat up, letting some wind back into his lungs. He glared at Harry and clenched his fists signaling round two would begin. The rest of us cleared some space, no one thought for a second about stopping the fight. But Seth failed to respond; he leaned against the wall and spit out some blood.

Harry rubbed his hand. "I'm not sorry for hitting you Slick, not one bit. You earned it a long time ago. But I will tell you something and I hope you take it to heart."

Harry walked around the room working his way toward some story, but I could not predict what was coming. "You all know I screwed up planning for this meet-up, scheduling it nearly a year late, but you don't know why."

Uh oh, I thought, *there is a lot of truth being told tonight.*

136

Harry glanced over at me and winked, so I knew he was ready. Harry sat down, arms on his knees, and began his story. "I got fired a year ago from my tech sales job for cooking the books. I was missing quota and not making enough to pay the bills, so I dumped inventory into the channel and fudged the numbers to make it look like I was exceeding my targets. I got away with it for a long time, and kept taking greater risk in order to get higher bonuses. I picked up the scam from another guy who had a similar job on the East Coast. Turns out my boss was encouraging a lot of us to do the same and five of us got fired, including the boss. We were all guilty and deserved it."

"The company was very reasonable with my termination since a case could be made about my boss orchestrating the whole thing. I didn't want to fight it; I just wanted to get out and start over."

"That's when I started drinking hard, at home, at the bar; it didn't matter where I was so long as Johnny Walker was with me. I spent a year drinking and thinking and not much else. The 15-year meet-up was getting close and I couldn't plan the event because I was not ready to face you guys. I could not tell you about getting fired and I was embarrassed about being drunk all the time. And then it hit me, the reason I was so ashamed. I finally figured out that I was trying to be like you Seth, caring only about accolades and money, not about the people. I couldn't stand myself, knowing that truth, so I drank even more until one night it all got away from me. I crashed my car on the drive home nearly killing a couple kids. That's when I called Bob and he got me set-up in re-hab. Mike took my case and kept me out of jail, it must have cost a lot of favors, though he never once complained. Luckily, the kids I hit were fine, just a few bumps and bruises so their parents did not sue."

Harry took a couple of breaths, no one moved. "Seth, it was pretty bad getting fired, but to me it was worse comparing myself to you and not one of these other guys. You see Seth, I took shortcuts just like you are and that's not who I set out to be. I was listening to our buddies at these meet-ups and I thought I was paying attention, but I was not letting their experiences impact me in a positive way. I did nothing to change my behavior and aspire to a greater good. Seth, you are on the path I was on and you don't see it, not yet. I am telling you my truth, admitting my failure, so that maybe it can help you get your act together before your life crashes down around you like mine did."

I admired my friend for telling his story, not holding back any punches. Seth's chin and gut would hurt for a little while, hopefully his conscience would feel this evening a while longer.

We waited for a reaction from Seth, the ticking wall clock the only sound in the room. Seth slowly got up, ignoring the helping hand from Kevin, and walked toward Harry. "Screw you Harry."

I didn't see the beer bottle in Seth's hand as he began his swing. Mike lunged and knocked the bottle to the ground while Kevin kicked Seth in the ass, sending him reeling toward the door. We watched Seth's back as he stumbled into the hallway, still hurting from Harry's one-two and Kevin's boot. Then he was gone and I wondered if he would ever be back.

Harry sat back against the wall and looked up at the

ceiling. "Damn, I messed that up."

"He had it coming," Kevin replied.

It was time to loosen things up, just a bit. "Damn Harry. Have you been working on the bag at home?" Kevin asked.

"Nah, I haven't hit anyone since high school. My fist is throbbing!"

I was concerned for my buddy. "Harry, you doing ok?" I asked.

Harry looked at all of us in the room and gave us a full-face grin. We smiled back and collapsed to the floor, laughing loudly.

Harry summed up all our thoughts, "Now that's what I call a meet-up! I knew we should have filmed these things!"

We were spent after all that storytelling and truth sharing; we were done for this evening. I was relieved that Harry found the courage, keeping his secret was wearing on me. Seth gave Harry the spark needed to lay his cards out, although I was shocked that Harry did it to help Slick. I hoped it would do Seth some good, but would not bet a nickel he would take any of it to heart. He was too small a man to learn a life lesson from a buddy.

◆◆◆◆

My benchmark scores after our 15-year meet-up:

Primary Yardstick: Money

Scott: Pass

Kevin: Pass

Mike: Pass

Harry: Starting Over

Seth: Pass

Me: Pass

Secondary Yardsticks:

Me: Kids Saved

Scott: Retirees Saved

Mike: Jailhouse Sentences Saved

Kevin: None

Harry: Buddies Saved

Seth: None

I gave Harry full credit for laying himself on the line to save a buddy, although trying to save Seth seemed like wasted energy.

Chapter 17

Coach Tom Norman

Amy, Taylor, and I had an easy time settling into our new surroundings at the state school in Michigan. The town and college campus were well integrated, each breathing life into the other. A lazy bike ride on a Sunday afternoon may start at home and before anyone realizes it, the bike is leaning against a wall, it's rider inside one of the many local establishments for nourishment, before the short pedal back home.

On occasion, the pedal homeward took a circuitous route, helping ensure a level playing field for the many business owners in town, eager to host the coach. It can be treacherous work keeping the peace among those who control the taps in town.

We purchased our first house outside of Illinois, not knowing how long we would be around. Crazy ideas went through my head as I weighed the buy versus rent argument, both sides scoring points, although there was no clear winner.

141

What if we lost every game that first year and the offense did not score any points? I worried. *How long would they let us stay around then? What if we won the Rose Bowl capping off an undefeated season and I fielded head coaching job offers from top schools across the country. How long would I want to hang around if that was the case?* There was so much to consider.

I stopped scaring myself with nightmares and dream scenarios and made a bet we were in for at least a five-year stint and put the money down. If nothing else, we needed that amount of time away from the U.

The best part of town was the people, mostly Midwest born and raised, hardworking folks rearing their own. They were avid sports fans, cheering the local team regardless of affiliation. A 500 hundred club that left it all on the field received great respect, and the coaches knew a return trip next year would be their reward. Beating archrivals during the season brought more local support than most bowl wins. That was the history I learned in talks across town, but I also heard something subtler, something from down deep inside, something only spoken after a few rounds at the pub. The town was desperate for a true winner, a conference title, a January Bowl game, and a top ten ranking at season's end. They knew the game was changing, shifting to high scoring offensive led teams. It went against the grain they had grown accustomed to, but they were ready to adapt, to do whatever it took to bring a real winner to town. Wins mattered and style was less important than substance.

I welcomed this pressure cooker, knowing I would thrive more so than most. I loved competition that was out in the open, honest, transparent, the better man winning a good fight. I did not fare nearly as well behind closed doors, where innuendo and deception were more valued than fact, where dirty tricks received high praise and subterfuge was a practiced art. The gridiron offered me a fair playing field to use my talents, those given and earned.

As my first day on the job approached, an honest self-assessment revealed a glaring gap in my skill set, something I had to address in this next role as offensive coordinator. I needed to up my political game, get smarter at sensing, responding, and even anticipating back room moves. I was not well versed in the black art of business politics, yet knew others who were highly skilled, including some of my corporate buddies. I had no intention, nor need for that matter, to torpedo a colleague, I just needed better antenna so I knew the plays others would attempt. I thought, *This offensive coach needs to play better defense or risk losing the coaching game.*

I entered the stadium to check out the field, a good first day boost before the new gig began. In the middle of the field on the fifty-yard line sat a man on a yoga mat. He was in some kind of pose, thankfully not a downward doggie or whatever the correct term. I sat in the stands and observed his peaceful routine, wondering who the heck might be doing yoga on the football turf, at mid-field no less. *He has some balls or nerve or both*, I thought. He finished the exercise, picked up the mat, and began to walk toward me. "You must be Bob, our new offensive genius. Welcome to State."

"Hi. Sorry, not sure I caught your name."

"It's Tom. Tom Norman, Special Teams Coach."

"Hello Tom. Did I interrupt your yoga exercise, Coach?" I stuck out my hand ready for a firm shake.

Tom laughed, more a chuckle than a laugh really. He took my right hand with both of his hands and moved in, nearly chin to chin. He looked me over; his eyes looked up and down then across from right to left, which seemed backwards to me. Then he finally spoke. "This is my one last chance for peace in this stadium, our battleground, our theater of play. Before each season begins, I warm up with a little yoga on the fifty-yard line. I take in the surroundings, and the quiet while I plan out my attack for the upcoming season. It's really amazing how peaceful an empty stadium can be, and it's unlikely you will hear this much quiet in the stadium for a while. I listen to the voices in the quiet; it's hard to hear at first, that's where the yoga comes in. It brings the voices."

"Huh, I never thought of it that way. Peaceful, quiet, a good fit for yoga to hear voices from an empty stadium? That's a new one on me Coach."

Tom grinned, then let out another chuckle. "The yoga is just to throw people off balance. No one would think of me being comfortable doing those poses and routines. I just like messing with the players and the other coaches. Gotta start the new season on the right foot, and the more people I can get off balance, the better my odds of sheer domination!"

Tom stepped away and finally released my hand; almost lending it back, as if it was his to make decisions over from now on. He had a warm sense about him, yet he was zany. I think that's the right word to describe Tom, zany. Then in an instant, his smile turned to a sneer; an evil character seemed to take over his body. I stood my ground unsure what to expect next.

"Coach, the peace won't last, not beyond today. Once practice begins and for the next five to six months after that, I plan to wreck havoc all over this place. That's our special team motto, wreck havoc! Grrrrrrr!"

And with that growl he was gone, up the ramp toward the lockers.

Wreck havoc, now that was a good motto for special teams, I thought. *Glad this guy is on our side.*

I spent a lot of time with Tom that first year, and each one after that. He was more of a hockey fan, enjoying the checking on the boards and the rough play in front of the goalie. But hockey did not pay very well so he applied the tenacity of hockey to football, figuring special teams was as close as he would get. He was a crazy person during a game; his eyes would nearly bulge out of his body as he yelled encouragement to his squad. Once in a while some hockey lingo would sneak into his vocabulary while he was growling at the boys to, "check him into the boards," or telling the ref the other team was hooking. His antics kept me in stitches throughout the season and our lifelong friendship that endured after our time together on the field.

There was a game in our second season that typified Tom's disregard for conservatism, and helped cement his reputation as one crazy coach:

♦♦♦♦

We were down by ten points with under a minute to go in the game. Our defense held the opposing team and forced a punt from their end zone. Most of our fans had left the stadium disappointed with the anticipated result against a team we were expected to beat handily. My performance had been subpar; the offense scored 24 points but turned the ball over three times. None of us were looking forward to breaking down game film of another loser. We had all but given up, players stared at their shoes or the empty seats, and neither provided any relief from the pain we all felt.

But Tom's mind worked differently than most. To him, we could make up the gap with just three good plays, a safety, followed by a touchdown, and then of course a two point conversion. That would put us in overtime with momentum on our side, the wind at our back. All we needed was a spark, or a miracle if we were being honest about it.

The opposing punter was a sophomore playing his first season in the college game. Tom pulled his squad together with a growl and went through his plan. He wanted to jam up the punter, force him out of his routine, make him adapt to pressure or surprise or both. Tom wanted, and even expected, the rookie punter to make a mistake, we just needed to give him a reason. I saw Tom's squad shaking their heads, not in frustration or disappointment, rather in amazement at the plan. These guys were stoked as they ran onto the field.

Tom ran up and down the sideline as the teams came to the ball, barking out orders to his unit. I could have sworn I heard Tom say something like power play, another hockey term, but was not sure. As the center gripped the ball ready to send it back to the punter, our team shifted student body left. Tom's plan was for ten of our guys to load up on one side of the ball, leaving only one person on the right. He was daring the other team to run or throw for a first down, challenging them to put away the game. A game that was already won, all the punter had to do was kick the ball forward, not even very far, just down the field, which was void of any player from our side. Tom had all eleven of our guys at the line.

Sure enough, as the punter grabbed the ball and saw all the daylight on his left, instinct must have taken over and he started to run. Just before the snap, Tom had three of his squad circle back around to our right side, now we had four on the right and seven on the left. The punter felt pressure on his right and ran toward the daylight he first saw on his left. But the gaps were closing quickly so the punter paused, a deadly pause in the end zone. He looked to throw the ball, but no one went out for a pass, so he opted for a punt on the run. He let go of the ball, expecting it to head for his foot and a punt down the field. But he was on the move, and to his left, away from his punting leg. Now it was all about the angles. Would his drop of the ball toward his right leg, while running left, come anywhere near his punting foot? Without much time to make the calculation, the rookie punter took his best guess. His leg came toward the ball and went high in the air past his right ear, but his body was torqued at a bad angle and he whiffed on the ball. The football bounded toward the side of the end zone and our players dove for the ball. This is where Tom's plan kicked into another gear. The defensive player's usual instinct is to fall on the ball and wrap it up tight into his belly for a recovery, but not this time. Tom had instructed his team to knock the ball out of the end zone, taking the two-point safety so we could get the ball back after the free kick.

Tom's squad went wild; they had executed the perfect surprise. The few remaining fans clapped politely, not knowing about Tom's three-part plan. Tom eyed me and walked down the sideline.

"One play done, two to go coach. Your ball!"

After the free kick we moved the ball to the opponent's 40-yard line with three seconds remaining in the game. We were out of time but not ideas. I was huddled with the QB and head coach as we worked out our play, ignoring the constant growls I kept hearing from Tom just a few yards away.

"Ok Bob, how do you plan to get us home?"

That was our head coach, putting the pressure on me. He was on borrowed time, as our season had not gone well, but I was eager to provide him relief, I had more time on the clock than he did.

I nodded to the coach and then looked at our QB

"Coach Tom taught us something with that safety, let's take a page from his book. Let's go trips right to the front corner of the end zone. Two of the ends go into the end zone, one stays back a few yards on the one or two yard line. Tell the two ends in the end zone to bat the ball pack to the one-yard line for a rebound play"

We got lucky and the rebound play worked, making me look like the hero for a brief moment, although I had only borrowed the idea from my buddy Tom. We were down by two points with no time on the clock, our point after touchdown try would be the last play in regulation. We ran a quarterback draw and the nose of the football crossed the line, our QB using every inch of the ball to tie the game.

Tom had nailed it. Three plays to close the gap in less than a minute to send us into OT with momentum now on our side. Too bad there were few fans remaining to enjoy the moment. We had the ball first in overtime and got to the five-yard line where it was fourth down and time to make a gutsy call. I wanted to go for the touchdown, putting everything on that one play. The head coach opted for a field goal, expecting our defense to hold our opponent to a field goal attempt to tie the game, and force a second OT.

We were back in Coach Tom's hands, the field goal unit ready to take the field. I could not see Tom, hidden from my view in the middle of his eleven guys. But I could hear the growling, it started deep and slow and grew into a blood-curdling yell. The field goal team took the field for a mere five-yard kick. Just like an extra point, which most teams make 99% or more of the time. Routine usually, but not when Zany Tom Norman is in the mix.

The snap from center was perfect, the hold was straight, the laces turned away from the kicker who moved toward the ball and planted his left foot. His right leg came down toward the ball and then shifted, hitting nothing but air, and he landed on his back with a thud. The placeholder had removed the ball and ran to the right behind two blockers who pulled on the snap. But the defense was ready; burned once before, they anticipated a trick. They were on to Coach Tom and wanted revenge. As the defenders swarmed around the placeholder at the four-yard line we knew the rouse had failed.

I glanced at Tom and did not see what I expected, he was not alarmed, nor concerned. Instead he was hyped up, jumping and running and of course growling. Our kicker had stayed on the turf after his whiff, but got up and ran to the left toward the end zone. The placeholder, our second string QB, heaved the ball high in the air across the field, toward the left side of the end zone. The toss was off mark, but our kicker was uncovered and easily adjusted to catch the ball at the three-yard line then walked into the end zone for the score. The remaining crowd went completely nuts, as did our entire sideline.

Our head coach did not react for a while, then shook his head and roared with laughter. That's when I knew. Coach Tom had not discussed the gamble with anyone; he just took the risk, a crazy bet with low odds. But that was Tom, not one to wear a belt or suspenders. He let it all hang out so to speak, always did and always would.

We won the game with a defensive stop and qualified for a bowl game with the minimum six wins that year, saving a few jobs for another round. Our offense had a great season, nearly doubling the points scored per game over the year before. Most people forget, or like me, choose not to remember, that my first year we scored fewer points than the prior season. In retrospect it was a brilliant move to set an easy baseline to beat in following years. I received a fair amount of credit, but always knew that second season belonged to Coach Tom and I made sure all the tap owners in town filled Tom's cup again and again. Of course I went to the pubs on a regular basis with Coach Tom, it was the least I could do to support a buddy.

++++

Coach Tom helped breathe life back into me through his crazy risk taking and overall zaniness. His zest for life showed on every play, in the locker room, and even in the office. He never cared what others thought, that's why he tried to throw people off with yoga on the 50-yard line. His zaniness was a mere reflection of himself as if he had turned a mirror around backwards so we could peek inside.

We all have a little craziness inside. Tom just let his out more than most, critics be damned.

Coach Tom Norman

Chapter 18

Offensive Coordinator

Amy and I spent seven wonderful years in Michigan and I learned a thing or two about management and the politics in the game I loved. I hate to admit it, but there was some backroom stuff going on, coaches trying to get a leg up to reach that next level and get a higher paycheck. I think it was the money that brought out the evil that resides in all of us. Most keep it in a bottle, but a few bad apples, well you know that saying, and we sure had some in the barrel. My challenge was to take a lesson from my buddies who had experienced or played the political game in the corporate world. *In other words, how do I not behave like Seth, or even Kevin for that matter?* Truth be told, I still had a lot of hope for Kevin. I admired his tenacity and respected his ideals, always did. I had a sense he was greatly impacted by our last meet-up and Harry's one-two knockout of Seth. Hell, Kevin was the one who had given Seth the boot, and I was betting they both felt it.

As for Seth, he became an important guidepost for me, as I learned the upper management game. When I saw or felt an underhanded move by another coach, I used Seth as my foil. I simply asked myself what would Seth do, and then proceeded to take the opposite path. It was a simple approach to a variety of complex problems, yet it worked consistently well and kept me on a positive track. I never thought I would say this, "Thanks Seth for showing me the way."

I created a list of challenges to overcome in my leadership position as offensive coordinator. I often asked myself, *how do I create a team-based environment that everyone buys into? How do I identify and weed out those bad apples before they poison everyone else? How can I help the head coach keep the competition on the field where it belongs, transparent, open, honest and away from the hallways and the locker room?*

Maybe I was too naïve for my own good, or maybe I wanted to believe too much in the good of my fellow man. I still had not figured that out, but I was driven, motivated by something good, never evil. I always aspired to win, more than I feared losing and am thankful for having that perspective. The other way around is to go through life looking over your shoulder all the time, being afraid of the hidden, wondering what evil lurks around the corner. I wanted to live with my windows wide open, taking in the fresh air, not closed and locked with the A/C blowing.

To me, open windows are a good metaphor for my coaching philosophy and style. That's how I would think about it when I couldn't sleep. If I were trying to solve a problem at the office, I would imagine the night breeze wafting through the bedroom. Yeah, I said office, that's how I felt about football for a while. It had become an office and no matter how much I resisted, I got sucked indoors where the windows did not open. It starved me of the oxygen I needed and I yearned to get out on the field and away from that office as much as I could. Windows wide open was how I thought of the gridiron. I was not a fan of the indoor stadium, which was becoming popular with professional teams. A natural turf field under sun or snow or whatever the weather brought on game day was what real football was about for me.

During the first few years in Michigan I kept my distance from the players, meaning I did not allow myself to get too attached to anyone in particular. I was still hesitant to open myself up as I had done with Jerrod and some of the other guys. I argued with myself to get back in the game with the kids, get closer to them, and get back on plan. But I couldn't make the dive; the water seemed tepid, and did not feel welcoming, which was my excuse. Truth was, I was being a coward. And although I only shared that truth with myself, Amy knew. She could always read me like a map and knew the routes and ramps I would take in life, often before I knew them myself. I think that's the sign of a good marriage, or rather a good spouse. I was not sure, just fortunate, since she's the only wife I would ever know, and that was more than ok with me.

I was not living up to my personal creed, with windows wide open, and it was suffocating me. But I did not know what to do about it. Amy shut the bedroom window one night and before I thought about getting lucky, she let me have it. "Bob, I never knew you to be one who waded in the shallow end of the pool, too afraid to get his hair wet. It's high tide and some of those boys need a man in their life. What are you going to do? Sit next to me and be protected by the coach's wife or get out there in the deep end and save some lives?"

Crap, I hated being read that easy, and Amy had the lingo down, challenging me with my own words. *That girl is gonna really get it one of these days, if I ever get brave enough to take her on*, I tried to convince myself. "Ames, I just don't know how to get things going again. I don't want to over reach and get between my coaches and their players. And, you know, I am not sure I want to get burned by a player."

"Honey, you are running away from the person you once were and it's eating away at your soul one day at a time. I can see it, sense it, and even smell it on you and it stinks."

"Ames, that's hitting below the belt."

"Yes it is, and I hope you felt it. I can't play the bad guy any longer, that's all I have left, but it needed to be said."

Ames got up and reopened the window and then looked back at me over her shoulder, and struck a pose that most men in the world would love to see. The good Ames was back, she had kicked me upside the head and I sorely needed it. Now she was signaling my favorite play, it was lights out time; we only ran this play in the dark.

I awoke the next morning a new man, well a refreshed man anyway, and drove to the office, I mean the field. Before joining the early morning meetings with the offensive coaches, I sat in the bleachers and listened to the quiet. I could not hear the voices Coach Tom felt; it must have been the yoga mat after all. However, I began to sense it was time. It was time for me to get back in the pool. Amy had challenged me last night, she took a risk and laid it all on the line just like I needed her to do. But she had one thing wrong. I was not in the shallow end afraid to go into deeper waters. Nope, that was not it. I wasn't even in the water at all was the problem. So my first step was to dip my toes and get wet. The deep end would need to wait until I had better bearings.

There were two people I selected as my projects, one a player and the other an assistant coach. It only seemed appropriate to work a deal at both levels, each with different types of challenges to overcome. Violence and politics were the issues I chose to face that season; some would say they were two sides of the same coin.

Marcus

Our starting running back was a stud, unfortunately he had more muscles than brains and he always led with his strength, while his mind played catch-up. Marcus was one of those players with "great potential;" if he could stay out of trouble he would earn his rewards. I'm not sure he looked for trouble off the field, but it sure found him and on a regular basis. Marcus knew how to handle himself and took pleasure in dishing out punishment; sometimes he even wore a helmet. He was the prototypical athlete attracted to the game so he could behave on the field as he did on the streets.

Violence was not becoming a problem in football, it had shifted from present tense to past tense a while ago but we failed to recognize it, or looked the other way, or both. It did not much matter, if we did not curtail the off field behavior we stood to lose control of the golden goose. Helping Marcus would be one of my contributions to the game. I knew we needed a good example of a turnaround play where a known violent person found a better path. This was a lot easier said than done.

Marcus was a fighter; he could have been a boxer, maybe a middleweight contender. He got in a lot of practice at the bars around town trading punches as if they were baseball cards. He was smart enough to not get caught, taking his bouts outside in the back alleys and streets. He drew a crowd on weekend nights, he thought they were friends but they just wanted to see some blood and it didn't matter whose.

◆◆◆◆

Marcus sometimes came to Monday football practice with his fists raw and bandaged from the weekend rounds. It never affected his running game; it was the passes dropped that hurt the team. I could not figure out how to help this kid, he would not talk especially not to a coach. So, I went out to the bars to meet Marcus on his other turf.

At the second bar I visited, I found him outside with three other guys. Lines had been drawn and the odds looked dim, three to one against. I pushed forward onto unfamiliar turf, and lowered my voice. "Hey Marcus, you doing ok out here?"

The three dudes turned to face me, and sized up the unwelcomed guest. Wearing school colors and sneakers gave me away; the dudes were not too worried about the intruder.

"Coach, what are you doing here? Not a good place to be man, I'll see you on Monday'"

I moved over to Marcus' side of the alley, and tried to keep cool. I slowly pulled my hands out of my jeans pockets and thought, 'What the hell am I doing here, about to get into a fight? I came here to stop Marcus not join him.' Then Mr. Ego reared his head and the words stumbled out of my mouth, "Got your back Marcus."

My voice pitched a few octaves higher than usual, revealing the inner strength of a teenage girl rather than a seasoned alley fighter. My instincts had taken over and demanded I behave as a man even though I sounded like a girl. 'Oh shit!'

Before Marcus could reply, two of the dudes went at him, the other glared at me. I had not been in a fight in years, well decades, it's easy to lose track of something you don't participate in, ever. But I was in great shape and if this is what it took to reach Marcus, then so be it. The third dude moved toward me, and all I could think of was Harry's one-two knockout of Seth. My mind yelled, 'one-two, yeah that's it. Chin then gut.'

Or was it gut then chin.

Chin then gut or gut then chin.

I was out of time and had to make my choice. I went for the gut with my left, an upper cut motion, making sure I kept my balance and pivoted off my right foot. As I began my move, I closed my eyes and hoped, well prayed, that I would connect. Luck was with me, the dude slipped as he approached and my upper cut that was aimed for his gut landed square on his right cheek, knocking him out cold. My only thought at the time was how much my hand throbbed.

I looked over at Marcus and saw him wiping the floor with both dudes who were on the ground. This fight thing was going much better than I expected and I turned to give Marcus a high five. Then I heard it.

"Coach, watch out!"

There was a fourth dude; he must have been hanging in the shadows. He moved quickly to my backside and smashed a bottle on the side of my head. I was out for the night and awoke in the emergency room with Amy at my side. Now my head hurt as much as my left hand but I knew there was a lot more pain headed my way.

"Hi Slugger. The doc says you will live, for the time being."

"Ames, I'll explain. Where's Marcus? Is he ok?"

"There's no one here but you slugger. Doc says some guy dropped you off then ran out before they could get his name."

Amy forced a confession from me and then extracted a promise. My fighting days were over; cut off after one punch, a knockout blow I might add. The judges would have scored it a TKO in the first round! I didn't tell anyone that I closed my eyes, why take a reputation hit unnecessarily?

What mattered is I scored some points with Marcus, and we began to talk. He gave up the fighting so long as I promised not to tell anyone about our evening together in the alley. 'Deal!'

I thought things were going well for a while, one banged up head and a broken hand was a price worth paying if I could save Marcus and help curtail some of the off field violence that was hurting our game. I felt pretty good about myself until Amy made it clear how lucky I had been and something about Taylor needing a father. Amy hit home with all her points, her eyes wide open, not closed like her slugger husband.

A few weeks later, Marcus robbed a store with a loaded handgun, the owner was ready and shot Marcus in the hip. He now wore an orange jumpsuit, every game a home game, at least for the next five years.

✦✦✦✦

I had failed in so many ways with Marcus and racked my brain trying to figure out what I could have done better or differently. Nothing came to me, other than how naïve I had been and how much I risked in that alley. I thought I was being a man when I joined the fight to save Marcus, but it was a very foolish move. I had risked too much, way too much as Amy reminded me. If I wanted to save a kid, I needed to do it on my turf where I could apply skills and smarts, not some back alley where Lady Luck might not show.

Amy may have had the best insight on my failure as she often did. "Bob, did you work with Marcus from his perspective or your own?"

"Not sure what you mean Ames?"

"Step back for a moment. It seems as if your focus with Marcus started with the football team and the possibilities and opportunities it brought to him after college."

"Yeah, that's right. What's wrong with that?"

"Nothing is wrong necessarily, I'm just saying you

don't take into account anything about Marcus before he joined the team. What was his family life like? What was school like for him? How did the community he grew up around shape the way he thought and behaved?"

"We check out the players we recruit very carefully." I was starting to sound and feel very defensive and Amy was only trying to help.

"Honey, I'm sure you do. But I bet most of your research is about their skills as players and their attitudes based on what their coach says about them. I know you meet with parents, and school friends as well, but do you truly understand these boys? A lot of them come from very difficult backgrounds, and honestly, we have no real idea how their environment affects them as people."

"You're saying I did not understand Marcus the person as much as Marcus the football player."

"I'm just saying it's very hard to get underneath the person, to truly understand what shapes them as individuals. Especially kids from troubled families, poor environments, and perhaps an upbringing around crime. We are so lucky to not have been exposed to that when we were growing up."

"Ames, a lot of the kids grew up in difficult environments, that's true. But I'm not a social worker, there's only so much I can do."

"I know dear, but when you invest in some of these kids, like Marcus, the ones you truly go to bat for, you might have a better chance understanding them, reaching them, and impacting their behavior, if you knew how they grew up."

I didn't know what to do with Amy's advice at the

moment; I filed it away for another day, still wondering what I would do differently.

Brian

Our quarterback coach was a young hotshot, (much like yours truly a bunch of years ago). He was jilted by the pros after seven years, riding the bench, coming ever so close to his dream. He was shook up by this failure and determined to make up for lost time in the coaching ranks, looking to move up quickly, doing whatever it took to make the grade. Brian was a little too proud of his QB heritage and his ego filled the empty stadium as players were told and retold heroic tales. Brian allowed his trumped up self-image to get ahead of his capabilities on a regular basis, or so it seemed.

++++

We were breaking down game tape one Monday evening, Brian, the other offensive coaches, our three QBs and me. We had lost the game and heads were bowed low. Each time our offense blew a play, Brian would say something such as, "I knew we should have run a different play", or, "I told Coach to try it my way." It was unnerving, but I let it go, no benefit would be gained ripping into Brian in front of everyone else. I would save it for our one on one later in the week. But Brian did not let it rest, he went to the head coach with his view of the tapes and how he would have managed the game, implying I was at fault for the loss. It looked like we had a back room maneuver going on in my football family.

I needed a plan of attack and my emotions stepped in to call the play. I visualized the potential play in my head, and it wasn't pretty. Brian was on his backside sucking air and there was blood on the floor. I enjoyed the moment, and then asked to see the next play. This one had Brian carrying boxes to his car, his office packed, his last paycheck in a back pocket. That sight looked pretty good to me, but it was not right. That's when I asked myself, 'What would Seth do?' I needed a teaching moment from a buddy and his name was the first that came to mind. Go figure.

I guessed that Seth would play a better back room game than Brian. My inner dialogue told me that Seth would meet with the head coach and spin a web about Brian's poor performance over a period of weeks and months, setting him up for the firing line. It would be a slow and quiet death for Brian, never quite knowing what or whom had hit him, allowing Seth to enjoy the process as much as the end result. I got sick to my stomach thinking of Seth's plan to handle Brian. Then I got inspired. I asked myself, 'What is the opposite of what Seth would do?'

Brian and I had our one on one's each Wednesday. Although I had to be patient for nearly two days, I held my breath and waited until we were behind closed doors. "Hey Brian, come on in, let's have a chat."

We did a verbal dance for a while and then I moved the conversation to the elephant that walked in with Brian. "Brian, I listened carefully to your criticism during the tape breakdown session on Monday. You did not hold anything back that night."

"No Coach, not my style. I call 'em as I see 'em."

"Yeah, that's what I thought too. But the thing that troubled me Brian is you don't make any suggestions at practice during the week. You keep everything back, and then let the criticism roll. Why is that?"

"Coach, can I be honest here? You don't listen to me. You don't seem to care about anything I have to say."

I didn't think that was true, but it didn't matter. His perception was that I boxed him out. I knew I had something to work with as a result. "Ok Brian, tell you what. Why don't we work on the plays together during the week at practice? That way, we will both have some skin in the game and we can be our own best critics afterwards. What do you say?"

Damn, that was not an easy concession for me. I felt as if I was giving in more than he was, but I was determined to pull him out in the open. I left it to him to make the choice to partner up and be a good teammate, or continue his deception.

Brian let my offer hang in the air, unsure how to respond. After a few moments he said, "Coach, why are you doing this? You must realize I want your job and I'll do anything it takes to get it. Why are you being kind to me, there must be a trick here I don't see yet."

'There we go, finally some honesty. This I know how to handle,' I thought.

"Brian, I hope you do get my job someday, but you are going about it the wrong way. You're too impatient, too egotistical, and not very trustworthy. Going behind my back to the head coach is not going to win you many fans."

He gave me a puzzled look.

'Did he really not think I knew about his deception?' I wondered.

"Listen, here's the deal. I'd love to teach you what I know, share my experience and knowledge and in return I'd love to learn from you. I never made it to the pros like you did, and I know you have a lot to share. But we need to be on the same side for that to happen."

I could tell Brian needed some time to decide if I was being genuine or setting him up. I was willing to give him some time, but not a lot.

It took a few days for Brian to make his move. He was subtle at first and wanted to test my offer before fully accepting it. He started calling out plays during practice, normally my role alone in front of the players. I supported him on the first three suggestions, letting it sink in a bit more with each play he called. On the fourth suggestion, I changed the play. This was going to be a partnership not a takeover.

We found a way to make it work and cemented a good working relationship based on respect and trust. We were not buddies; our styles and tastes were too different for that to occur. The best outcome from our teaming up approach was that our offense got better, a lot better. The players fed off the good vibe from the coaches and Brian's creativity. He had a lot of great plays stuck in his head and only needed an invitation to let them out. He was good, damn good.

✦✦✦✦

I took a lesson from the experience with Brian on how to be a better manager, a better leader, how to adapt my style and thinking so others could participate more fully. I learned to share the spotlight, giving credit to others for the benefit of themselves and the team. Initially, I viewed Brian as a competitor, someone to knock down, to keep away from the things I wanted. Over time, through some peaks and some valleys, I learned to treat Brian as a colleague, someone to trust, to work with for the betterment of the team.

After a few years together, Brian and I had the offense in a groove. We went through a very innovative period and put a lot of points on the scoreboard. We opened up the playing field with our no-huddle approach, and our team was always in better shape than the opposing D. Brian deserved a lot of the credit and he had earned my job.

Chapter 19

20-Year Meet-up

Mike had the ball for our 20-year meet-up and surprised us with his hosting site selection, Austin, Texas. We did not know much about the Lone Star State and its capital city, but we were sure fired up about the trip. We stayed downtown on 6th Street in an old historic place called The Driscoll Hotel. I was pretty sure that most of the guys had forgotten Mike had dated a girl in high school named Barb, a tall, slender beauty who went to the University of Texas, taking Mike's heart with her.

We played a few rounds on a riverside Golf Course, and also took full advantage of Austin's reputation as the Live Music Capital spending most of our time in the bars, clubs, and theater venues. I was in my element in this town; music had become a passion of mine over the years, my interests and tastes expanded almost as fast as the size of my stereo, as Amy often reminded me. Developing a deep interest in a hobby is not much different from a career; it requires attention, hand-holding, and a lot of investment. That was my argument and Ames let it slide, she enjoyed the tunes almost as much as me.

After our previous reunion, we were all surprised that Seth joined us for the meet-up. We were tentative around him all weekend, unsure how to make him feel welcome. As we approached the final evening, we knew he liked going first, so Mike asked Seth to stand and tell us a story.

Seth told us a different type of failure, not really a personal story, rather a failure of his company. Seth tried to save the job of a friend who had been laid off, or to quote Seth's corporate speak "he was surplus." Fred, Seth's friend, had recently returned to the United States from an overseas assignment where he ran the IT operations for a large national bank. Fred and his wife lived in Paris for two years, enjoying the experience, and came home when the company needed him back. Fred did a bang-up job on the overseas assignment as expected. He had been a strong performer his entire career. A few short months after returning home, Fred was working a variety of tasks, awaiting a permanent role. And then it hit. Fred found his name on some list with a 30-day clock ticking, the amount of time given to find a job somewhere in the firm, or be out on the streets. Fred had given 32 years of top-notch service, a loyal employee who had defended the company when it was down, and stayed true to the firm when it needed him most. The 30 days went by quickly and Fred was out of luck, sitting at home wondering what had hit him. Fred learned a hard lesson: trust is only between people who have good intentions for each other.

Mike shook his head, a common reaction to a Seth story. "I don't get it Seth, how does your company layoff a valued employee like Fred?"

"It's part of our cleansing; every few months there is a layoff somewhere in the company. We got the process down pat after years of practice. It used to be a big thing, but that was ten years ago. Now, it's like getting the morning coffee and reading the paper."

Harry refused to buy that nonsense. "That's absurd Seth. It's not like Fred was some flunky, you said he was a top performer. Why let one of the good ones go?"

"In theory, we let go of the poor performers years ago when our company was in the ditch for a decade. Now that we are healthy, it's all about managing the bottom line. If we have too much resource in a particular part of the company, we pull the layoff trigger. The surplus guns are always loaded; it does not take much for a division CFO to call a layoff play."

Scott was curious about Fred, "Have you stayed in touch with Fred?" he asked. "What's he doing now?"

"Well, that's the ironic part. About six months after being laid off, Fred received a call saying we could use someone with his skills on a project. Fred was hired back as a temporary employee; I believe it was a three month project."

Kevin could not believe what he was hearing. "Wait a minute, let me get this straight. Your company laid-off Fred and just six months later he was hired back as a temp, not a full time regular employee?"

"Yep, that's right. You see, the company had no one available with Fred's skills and we needed someone like him for a critical project. So we were able to hire him back solely for the duration of the project, and only pay him a fraction of his prior pay as a full timer, and with minimal benefits. It's a great trick to keep the costs down, the margins high, and increase the stock price."

I could not believe Seth made that last statement with an egotistical edge and an aura of pride. He knew the ongoing stream of corporate layoffs buttered his bread and stock options, giving the CFO ammunition at the quarterly earnings call. It seemed a shallow game to me, one played with jagged knives and an unaware conscience. *Watch out Seth boy; keep honing your political skills, or you could be the next one kicked to the curb*, I thought.

I wanted to know why Seth's company behaved this way. They had such a great reputation. "Seth, do you really believe toying with good employees like Fred makes any kind of sense? I thought your company had a set of values, or beliefs, and one of them was something like respect for each person. How is this example consistent with that belief?"

"I joined the firm through an acquisition, so that history does not mean very much to me. It could be that we had values or beliefs like you mentioned, I just don't know. What I do know is today it's all about the numbers. And Fred was just a number, it's not personal."

That's when I wondered how hard Seth really worked to help save Fred's job. Once Fred was on the list, his destiny seemed predetermined, down the chute and watch out below.

Scott opined, "Well, I think it was very personal to Fred."

"What's next for Fred, have you kept up with him?"

Mike asked.

"He'll finish out the temp project and then probably get a bunch of offers from our competitors. He's that good."

Scott had studied a lot of firms in his job and wanted to know more. "Why all the layoffs Seth? Your firm has axed a lot of people; does anyone know how to right the ship?"

"Our strategy is pretty clear; we buy it rather than build it. So long as we keep buying revenue streams and customer bases we don't need to grow our own."

I could not believe this approach would be favored by the loyalists who had stuck with the firm all these years. "If you've given up on the aging businesses, why would any employees hang around and wait for the axe to fall?" I asked.

"Good question. There are a lot of stupid people who are blinded by their loyalty to the firm and never see it coming. They actually believe their dedication to the company is valued and fail to realize the transition we are going through will cost a lot of them their livelihoods. They don't realize a lot of general managers are running these aging businesses into the ground because they have no idea how to develop a new strategy or new business model. Instead of fixing the old, they buy something shiny and new. It may or not work, but it gives the general manager another few years at the helm. That's why I keep moving around."

Harry smiled and offered a thought, "Seth, you and your firm remind me of a story I once heard, but I don't know the author.

"A man was flying in a hot air balloon and soon realized he was lost. He reduced his height when he spotted a man

below. *'Excuse me, can you tell me where I am?'*

The man below said, 'You're in a hot air balloon hovering thirty feet above this field.

'You must be an engineer,' the balloonist said.

'I am,' the man replied. 'How did you know?'

'Well,' said the balloonist, 'everything you have told me is technically correct, but it's no use to me.'

The man below said, 'You must be in management.'

'I am,' replied the balloonist, 'but how did you know?'

'Well,' the man said, 'you don't know where you are or where you're going, but you expect me to be able to help. You're in the same position you were before we met, but now it's my fault.'"

We had a laugh and another round, even Seth seemed to acknowledge the shallow truth in Harry's tale.

Kevin stood; his turn was next; he was still shaking his head about Seth's story. He was acting president for a firm in Atlanta, owned by the private equity company he worked for. Kevin's role was to swoop in, reduce costs, improve margins and "pretty up" the firm to be sold at a profit. Kevin was very good at this role; it required brains and balls, some would say his best traits. I expected another success story with the PE firm raking in a substantial profit on the backs of laid off employees. Kevin had inherited a mess; the firm was in the red from years of bad luck and worse management. His team had prepared the customary proposal, using an axe to bludgeon the bloat; quickly improving the bottom line for would be suitors. Another easy path lay ahead for Kevin and his team, the pattern set from prior deals.

Kevin stared at the list of names, 187 victims whose lives would suddenly change, perhaps forever. Pen in hand, the layoff pronouncement ready to go; his team was anxious to get started on another "Black Friday." But Kevin paused; perhaps it was guilt that piled up for years, he knew deep inside there was a better way. Kevin was not ready; he hesitated then laid down the pen. Rather than taking the quick hit path to improving margins through cost reductions, Kevin thought he could take a different route by increasing revenues. It would take longer; require more work, more risk and more patience from investors. It would also require many of the 187 pink slippers to remain on the payroll, their skills needed for the revised road ahead.

Kevin commuted to Atlanta every week for a long three years to implement the higher risk plan. He convinced the private equity company to take the revenue route and was logging miles, paying the price of his own proposal. The 187 pink slips had been reduced to 70 unavoidable hits, each with a severance and job-hunting assistance. The revenue route had worked, the employees rallied under Kevin's leadership, the change in management somehow inspired good luck. The company had recently been sold at a solid profit, higher than the cost reduction path alone would have derived. Kevin was fully spent after his story, and I proudly led our buddies in a toast to his new approach.

Seth and Kevin both discussed corporate layoffs, a common event occurring around the country. After their stories concluded, the guys in the room grilled Seth, yet Kevin was cheered. Both of them talked about impacts to the bottom line and expectations of their firms, with layoffs an everyday tool to achieve the needed monetary benefits.

Seth's firm had used a blunt instrument with no regard to human impact, and then toyed with their prey to gain a financial leg up. Fred was a mere convenience, an abled body who was expendable for short-term gain. The firm had no embarrassment in rehiring Fred as a part timer; they simply added a pawn back on the board for a temporary period of time. Kevin had bucked policy norm and taken a longer-term view at great personal risk. He did not take the revenue route solely to save employees; rather he visualized a better outcome for everyone involved by growing the business and pruning costs where necessary. He displayed compassion along with brains, although he certainly knew which of his body parts were on the line.

I was proud of Kevin, he chose to shape the environment he worked in; Seth was content to live in his.

During my turn at the mic, I talked about my 1-1 record in handling Marcus and Brian. I thought of Marcus as a bad loss and Brian as a solid win.

As I described the challenge with Brian, Seth interrupted, "Did you ask what would 'The Mayor' do?" he chided.

"Seth, it's only a burn if you are creative about it. Asking me what The Mayor would do is just too easy."

Seth just sat there with no comeback. I had to give him credit for showing up; if nothing else this guy had some guts, even though he kept leading with his chin. *Silly boy.*

"I didn't ask what The Mayor would do, instead I asked a much better question, something you taught me Seth."

Seth was having an uh-oh moment and I hate to admit,

I was thoroughly enjoying it. I chose my path and let him have it, again. "I asked what would Seth do?"

Harry could not believe what I said. "What would Seth do? Are you nuts?" he asked.

"Yeah, I asked myself what would Seth do, and then did the opposite. See, Seth you have influenced my behavior and I thank you."

All the guys cracked up; they tried to hide it at first, but were spitting out their beers in no time. Seth was not a happy camper, but he took it. After all, it wasn't like last time when he ran into Harry's fists. This time he just listened and it dawned on me he was trying to figure out a new path for himself, but he had no idea how to change. I had struck a low blow, which felt great at first, then the guilt washed over me and I needed to atone. But not now, I took a mental note for later, maybe much later.

Harry was up next and edged past Seth a bit too close, we braced for a rematch. No such luck, we would need to make our own entertainment for the evening. Harry had finally tied the knot, marrying a girl he actually had to chase, a new experience that resulted in a clear success for his bride and him. In the months following his marriage, Harry kept in shape by eluding the office chase, turning down what were once sure bets. I never asked, but was fairly certain Harry saved a lot of marriages by taking himself off the playing field. It was not much of a sacrifice for Harry, he had chosen well.

"Boys, marriage is a wonderful elixir for me. It's early, but I can already tell it will be a potent drug. I would have given up all those chases long ago if I only knew."

Scott laughed. "Atta boy Harry, welcome to the club. Let's see how you feel in a few years. Hell, what am I saying, we are nearing 20 soon!"

I could only think we were witnessing a real milestone. "Harry off the board, there's something kinda sad about that." I said.

Kevin said, "Wilt had nothing on you Harry; I bet you could have beaten his record if you stayed in the game."

Mike pulled us all together, "Gents, this calls for a toast. Harry, may your best years be ahead of you!"

Cheers for Harry went around the room, even Seth got in on the action.

✦✦✦✦

Austin was a grand host city, imprinting a lasting image in my mind, a town of great character now being weighed down by concrete and steel, trying to resist, or perhaps balance, its shift into a big city. It was a struggle worth watching, as both sides, town and city, seemed to be winning.

Here's the tally after our 20-year meet up:

Primary Yardstick: Money
Scott: Pass
Kevin: Pass
Mike: Pass
Harry: Pass
Seth: Pass
Me: Pass

Secondary Yardsticks:
Me: Kids Saved
Scott: Retirees Saved
Mike: Jailhouse Sentences Saved
Kevin: Jobs Saved
Harry: Marriages Saved
Seth: None

Kevin came to play at this meet-up and I gave him full credit for saving jobs. I'm not sure what brought about the change in him; maybe he was taking some lessons from his buddies. I realized that all of us could learn a lot from these meet-ups.

To me it was the real Kevin finally getting back out in the open. Those sharp elbows were not retired by any means, now they were balanced by a softness I had not seen in a long time. It would not surprise me if he started writing songs again, I bet he had a lot stored up.

Chapter 20

Head Coach at the U

We dropped the ball.

I was back at the U, now as head coach, reviewing player personnel for the upcoming season. Late summer practice started in two weeks, our defense was in great shape with seven returning starters and talented underclassmen competing for the open spots. The offense was a bit porous, only three starters were returning, with one true quarterback. We had a gaping hole at the helm and were scrambling to fill it.

Alice flagged me down and said, "Coach, Mike Harding is on the phone for you. Says he is a buddy from school days."

"I'll call him back Alice; too busy looking for a QB now."

"Mike says you will want to talk to him."

I relented and went in and took the call. "Hi Mike," I said.

"Hey Bob. You gotta get up here. One of my clients is headed to the slammer, I have a chance to keep him out of the hole, but need your help."

"Mike, I'd love to help you, but I'm kinda busy build-ing my team for next year. We start practice soon and I got some holes to fill."

"Coach, it's time for a favor."

"Come on Mike, I'm flat out, can't do you a solid right now. Can I help you with the next one?"

"Coach, you don't get it. I am doing you a favor. Your future QB is sitting right here in front of me. Get on up here and let's work this one out. Trust me on this one."

I hung up and called for my QB coach to send him to Chicago. Then I replayed the phone conversation in my head. I could not think of the last time, anytime for that matter, that Mike said, "Trust me." If Mike were hoisting a baseline shot to win the game from the corner, I would have trusted him. Judg-ing football talent, especially at QB, where character and lead-ership mattered as much as talent, there were very few people I trusted with that.

Three hours later I was in the city, looking for Mike and his QB. I found them in the county courtroom, Mike was argu-ing with the judge, waving his arms in the air. Mike's client sat at the table, crammed into a chair not up to the task of containing him. He turned to the side and I recognized Mike's QB.

We knew about Vince, had a file on him and threw it in the trash. His reputation ran ahead of his fast legs, preceding him like a shadow early in the day. He lacked discipline, was unresponsive to coaches, ran into trouble with the law, and was rumored to be a father twice over. His off field antics stopped recruiters from viewing the game tapes, where Vince excelled when he showed up. His was a game of beauty, running and throwing at will, the defenders were mere pawns for Vince to move around the board as he pleased.

Vince was trouble, a red X on recruiting boards across the state and Midwest. He was not even lightly recruited by the big schools, and probably did not care. Vince had no parents to guide him, living with an uncle more interested in the dogs at the track than the kid in his house. Vince mostly raised himself, shaped by the streets, ready to live and die in the gutters.

Mike turned and saw me in court with my arms out wide, my mouth agape, saying 'what the hell?' I tried to turn and run, my head was yelling, *Fire, please escape to the exit, pronto.* My feet felt differently, sticking to the courtroom floor, choosing not to respond, not yet anyway. I was conflicted, losing an argument with myself, not even knowing which side I was on. Mike asked for a short recess, which was granted by an irritated judge.

"Bob, hear me out on this."

"You gotta be kidding me, Mike. This kid is a jailbreak away from his next meal."

"Listen, I know Vince, he's been at my table more than once. He's got no one in his corner, been that way most of his life. No structure, no discipline, and no rules to guide him. We should not be surprised that he's in the system."

"Then you take care of him, what do you want me to do?"

Mike looked at me, as the judge called him back to court. "I want you to give him a scholarship Bob, and teach him how to be a man. He needs someone like you, someone more than a father figure. And from what I hear, you need a QB."

Bang. Bang. The judge's gavel had no patience.

"And Bob, here's the hardest part. You have to decide now, right now, or the judge will lock Vince up. So you know, I would bet on this kid. Put him in the right environment and he's an all-star waiting to happen."

Mike turned and headed back to the judge and his client. He had passed me the ball and my feet were still stuck in the same place, not able to budge in any direction. The internal argument in my head pounded back and forth. The low risk route was out the courtroom door, no blemish on my recruiting record, no hassle from the alumni or the administration. I could sleep at night knowing my job was safe, probably winning the minimum six games to squeeze into some potato chip bowl in mid-December. The high-risk route was the opposite, attempt to save the kid, break him down, build him up, and pray he stays out of jail. This path would result in a great deal of criticism from alumni, the school president, and the talking football heads at ESPN. I could be a laughing stock, risking my reputation and the school's on a down and out kid who no one wanted. But, and it was a big but, we probably had a better chance of winning more games if Vince became our QB.

The head pounding continued. *Save the kid or keep my job. Risk the kid or risk my job. Potato chip bowl or Rose Bowl. Who was I kidding, Rose Bowl?*

"*Bang. Bang,* the gavel reverberated. "Is there anyone present who will speak for Vince?"

Mike looked over his shoulder, urging me to step forward. "Bob, it's now or never."

Bang. Bang. "Vincent, please rise."

Save the kid or risk my job.

"Vincent, the court finds ..."

It would be in character for me to make the safe play, just like on the field, to punt on fourth down, or kick the extra point to seal the tie. *Make the safe play,* my head screamed to my feet. *Turn toward the door, do not pass go, and get the hell home. Don't be an idiot* rang through my head.

There was a lot more at stake in the courtroom than I encountered on the field. A kid's life was in the balance and I wondered if I had the character, the courage to go for it, to risk it all for some kid I did not know. All I had to go on was Mike's trust, and the game tapes. I did remember Vince on those tapes.

The judge paused, gavel in hand, ready to rule. *This whole charade has to be a set-up,* I thought. I was convinced that Mike and the judge were in cahoots. Nothing else made sense. Truth was, I need another QB on the team and everyone in the room knew it. *Damn, I never did like potato chip bowls.* My feet moved, telling me which way we had decided to go.

"Your honor, I am here to vouch for Vince."

I thought the judge would be more surprised, and knew for certain Mike had set this up in advance, telling the judge there was a good chance I would speak on behalf of Vince and give him a scholarship to the U. That meant Vince would not be on the city streets, he would be 200 miles away, which was all the judge cared about. Of course Mike had worked a deal behind the scenes, otherwise there was no way a judge would let a stranger vouch for a kid he didn't know. That was the only scenario that made sense to me.

Vince never looked at me during the proceedings; his

stone face masked any attempt at emotion. He stared straight ahead, hands clasped, back straight in the chair. He did not seem nonchalant, more perturbed that others would be deciding his fate. He was not accustomed to anyone caring, or spending time on his needs. His biggest concern was probably his next meal, not the rest of his life.

Outside the courtroom, I huddled with Mike and he introduced me to Vince. We did not talk at first, simply shook hands and connected eyeballs, sizing up each other's manhood. I took Vince home to his uncle's apartment, to collect his things. A small bag of clothes and a pair of gym shoes later, we were back on the road headed to the U. We both needed the quiet drive, to gear up for the battle ahead.

As we drove on in silence, I thought of Mike. He had made another jailhouse save, I could only feel that I was aiding and abetting. The potato chip bowl was starting to sound better by the mile, as I rehearsed my speech for the athletic director and his boss, the university president.

My chances were good with the AD; he used to serve me cold ones back in the day. Big Willy had attained his dream gig a couple of years ago and then recruited me to join him at the U. I did not make him work very hard, we both knew where we belonged and wanted to be. I knew immediately that working for Willy would be a treat. *If I played my cards right the tap would continue to flow*, I told myself.

My bigger concern at the moment was explaining how Mike was involved in this transaction to give Vince a scholarship. Mike and Willy had a history and they bet on everything. They bet on basketball shots. They bet on card games. One day they even bet on who could eat the most hamburgers in a single hour. Mike took that one, although Willy lodged a protest since Mike conveniently went to the men's room clearing his plumbing to win by two. I could never tell who was ahead from all their wagers, and doubted they really kept score, the only thing that mattered was who won the last bet.

I called Willy the next day. "Hey Willy, we need to talk. You got a couple minutes?"

"Sure, what's up Bob? But you gotta start calling me Tom like all the other adults around here."

I thought, *Tom instead of Willy, fat chance. I'm fine removing the Big from his real nickname, Big Willy, but Tom is just not gonna happen.*

"Willy, I have good news and bad news. First the good, we found a QB and he's here on campus under scholarship."

Willy knew better, he let the Tom request go by the wayside. Calling a buddy by his old nickname is like muscle memory. Not only was it earned; it was well worn and practiced. "Ok, that's great, now give me the bad news."

"The bad news is I had to spring him from Cook County Court yesterday. Mike gave me the lead on this kid." I took Willy through Vince's story, his troubled past, and his football skills.

Willy listened politely and when I finished, he hit the roof. "I can't believe it! No frigging way. This is not happening!"

"Calm down Willy, this will work. I will handle Vince, you don't need to get involved in this at all."

"I'm not yelling about Vince, damn it! That's your decision Bob, I promised to never get involved in recruiting. I'm pissed because I lost a bet to Mike, the son of a bitch called me a week ago and bet me a C-note he would find our next QB. How the hell did he know? He's going to lord this over me all season!"

Willy was still cussing up a storm as he slammed down the phone. I just shook my head and laughed, thinking of Mike scheming for a week to win a bet from Big Willy. I made a mental note to be in the vicinity when Willy paid off the hundred he owed, knowing Mike would spend it freely at the nearest bar around.

Chapter 21

Vince and Zach

It was a brilliant idea, one of my very best. Or it was crazy, one of my worst. I was determined to get ahead of the V train and after careful deliberation, all ten seconds of it, I put Vince and Zach together in a two bedroom dorm. They could be Yin and Yang, or a bull and bear, any opposite pairing seemed to work. To me they were just V and Z, both at the back of the alphabet, with a lot to prove. The polite suburban kid, all work and no talent with the street city kid, skills galore yet no discipline. If nothing else, the entertainment value for me and the other coaches would be well worth it. I tried to ignore the side bets being placed by the assistant coaches, not wanting to know the odds given for this pair's survival.

I had a small wooden sign built and hung it in Vince's locker. It was a famous John Wooden quote that seemed appropriate:

Talent is God given. Be humble.
Fame is man-given. Be grateful.
Conceit is self-given. Be careful.

It did not matter to me that John Wooden was from a different sport, the man had game and showed his brilliance to anyone who would watch or better yet, listen. I checked Vince's locker the next day and saw it still hanging, a good sign. I did not put anything in Zach's locker, uncertain how long he would be around, yet hoping to see him succeed. The offensive line coach was reluctant to give Zach a shot and for good reason, it was against my rules and reeked of favoritism, something I railed against. I tossed a hot one in the coach's lap and walked away, hoping he would do the right thing.

V and Z were more than roommates that year, they were QB and Center, and no closer relationship existed on the field than those two positions. Vince had large hands, very large hands with very long fingers and he would use them ever so craftily to annoy Zach. Vince was a practical joker and could get under Zach's skin, figuratively and literally, much to the delight of the other players.

++++

During one practice that first season, the offensive line coach was berating the offensive lineman about offsides penalties. We were having some trouble getting off the ball together, wrecking our rhythm and the penalty yards were piling up. I brought this item to his attention in my usual snide way, said something to the effect that our offense was the only one in the conference that had to get 15 yards for a first down since we always started each series with a damn offsides penalty.

It didn't matter that Zach was fighting for third string; every lineman was getting the treatment that day. Vince was in at QB for a few plays and Zach gave our first stringer a breather. Zach was more than excited to get in on the action and tripped on his way to the huddle, causing a stir from the coaches and muddled laughs from the other players. Unfortunately, he hit the turf right in the middle of the offensive line coach's rant. Not a good start for Zach.

Vince saw an opportunity and took it. The offense came to the ball with Zach at center and Vince at QB. Vince yelled out the formation and just before the snap, his right pinkie twitched along Zach's upper thigh. Zach exploded forward before it was time to hike the ball, as clear an offsides penalty as there could be. The line coach went ballistic, yanking Zach's helmet right, then left, then up, and then down. It was a mess.

On the next play, Vince shook things up, this time grazing Zach's left thigh causing another stir and Zach plowed ahead once again. The line coach let Zach have it, finally asking him what the hell was causing him to always be offsides.

Zach just stood there, not wanting to respond, he just wanted to escape back to the huddle where it was safe.

"Damn it Zach, I asked you a question. Why were you offsides two damn plays in a row? Give me an answer."

Now Zach had to reply, though he still wasn't sure what to say. Finally he let it out, "He's tickling me coach."

"What? Tickling you? Who's tickling you?"

"Vince is tickling me on the thigh. First the right thigh then the left."

Now the other players were on the ground, no longer trying to hide their laughter. Everyone but Vince; he was just standing there tossing the ball from one large hand to the other

"First the right thigh, and then the left thigh. Huh, are you saying Vince is an equal opportunity thigh tickler Zach?"

That's when the coaches lost it and the laughter became a roar. The line coach went up to Vince, and eyed him over. "Vincent, I am glad to hear you do not have an aversion to Zach's thighs and that you treat both of them equally. Now are you ready to get back to work and stop tickling Zach here? He can't take that kind of punishment."

"Yes sir, Coach, I'll be more careful."

"Alright let's go again and this time no damn offsides, or every player is running steps until they puke! That includes you V."

Steps were the stadium steps, a punishing drill when needed. Players who needed a little extra care and attention, meaning some discipline, would be forced to run the stadium steps, up and down until the coach felt the lesson had been delivered effectively.

I heard third hand about the noises coming from V and Z's room that evening, there were a few bruises on both boys the next day at practice, though only one ego had taken a hit. I was starting to regret my decision to make them roommates, but said the heck with it and let it ride. Over the ensuing days and weeks ahead the coaches doubled down on their bets, the easy money on a break-up.

◆◆◆◆

Another issue the two of them had to overcome was, of all things, music. Teammates would approach V and Z's room only to hear dueling genres blaring from each side of the room, neither roommate willing to acquiesce to the other's taste. V was a city boy and rap music was his thing while Z was more a country boy, and he enjoyed some twang. It was worse than oil and water, these opposing tastes played at full blast, not quite mixing as well as the budding friendship. Luckily, Apple released their initial iPod that fall and both boys learned to "plug-in" and escape "the awful music" that the roommate liked to play.

It didn't take long for me to realize I was drawn to V and Z and would make them my projects for the next three or four years, if they would let me. I was still a bit rusty with the coach/player relationship thing; the failure with Marcus was still a sore point every time I cracked my left knuckles. This time I wanted to wade deeper, perhaps much deeper into the waters. I could feel it in my bones that my mission would begin soon. Much like I had with Jerrod, I probably needed this to work as much as they did.

Vince and Zach

Chapter 22
Freshman Year

Zach overcame Vince's tickling and made the squad. It wasn't easy and it often wasn't pretty, but this kid brought it every day to practice, holding his own against the first team defense. It took Zach a month to get in football shape and once there, he never let up. He was handling the defense better than his new nickname; the boys called him Elmo, and threatened to unleash a tickling attack on any given day. As a "frosh," Zach had to take it and he held up pretty well. I did not much like the Elmo name, to me he was simply Z and I let everyone know it. As the season wore on the boys dropped Elmo for no other reason than Z was only a single utterance. It's always been amazing to me how laziness is the trump card for a life decision.

We did not have a file on Zach since he was a walk-on, and a late walk-on at that. I called his high school coach to get some background on the kid and to ensure he wasn't a bad guy, didn't have a rap sheet, that kind of thing. I could handle that he liked his twang, though it was hard to watch him dance to that music in the locker room. We all have our faults, Z just showed his every time he broke a move. Mostly I wanted someone to validate what I already knew, we got lucky and found ourselves a really good addition to the team. Zach had slipped through the cracks into our hands and now it was my job to take care of him.

"Hey coach, it's Bob down at the U. Thanks for taking my call."

"Coach Bob, great to hear from you."

I could tell he was pretty surprised to be getting a call from me. Recruiting season was behind us and we were both getting ready for our upcoming seasons.

"Coach, I called to ask you about a player from your school that graduated last year. A guy named Zach ..."

Before I could get the last name out he knew exactly who I was talking about. We chatted for a few minutes, all good news about Z. Zach was a leader on the team and a terrific center who was recruited by mid tier schools, but no big names. Zach was tough enough for the college game, but not big enough was the typical slam on his ability. The bet was he could not handle the beefy defensive lineman who had 50+ pounds on him. And then he told me a story:

◆◆◆◆

We went undefeated last year on our way to the state title. We had a lot of close playoff games, not winning any by more than seven points. We were banged up and bruised and had just enough in the tank for one last game. Our opponent was heavily favored to repeat, they had blown everyone out in their playoff run by 20 or more points, usually closing out by halftime. Their starters were well rested.

It was our first time at the dance and it showed in the first half, we were down three scores after only ten minutes. I saw the panic set in, initially with the players, then the coaches, and then in the mirror. Our kids were smaller, slower, and a lot more tired than our opponent. We were in desperate need of a game changer, something to shake us all up, especially on the offensive side.

Our right guard, Keith, was an all-state, big kid with big hands, quick feet and about 275 pounds. He beat on the defense all season long, but not this game. The defense was bigger, stronger, and too fast for him. We lost two fumbles due to his missed blocks and would probably have lost more. At half time, Zach pulled the line together to figure some things out. And then Keith's father stormed into the locker room and ripped into his son. He was yelling at him about losing his scholarship, embarrassing the family and the school. This guy had a mean streak and Keith just backed away unsure how to handle it.

Not Zach. He stepped right up to Keith's dad, nose-to-nose, and politely but firmly told him, "We got it." Keith's dad was a big guy, about three inches taller than Zach and a lot wider. So, they were really nose to chin rather than nose to nose, but that didn't bother Zach. Before Keith's father could speak, Zach said again, "Sir, we got it."

Keith's dad glared at Zach then said, "Well then get it done! I'll have your ass too after the game if you don't." Then he stormed out of the room as our coaches moved in to take him away.

Zach sat with the lineman and created a new blocking scheme to help out Keith whenever he needed it. There were a lot of double teams and cross blocks the rest of the game, and it worked. We came back and won that game, no more fumbles lost and Keith escaped with some self-respect, thanks to Zach.

Coach, Zach is a 'quiet strong.' He's never one to back down, and will do anything to help a teammate. He showed a lot of smarts too by changing our blocking schemes on the fly. And, after the game, he never talked about the halftime uproar, never said a word about Keith's inability to get the job done. He never even talked about Keith's father behind his back.

Zach just stepped in and made things better.

◆◆◆◆

"That's quite a story, Coach. Tell me, how did you find out what happened if Zach never spoke about it?"

"Keith told me. He knew the schools Zach wanted weren't recruiting him, and Keith thought the truth might help Zach someday. Keith was a standup guy, he was just getting beat that day and fortunately got the help he needed from Zach."

I hung up the phone with Z's high school coach and looked out my office window onto the field below. Quiet strong seemed an apt description of Z, from what I had observed in practice. The smarts to change all the blocking schemes at halftime and then execute it against a stronger opponent, was something else altogether. I liked what we had been seeing from Z and I especially liked what his coach just shared. *Quiet strong,* I liked that, much better than the nickname Elmo implied. I typed up the story and put it in a new folder labeled "Z."

Vince, on the other hand, had a folder, well that is until we tossed it in the trash. I had to dig deep into the computer archives to find the analysis we had run. V had high marks for athletic skills; a pocket passer with a strong arm; he could also throw on the run, or carry the ball himself. He had speed to get end around, and quickness to elude defenders. But, and it was a very large but, he had problems coping with authority, broke all kinds of team rules, came across as a selfish kid and had a history with the local police. The things I wanted to rule out about Zach were staring me in the face with Vince.

It took me a few days to track down V's high school coach. He was hesitant to talk, the scars from V had not yet healed, but he found a way to give me some insights.

✦✦✦✦

"Coach, Vince is a team buster. You and the players will put your faith and trust in him because of his abilities, his charisma, and his smile. And just when you think it's a two-way trust, he'll do something to hurt the team. He'll bend a rule once too often, he'll talk behind the coaches' backs, he'll pit one player against another for his personal enjoyment, he'll get in a fight in a local bar and spend a night in a cell."

He paused to collect himself and I could tell how painful this conversation had become, and we had just started. "Coach, it's hard for me to talk bad about Vince. I put a lot of myself into Vince, my family too. We thought we were close, a pseudo family watching his back. He only has an uncle, no parents as you may know. He not only broke up my football team, he tore the heart out of my wife and my kids who looked up to Vince. And the saddest thing is I don't know why. Part of me believes Vince is afraid of relationships, he can't allow himself to get too close because no one has ever taught him. Another part of me believes he is devious and hurts others willfully, for personal gain."

He paused again and I counted to five before asking the one question I had planned for this call. "Coach, if I decide to dive in with Vince, like you did, what did you learn in hindsight that might help me? What would you have done differently?"

There was no hesitation; the answer was immediate and immensely helpful. "Don't give into him too early. Don't let him take over the team before he's ready. Don't let him start any games the first year; don't even let him play for a while. Don't get blinded by his football ability, make him really earn it, off the field more so than on the field. Good luck Coach, for yourself...and for Vince." Then he hung up the phone.

✦✦✦✦

I started a new file on Vince that day, with instructions and reminders for myself, knowing I would return to these notes, and this conversation a number of times over the next few years.

These two boys were indeed complete opposites. My suspicions were validated, my fears accounted for, but my plan was hardly underway. I needed some help and picked up the phone and called the one person who might make a difference.

"Hi Tony."

Tony had become a close family friend. He finished the engineering degree in the minimum four years and followed that up with an MBA, both at the U, where he now worked in the Athletic Department, reporting to Big Willy as VP of Operations. Tony was overseeing the expansion of our football stadium among other things. Sometimes the circles we live in are indeed small.

"How goes it, Coach?"

"Tony, I need some help with one of the guys on the team and I think you might have the right touch. Any interest taking on a project with me?"

"You can count on me, Coach"

There it was, the automatic response to a coach's request, which was now working for me rather than against. *God, I love this gig!* Besides, Tony was always hanging out at our practices every chance he got; now he would have something productive to do. He never lost passion for the game, and I know he missed being with the guys.

Tony and I hatched our plan, a balance of risk and reward highly dependent on Vince and Tony working together as a team. Besides, I thought it would be helpful for Vince to spend some time with a successful black man, an executive at the U, who understood the mindset of a player and also the chairman in a boardroom. I figured V had not had that type of role model in his life and I wanted every lever available to me. It's not that I shied away from any racial barrier, hell I befriended Tony, Jerrod, Marcus, black, brown, white, color never mattered to me. But I knew, or thought I knew, it might just matter to Vince. I hoped I was right.

First Game

I looked at the kids in the locker room. These weren't my kids; they were my inheritance from the prior coaching staff, most of whom were long gone, a one-way ticket from Big Willy. He had cleaned house; even the equipment manager was new. I didn't spend any time in living rooms convincing these kids to come to my school, my team, and my program. I had nothing invested in them, and they had nothing invested in me, nothing at all. We were stuck with each other and had no alternative, no other options than to play out the season. They were my excuse for a poor first year, they knew it, the press knew it, and I knew it. It was understood, words were not necessary to explain our position with each other.

And yet, they were my kids. We slaved and toiled together over the summer, slowly getting to know each other, able to predict one another on occasion. I liked and even admired most of these kids. They lacked some skills, and would not win many games, but they had a toughness about them and a damn fine attitude. They didn't complain when the coaches barked orders and made them do drills. Hell, they even put up with my speeches and slogans. Now that was loyalty, and it went a long ways toward gaining my respect. Yep, my friend ego was back and was riding in the front of the bus, blaring the horn and revving the engine. I was head coach again and I loved my job. I especially enjoyed motivating the kids before, after, and during ball games.

I made eye contact with the three most important people to me in the locker room as the big speech commenced. Vince was in the corner sitting alone, tossing a football in the air. Zach was with a group of offensive lineman slapping each other on the pads, hoping for encouragement with each hit. And standing in the back of the room, pacing between the lockers and showers was Coach Mac. He was my first call after coming back to the U. I needed him on the staff to head up the defense, be my confidant, and kick me in the ass now and then.

Coach Mac could have been the ball boy and I would still drop and give him ten whenever he commanded. He had retired two years ago but it didn't take much to convince him to return to the game. I gave him free reign on the defensive side as long as it fit within my overall game plan. We convinced each other it would work during our ten-minute phone chat. He did not ask how much the job paid; he never much cared about small matters. He only had a single question for me, "When do we get started Blur?"

These three, Coach Mac, Vince, and Zach formed the nucleus of our future, four of us including me.

"Gather round men. We'll be taking the field soon for our initial game of the season, our first together as a team. In many ways it feels like we're still getting to know each other, still wondering why and how we got here together, in this room on this day. Some of you seniors are certainly thinking that way, hell I don't blame you one bit, 'cause I'm wondering the same damn thing.

"But when those thoughts come across my mind, they just keep going on out through the open window. It's easy for me to dismiss the questions, the worries, and the fears about this team, this year, my first as a head coach at the college level, and your first with me. You men gave me the reason, actually the many reasons to be here today. Each one of you is my motivation to come to work everyday, to be part of this special game, to spend my time running steps and eating turf." (I threw the turf line in for Coach Mac.)

I paused and looked at the many faces looking back at me, waiting to hear something from me that mattered, something smart, maybe something from the heart.

"Winston Churchill said a lot of smart things over the years and one of them is appropriate for today. 'Attitude is a little thing that makes a big difference.' Think about that men, attitude is what makes all the difference in the world and that's what you have shown the coaching staff and me these past few weeks and months. You never once complained, never whined about the change in coaches. You learned a new system on both sides of the ball, studied hard, and worked harder. And for that you have my respect. Gentlemen, I am proud of each one of you for putting in the work. "Now, what's our goal for the season men?"

"Win the game we are playing today."

"That's right, win the game today, not the one tomorrow or next week. Not the conference title and not the peanut bowl or the Rose Bowl. Just win the game we are playing each day. "How are we going to get that done?"

"Together, one team."

That's right men, we are not individuals, and we are not focused on selfish statistics. We support each other, help each other, and play together as one team. "And how do teammates treat each other?"

"Respect, Openness, Kindness."

"That's right. We show respect, we are open to one another's thoughts and ideas, and we are kind to each other. We always assume our teammate has a positive intent in his actions, especially when we don't understand what or why he is doing something. And men, what do you expect from yourself today?"

"I am accountable!"

"Each one of us is accountable to do our job and help a teammate when needed. The players, coaches, all of us are accountable!

"Ok men, if we are each accountable, and treat each other with respect, openness, and kindness, and we play as a team not a collection of individuals, then we stand a very good chance of achieving a good outcome today. "We are going to win the game we are playing today!"

Throughout the season I kept wondering if we should add a C to ROK, but four words seemed like a lot and ROK still sounded like ROCK. Yeah, it was a small thing, but small things can make a big difference. I liked respect, openness, and kindness as they summarized the behaviors I wanted and expected from the kids on the team and the coaches as well, plus I could not think of a fitting C word, so we let it roll.

The first word, respect stems from kindergarten where we learned take direction from our teacher, more often than not the first authority figure outside of our mom and dad. It has always amazed me how much we apply what we learned at age five throughout our lives. Respect your mates and the teacher, listen before you speak, tie your shoes, and look presentable so you also respect yourself. All of these are fundamental, simple, and easy if you learn them early in life.

The second word, openness, is a simpler way of saying transparency, which at four syllables are too many to be useful. I believe in keeping messages as simple as possible, and sylla- bles count. Being open with the team and with each other re- moves suspicion from the equation. It's a posture that allows us to assess and solve problems and gaps much faster. A great example, our left offensive tackle was having trouble handling his man one game, resulting in two QB sacks and little running yardage for our backs. Based on his admission that he could not handle his man, we could solve the problem. We put to- gether a new approach that included some double teams, and our tight end would chip the defensive player on occasion. It worked, but only because our left tackle did not hold back, did not get lost in self-embarrassment; he put it out in the open so we, as a team, could deal with it. It's a bigger man who can honestly admit his failures than one who hides the truth from plain sight.

The third word, kindness, might be the surprise of the three. Most people don't imagine football players being kind to each other, certainly not on the field of play. And that's the whole point; these words and messages transcend the gridiron and help establish behaviors to follow off the field and beyond the game. How much could we accomplish in life if our first instinct was to be kind to each other? How often have we seen the opposite, where people are defensive, protective, afraid of interaction with the other guy or gal? Being kind to a team- mate is not hard; sadly in our culture it has become the excep- tion rather than the norm. I was doing my part to reverse that, one player and coach at a time.

I usually did not focus too much on our opponent in these last few minutes before game time. It always seemed to me people get carried away with "the other guy," rather than taking care of your own business. I wanted the players and coaches concentrating on their roles, their responsibilities, and their teammates. Not the other guy. It's another small thing, but they sure pile up.

We took the field that day to a sold out home stadium against an easy opponent, the schedule determined years ago. We won that first game, though it was closer than I would have liked and we won the next before losing two difficult conference games in a row. We battled well in all our games, losing to teams more skilled but not with deeper heart than our kids showed on the field.

Vince was having a good year, in practice. I heeded the insight and advice from his high school coach and had not played V in a single game, though everyone on the team, from the coaches to the ball boys, knew V was a secret weapon waiting to be unveiled. His fundamentals were weak and he was out of shape, yet each day he got better and everyone could sense a leader was among them. V had a presence about him that oozed confidence, with an eerie calmness. He was not aloof, never seemed in a hurry, and had a coolness factor difficult to describe. He drew people to himself without trying and easily handled a crowd as he had been doing his entire young life.

I was still feeling my way with V, we had not yet developed a meaningful relationship and I had not pushed it very far. It felt as if we were playing a chess game, making board moves against each other, not yet checking the king and nowhere close to mate. It was a quiet duel between two strong wills, neither knowing when the real game would begin.

In our fifth game, another tough conference foe, I changed quarterbacks. We needed some new energy, a spark, hell we needed to score some damn points. Our offensive output was second lowest in the conference, and we read about it and heard about it every Monday. So, I rolled the dice and took a risk, the result couldn't be any worse. To no one's surprise, the back-up QB was not much better than the starter, tossing an interception, fumbling two balls, recovering one, and playing uninspiring ball in the first half. The defense kept us in the game as they did all season. Mac sure knew how to get his side of the ball ready.

The locker room scene wasn't pretty at the half, it got rough, and it got ugly. I like a little bit of tension on the team: starters worrying about second stringers gunning for their roles, offenses and defenses putting pressure on each other; the competition is healthy and damn fun to watch. The other coaches and I encourage the competitive juices to flow and everyone knows that. But things got a bit out of hand during this half time. There's a lot of testosterone on a college football team and when it explodes in a cramped locker room space there could be some pain involved. The defensive team had had enough, tired of keeping us in games only to lose a close one because we could not put any points on the board. Coach Mac usually knew how to keep his boys in check, but they unloaded the pent up frustration on the offensive lineman nearly coming to blows.

Zach flew into the melee to help the first team offense, a rookie mistake among his elders. He got tossed into a pile of towels, the soft landing unintended. Zach pounced up to rejoin the scrum until a hand reached out and gently but firmly pulled him back. Vince released Zach and took the baton but did not race out of the blocks. He walked calmly into the midst of the storm and quieted the offenders without saying a word. His eyes spoke volumes, his hands pulled mates away from each other and then down into a kneeled position. V knelt down too, keeping eye contact, always moving his eyes from player to player. At last he spoke, his voice soft and steady, and difficult for me to hear. I hung back not wanting to interfere, yet my curiosity peaked as the tension released from the room. It sounded like three words repeated over, and over. I leaned in to hear Vince:

"Respect. Openness. Kindness."

"Respect. Openness. Kindness."

I skipped a breath or missed a heartbeat or something grabbed me, it was one of those moments you felt physically and emotionally. Part of me was in that huddle, where large men were on knees, holding hands, repeating the messages I drilled into their heads, almost as if they were in church. It was surreal and I did not know how to react so my body parts took over and made sure I would remember the moment long after it had occurred.

V's fundamentals as a QB might not have been ready, his leadership skills honed on the streets certainly were. Vince took over the team that day; it was not discussed, just understood. And he did it by following the attitudes and behaviors I had preached to the team, though I had to admit, he expressed them a lot better than I did. Vince was learning and changing himself, allowing the discipline he lacked and craved, to mix with his raw traits, into a new type of man. Our new leader was born, recognized by everyone in the locker room as someone who had arrived to his rightful place. It was the only time in my career as a player or coach when a clear leader was anointed without ever playing a single down. V was ready.

In the far corner of the locker room I saw Tony nodding his head in approval and knew he was having an impact on Vince as I had hoped. I became more interested in Vince the person than V the Football player that day and finally knew for certain, it was a good decision, a very good decision, to bring him to the U.

We came back strong and won that fifth game, finishing the year with six wins and five losses, then lost a nail biter in some potato chip bowl before Christmas. It's never a good sign when your bowl invite has a date prior to the holidays. Vince never played a down that season and it didn't matter. We all knew V was a fine wine; his cork would pop at the right time, if I had any idea what I was doing.

I ended the year as always in a discussion with Willy, a review of my performance and an accounting of the team objectives we had set for the year.

"Well Bob you were the highest paid employee at the U again this year. Let's see if we got our money's worth."

That's Willy, always giving me grief and reminding me how much more money I make than he does. He likes being the boss but we both know who really wears the pants. It's the same dance played at all tier one colleges across the country, the head coaches rule their roost and the ADs have one and only one lever, hire or fire the coach. It's a very big lever, but can't be used very often.

"You know Willy, I will gladly volunteer for a pay cut if I can give the money to our players. All they really need is a small monthly stipend, an equal amount for all scholarship players. We couldn't manage anything more complex that that and it would make an impact on their lives while at college."

"Don't get going on that one again, it is not going to happen no matter how much you whine about it."

I let it go, this was not a fight I could win on my own. The time would come one of these days when the players who made their schools rich, participated in some of the upside. Besides, Willy agreed with me, he just didn't want to admit it.

"Six wins and six losses including the bowl game. That 's not bad for a first year coach, better than what most everyone expected. What's your take Bob?"

"We met some of our goals and badly missed others.

We should have finished 7-5 at minimum, with a late December Bowl game. Too many of our wins were against easy opponents, we must improve conference play next year."

"Yes, I'd agree with that Coach. Are we positioned for the improvement? Can we win seven or even eight games and compete for the conference title? Or is that just wishful thinking?"

I let Willy's question hang in the air for a bit. He and I both knew the one and only answer to his question. We were not a top 20 football school, not even close. We hoped to be in the top 50 with a respectable bowl and positive cash flow to fund other sports. Once in a while we had a chance to get lucky if we recruited the right couple of players.

"Willy, next year will be greater highs and lower lows than either of us have ever known. We are opening the Vince show and it could be ugly, real ugly, or we are in for the ride of our lives!"

"How do you know Vince will be ready? You didn't play him at all this year."

"Willy, honestly I don't know yet. It's more gut instinct than proven ability at this stage, but I like the horse we are riding."

Chapter 23

Sophomore Year

In my book, the next season began the evening of our bowl loss. No time to look backward, and certainly no time to obsess about what could have been. Winners get back to work right away was my style and I showed up in the weight room on Christmas Eve for a badly needed workout. My plan that day was threefold, first the workout, an hour of weights and another of cardio. I would try to make up for the past four months in a single day. If I survived the workout some shopping would follow. I was a last day shopper and loved the Christmas Eve rush. Decisions came quickly and I spent as little time as necessary in the stores. I already bought a few items from Amazon, every lazy guy's dream website. For me, there was a spirit of Christmas in the air; people were hurried, but friendlier and more aware of the other guy. I ate that up as presents for my two ladies were bought, wrapped, and bagged. The last item on my to do list was a nice dinner with the family. There's just nothing like Amy's cooking and hanging with her and Taylor for a feast on Christmas Eve, followed by at least one holiday movie. It was hard to beat this day of the year, unless of course we were practicing for a January bowl game.

Most of the players had hit the road, families eager to have their kids at home, so I had the facility to myself that morning. It was a very large weight room and I didn't see him at the other end, not until I heard the clink, clink, and clink of the weights moving up and down. The one person I least expected to see that morning was Vince.

"Morning Vince. What brings you here on Christmas Eve?"

"Hi Coach."

Vince evaded my question and moved on to his workout. We kept our distance for the next hour, both working on our muscles and our thoughts. I was trying to plan out my shopping spree, minimizing time in the stores, but Vince kept intruding, taking my mind away from the day's game plan. It finally dawned on me why V was still on campus hitting the weight room, he had nowhere to go. I wanted to punch myself upside the head for being so slow to figure things out.

A flashback raced through my mind of the day I drove Vince to his uncle's apartment to pick up one pair of shoes and a small bag of clothes, everything V owned for his move to the U. The place was a real dump, a single bedroom and a broken down couch. It reeked of beer, the open bottles strewn across the floor. The apartment was on the fourth floor, steps the only option as the elevator looked as if it had retired long ago. Vince hurried me out of the place, but a quick look was all I needed to form my conclusions. It was miraculous for V, or anyone for that matter, to survive these environs, and hard to imagine anyone calling it home. It was just a place to go, a place to hang, a place to hide.

I quickly recovered and added a fourth item to my plan for the day. "Hey Vince, do you have plans for dinner tonight?"

"Sure coach, I got plans. I'm set." V responded quickly to my question, too quickly.

"Well Vince, Amy and I would love to have you over to the house for dinner. It's Christmas Eve and Amy does Christmas better than anyone I know."

"Thanks Coach, but I'm covered." V moved on to the other side of the room, pumping more iron.

I followed. "Vince, dinner is at seven so be there around six. Amy hates it when people show up late, don't get on her bad side."

Vince did not reply; we looked at each other wondering who would make a move. Finally he nodded his head, a slight up and down motion. The deal was done and I got the heck out of there. When you get to yes, it's time to shut up and take the order. As I showered down from the workout, I started planning a new route for the afternoon.

My first stop was to see Jerrod. It had been a while, not that I counted the days, I could feel it, sense it, that I had not talked with my pal for some time. And I needed his help, or the help I imagined he provided. Maybe it just helped me to talk out loud, share my thoughts and innermost feelings even with a piece of stone. I don't know if psychiatrists are over or under paid, but I felt I was getting 80% of their benefit for free.

✦✦✦✦

I walked up to Jerrod's Place; I did not like calling it a grave as that felt too final, although years had lapsed. There were fresh flowers on this cold day and I could tell Amy's touch. We never talked about my visits to see my "shrink," but Amy knew. And once in a while she could predict the day and she would get out here and tend Jerrod's place before my arrival. There's something special about spouses and their nonverbal communications, when nothing need be said, yet full and deep meaning is sensed and understood. Some people call this soul mates, I don't know, to me it was a bit simpler. We just got each other. We could look across the room, whether empty or full of people and with a slight nod or twitch of the face send and receive messages that were instantly recognized and understood. That morning Amy knew I would visit Jerrod before I did, let's call it a good guess.

"Hey Jerrod."

He never said hi back, which was probably a good thing.

"This will be a shorter visit than most, being Christmas Eve, I bet you got some things to do, same as me."

I pulled my jacket closer; the winter air was sneaking in.

"Let me get right to the heart of things. I invited Vince to dinner tonight, it was more of a command really and I put the odds at better than 50% he shows up.

"I'm trying to find the right way to build a closer bond,

but I just can't figure out how to make the leap. I don't know what's holding me back. With you it was so easy, I think you were the initiator and we moved into a rhythm that just felt right."

I paused to hear myself think, hoping for a flash of some kind. But the tombstone just stared back at me, daring me to continue. "Why was it so easy with you and so difficult with Vince?"

The wind whipped up a little and some leaves flew through the air, one grazing the tip of my nose.

"Easy with Jerrod, hard with Vince. Easy with Jerrod, hard with Vince." I kept repeating this phrase looking for an opening, some entry point I could use with V.

Jerrod and I were closer together in age; I was more of an older brother to him perhaps. Was that it?

I kicked at the ground and paced back and forth seeking some direction from my friend. I was about to give up when that flash finally hit. "Jerrod, we went to the same high school. I knew your mom and dad. We were raised in the same community."

I stared at the stone, walked up to it and moved my hand over the engraved years Jerrod had lived.

"We have a history together Jerrod. That's it. We were not strangers. Vince and I have no history, we don't know much about each other's backgrounds. I have no idea how he was raised, the influences in his life."

It almost looked as if the stone smiled back at me and said, 'You dummy, you finally got it. Now go do something with that knowledge.'

"I need to better understand where Vince is from."

That realization hit me hard. Where is someone from seems a simple question, yet the answer can reveal deep meaning. Where are you from is the beginning of the onion, layers can then be peeled, and peeled some more.

"Thanks pal, I owe you again."

I said goodbye to Jerrod and wished him a Merry Christmas. As I turned to walk to my car, I heard or thought I heard, something or someone behind a clump of trees. The biting wind pushed me toward the car, away from the trees, so I moved along. I took one look over my shoulder and saw a human figure moving quickly in the opposite direction. I could not tell if it was a worker or another visitor or something else entirely. More importantly, my watch indicated shopping time was coming to a close.

++++

Christmas Eve at Home

It was 6:05 p.m. and I found myself pacing around the house like an expectant father, nervous energy combusting with excitement, causing more than a few trips to the men's room. Ames and Taylor were very gracious in allowing a complete stranger into our home on Christmas Eve, and I thanked them more than once. They were having a much easier time than me, giggling and laughing as they put the final touches on our evening feast. They booted me out of the kitchen, having grown tired of my walking back and forth, no longer interested in hearing the mumbled words spewing out of my mouth. Hell,

I don't even know what I was saying, though it was pretty good odds there was some cussing going on.

I was not worried about Vince coming to dinner, having him over was the easy part. The thing that concerned me was disrupting a family ritual, taking a special day away from Amy and Taylor. I should have realized they were much more adult about the situation than I was acting. If I was totally honest about it, I was mostly worried about sharing my family on this holiday. We treasured this time together, Christmas more so than other holiday. It was not much fun being this honest with myself, and my shrink was way too quiet to offer any words of wisdom, so I just let it go.

At 6:10 p.m. I looked out the window and all I saw was a squirrel scampering away. I scanned the house to ensure all was in order and noticed something I should have seen earlier, much earlier. The Christmas tree was stocked with presents all around, three feet high in some places, most of the tags with Taylor's name. *Damn, that's not the right image to portray for Vince.* At least he had two nicely wrapped gifts under the tree; I tried to make them look more important but failed miserably. I could not understand why I was feeling so self-conscious.

The doorbell finally rang at 6:17 p.m., and the entire house let out a heavy sigh, normal breathing was allowed to commence, well at least for me. *Here we go team, ready break!*

"Vince, you made it. I mean it's good to see you, again. Get on in here and come meet the women in my life! You are going to love the feast they've cooked up."

V stood on my front stoop, taking everything in. It was a lot to take in, this command performance to show up at

Coach's house, meet his wife, his daughter, and share his Christmas Eve feast. I could not begin to imagine what was running through the man's head, so I reached out my hand and pulled him into the house.

I marched Vince to the kitchen where Amy and Taylor were dancing; the loud music had shielded the sound of the doorbell. We were known to get a little crazy on the holidays, that is Amy and Taylor got crazy. At that moment they were kicking it hard. I turned the volume down and began the process of introducing everyone.

Amy saw the awkward moment approaching and batted it away as she moved effortlessly over to V and greeted him with a smile and a warm hug. Ames knew how to hug, a genuine embrace, full of charm and kindness. "Hi Vince, welcome to our home. We are so happy you could be with us for Christmas Eve. Please call me Amy, none of this Mrs. this or that and certainly not Coach's wife. Amy will do just fine."

"Pleasure to meet you…Amy." He stood there stiffly, his arms anchored behind his back.

Taylor took her cues wisely from the nurturing parent and moved in for the kill. "Hi Vince, I'm Taylor."

Taylor was not quite up to snuff on the warm hug part; she did the half arm around the shoulder thing, but pulled it off with a ton of grace. I preened.

"Hi Taylor."

Taylor wore her sly smile well, her head tilted just a bit to the right so she could see the hard object in Vince's jacket she felt during the half hug. Yep there it was, a flask, which she guessed was about half full. Vince had drained much of the original pour to hide his nerves, or boost his confidence, it did not matter which. This evening might provide Taylor a lot of entertainment, more than she had expected.

Vince pulled his right hand out from behind his back and placed the package on the counter. He handed a pink rose to Taylor, and a red one to Amy. His delivery was performed with such fluid movement, an easiness that quieted and calmed the room. Both ladies were in a semi trance and thrilled to be given a simple and thoughtful surprise. They smiled at each other and then at Vince.

"Vincent, how wonderful to receive a rose on Christmas Eve. Thank you," Amy said.

From that moment Amy always used his full name, Vincent. Never V or Vince, always Vincent. Her motherly instinct was more needed than any of us knew or appreciated at the time.

"Thanks Vince, I love my pink rose," Taylor chimed in.

The rest of our evening was a real delight. We kept our chatter light, not delving into V's family life or why he was on campus for the holiday. That would come later when we were alone. After dinner Amy decided Vincent was staying the night. He looked to me for help and I threw up my hands. Once Amy has made up her mind, a tank would have trouble getting her to move.

We moved to the living room for our next tradition. One and sometimes two presents were allowed per person, the rest were reserved for Christmas Day. We never broke the one present rule, though Taylor was always persuasive. Taylor had gift giving duties, selecting a package for each of us to open, including Vince who seemed a bit surprised.

We all waited for our "guest of honor" to open his gift but he did not make a move. I realized we needed some encouragement to get the party going again. "V, it's a family tradition that we open one gift on Christmas Eve, which this year includes you."

"Vince, let's see what Santa brought you," Taylor said, emphasizing the word Santa. Her mischievous laugh lightened the mood.

"Coach, I didn't bring any gifts…"

I cut him off midsentence, "V, don't mess with a family ritual, especially when the ladies are involved. And you did bring gifts, I'll be hearing about those roses for a long time."

Vince smiled, just enough to release the pressure. He clearly was not on familiar turf, sitting around a Christmas tree, present in hand. He went first as required, revealing a pair of leather gloves, extra-large. I wanted those hands protected and did not blink an eye about using the holidays as my cover. We opened the remaining gifts, enjoying this special moment, made even more so with Vince at the house. The evening was going better than I had hoped.

Taylor got up and returned with a second package for Vince. She played the elf role well and enjoyed the giving nearly as much as the receiving end of Christmas. Vince hesitated once again and then buckled at the peer pressure we generously applied. The book was a personal favorite and I hoped he would find the time to enjoy the read and learn about life from one of the greats—Mr. John Wooden.

I twitched my nose and the elf responded with two

DVDs, and put them out for Vince to inspect. It was his night to choose, *A Wonderful Life* or *White Christmas*. It was a difficult choice, and thankfully not mine to make.

"Which do you like best Vince?" Taylor asked.

Vince was speechless; this was clearly a night of firsts for him. How could he have a preference? It was unlikely he had seen either movie.

I stepped in for the save. "Taylor, I bet Vince would like *Wonderful Life.*

"Great pick Pops; movie starts in five."

"You're getting the full family baptism V. Taylor makes sure we get into the spirit of the holidays with one of these corny old movies." I gave him a wink and wondered what he thought about the evening thus far. I could not imagine how he viewed my family compared to his own.

I was feeling good about things until it dawned on me, those old movies were made a long time ago when there were few black actors, certainly few leading black men or women. I wondered if that mattered to Vince; I had never really thought of it this way before. The little things in life are the ones that grab you the most.

Taylor led Vince to the TV room, while I helped Ames clean up. "Hurry up," she yelled, "the movie is starting.

After the film Ames and I were tired and opted for bed, ceding hosting duties to our daughter. I trusted both of them, but was pleased that my daughter volunteered their conversation to me the next day.

Taylor waited a few beats until she knew for sure they were alone and threw out the question she had been scheming to ask. "So Vince, have you drained that flask or did you leave any for me?"

Vince had been thrown curves all his life so he knew how to keep his reactions at bay, but she could tell he was surprised by her boldness.

"Just a little picker upper on a cold night. No big thing."

Taylor put some music on, sat on the couch across from Vince and stared at him. She was a very pretty girl, with a new driver's license, taught thankfully by her mom. The old Driver Bob had retired long ago.

"Vince, may I ask you a serious question?"

Taylor played the shy girl type when it suited her, usually to unarm a target. Underneath she had a razor sharp mind, a very sly wit, and a whole lot of charm. She deployed all these skills with both her mom and dad on a regular basis, heck she learned them from us, but had perfected her own unique style. She made me damn glad I was not on the dating circuit. No way I could keep up with the ladies if they possessed her weapons.

Vince eyed Taylor for a second then replied, "Sure, I might give you an answer."

Taylor took her cue from V and did not dive in right away, letting the music fill the room. "Normally I would spar with you, toss a few verbal jabs around the edges, you know, soften you up a bit before I asked the hard-hitting question. But I'm not going to waste your time with games; I'm going to get right to the point. Vince, how did you feel being at our home tonight, sharing Christmas Eve with Coach and his wife and kid?"

Vince gulped.

Taylor had not meant to make him nervous. She was not flirting or prying, just curious.

"That's a deep question'"

As Taylor watched Vince, she imagined he had a Ping-Pong game going on in his head, debating whether to run for the door or be straightforward with the Coach's daughter.

"I felt a lot of emotions tonight. At first it was odd being here, a place very unfamiliar to me, all of it unfamiliar."

Before Taylor could comment, Vince waved his arm, indicating he had more to say.

It was surprising that he wanted to keep talking. Taylor anticipated he would avoid entering into a discussion, based on what her father had shared about the QB.

"I can't remember the last time, the first time, there was a Christmas tree in the living room with presents under the tree and one of them for me."

Taylor bit her lip. She knew what she had started, but was smart enough to know Vince would decide how far they would go.

"There was one surprise tonight, well two actually. Most stuff I could guess, it's all very upscale and suburban, no shock there. Part of me was secretly hoping to see a dysfunctional family with people who hated each other and their own lives. That's what we wanted on the streets when we saw the rich white guys drive by in their fancy cars."

Taylor's lip started to bleed, just a little.

"I was surprised you and your family did not fit the stereotype I grew up believing, maybe hoping is more accurate.

It's not that I wanted anything bad for you, it's something deep inside of me, a hatred of some kind that's been there a long time."

Taylor did not move, it was her turn to gulp, a short quick one she tried her best to hide.

"Taylor, you got a good family life, it's something to really treasure and I hope you never take that for granted." He obviously liked Taylor and her family.

Taylor nodded.

"What's the second surprise Vince?"

Vince smiled, and then laughed a little. "Your family has the worst movies, I can't believe you made me watch that thing."

They both laughed out loud, loud enough for me to hear and to check my watch. It was getting late and I started to get up. Ames held me back, she knew better.

Taylor and Vince stayed up all night. The discussion was honest and fluid, willingly sharing details about their different lives. It was a first for both, the give and take between two opposites on the outside, and yet two similar spirits within.

Vince also volunteered his assessment of the conversation with my spirited, thoughtful daughter.

Vince achieved an awareness about himself he had not known before. He felt an inner strength, he wanted to hold and protect Taylor like the sister he never had. V knew it was an emotional bond, that's what his head told him, it just took his heart a little longer to realize it.

Vince had been on guard his whole life against the shadows in the streets, the crime around the corner, the drugs, the gangs, everything. He played defense all damn day, every day and it was exhausting. He had learned to show coolness on the outside, a steady hand and a gliding walk were disguises for the turmoil within. A mix of hatred and fear of unknowns haunted his thoughts and shaped his soul. With no one to guide him, to teach him about the good in life, he only understood the bad. He could not escape the bad; only try to avoid it during the day and once in a while the night, only to see it again in the morning, every morning.

Vince sat there in the overstuffed chair, staring at Taylor on the couch. He shook his head. *How was it possible for a girl, a teenage white girl from the suburbs to disarm me so easily?* he wondered. Taylor broke him down with her wit, her charm, her honesty, and her innocence. She did not pretend, did not hold back, she dove right into the heart of things, pushing, pulling, probing, always probing, and asking 'why' countless times. It was not an inspection, not an interview, not a cop looking for a reason, any reason to throw the black kid in jail. There was concern and care in her questions; she was exploring the unknown for herself as much as opening up Vince to some of the good.

Her words dissected him like a frog in sixth grade biology, splaying him open on the table to peek inside and make her observations. It made him uncomfortable and curious at the same time.

"Vince, you have a hatred of something you don't understand. Why do you think it is hate and not ignorance?"

Bam, V felt that one in his gut. He opened his mouth to explain the real world to the privileged white girl from the "burbs," but nothing came out. He knew she would just poke and prod some more and challenge him in some new way he did not anticipate, again and again. He had no choice but to formulate an answer. "Tell you what, let's call it ignorance for a minute, my ignorance of not knowing there might be a cool kid living on the right side of the tracks. But let's flip the coin on the other side and look at your ignorance. What do you know about the streets, the poor, and the way they live? Huh, tell me what you know."

Taylor did not blink her eyes, did not look down at her feet, she kept her face frozen and locked onto Vince. "Vince, I don't know anything about that and I freely and openly admit it. Next question."

"What do you plan to do about it? Anything?"

"Vince, my plan is pretty simple. I want you as my teacher, you need to set me straight, show me what I don't know, and don't understand. Help reveal my ignorance, take away some of my innocence, rough up my edges a bit and let me see the real world. I want to know more about life, not just the bad you have seen and grown up in. I want you to show me that you know how to enjoy the good side of life. And if you're having trouble with that then it's my job to help you."

Vince did not have a reply

"Vince, can't you see how we can help each other? I know you see it and feel it and you know I know it. You just have trouble admitting it. You're not used to having a friend, someone who knows you better than you know yourself. Vince, I can be a good friend if you'll let me."

Vince just sat there unsure how to respond.

"Vince, I bet you don't ever let your guard down, not even tonight. You don't trust many people, maybe no one. You never allow yourself to rely on anyone. You don't know how to depend on someone. Isn't that right Vince?

Vince replied with an up and down nod of his head, the only communication he could achieve at the moment.

Taylor knew it was now or never with Vince. He might not be this vulnerable again, not with her anyway. She rose from the couch and slowly moved toward Vince a half step at a time. Vince watched her walk the few steps to his chair, her arms reached out and pulled him upward into a hug. She lay her head on his shoulder and let him support her. It was the most comfortable connection Vince had made with another person in a long time. Vince hugged Taylor and she hugged him back, both wanting and needing to feel the closeness.

Taylor heard me first. It was time to beat the coach off the field. She whispered into V's ear, "If he makes you do stairs, that means he likes you. It's a family secret."

Vince liked the sound of that. He did not have any family secrets and no one to share them with anyway. A split second later Vince realized there were more than two people in the room and one of them was hugging Coach's little girl.

"V, Taylor, have you guys been up all night? What's going on here?

"Pops, Merry Christmas."

"Uh, Merry Christmas Taylor. Now kindly tell your father what you and V have been doing all night."

"Dad, we watched the movie, listened to music, and sat up talking. Vince is quite the storyteller, you boys should spend more time together." With that, Taylor kissed Vince on the cheek and then slipped away for a catnap, leaving the two of us in the room.

"Coach, let me explain."

I held up my hand and stopped Vince, trying to think of my next action. I trusted my daughter completely, but V did not know that so I took full advantage of his concern. "V, I don't care if it's Christmas, you and I are doing stairs today. After breakfast, we are heading to the stadium. It's time to count some steps."

That was the first time I saw anyone grin when threatened with running stadium stairs. I didn't understand the grin, but I knew for certain it would be gone before the day was done.

Football Season

We entered the season with a number of new starters on both sides of the ball and Vince at the offensive helm. It was no surprise to anyone that V was now our quarterback; many felt I held him back much too long. The critics might have been right about that, but it was finally V's time and I planned to enjoy the hell out of it.

I was delighted and secretly proud to see Zach working his way up the depth chart. He came to spring practice a few months earlier with 15 more pounds, all in the right place. His new size and strength allowed Z to handle the bigger kids, winning more battles than he lost. He was not a starter, but he led our second team offensive line and I expected that Z would move up another notch next year.

I called Zach into my office a few weeks before the season opener.

"Hi Coach, you wanted to see me?"

"Have a seat Zach, I'll be just a minute."

Zach squirmed in his chair, not knowing the reason for meeting. He had no idea the fun I was about to have, at his expense, yet paid by the U. The offensive coordinator walked in along with the offensive line coach and we had Zach surrounded. I asked the other coaches if they would give me the honors to lead this meeting; they quickly agreed and allowed the head coach to have his fun. But they knew I had earned it, not because I was head coach, because I was the one to take a risk on this kid.

Zach looked a bit worried, so I broke the silence.

"Zach, I wanted, all of us wanted to spend a few minutes with you today. Son, you have impressed the hell out of us the past few months. You have moved up the depth chart and have led our second team offensive line admirably. That's quite an achievement for a walk-on and we are all damn proud of you."

Zach's shoulders eased a bit as some of the tension left his body.

"It also means we are relying on you this year to be ready. With no warning whatsoever you may find yourself on the field pushing a 300 pounder out of the gap so we can make a few yards. And maybe, just maybe if you keep up your weight and stay in shape, you just might make the starting team next year."

Zach took it in and nodded, a short up and down motion, still unsure why he was in my office and not knowing how to respond to the compliments.

"There I go getting ahead of myself as usual. Zach, the reason we asked you into the office today is an important one. It's not often that a walk-on makes the team, much less second string as a sophomore. Zach, it's my pleasure, our pleasure, to award you a scholarship to the U. A full ride scholarship effective today."

I stood and walked over to Zach, my arm outstretched ready to shake his hand. Zach had other ideas in mind, and put his arms around me into a bear hug and then lifted me up in the air. It had been a while since the bottoms of my feet had achieved air, at the same time. "Ok son, down boy, down."

Zach set me down gently with a big smile on his face, but he was still speechless. He shook hands with the other coaches and then turned to leave. On his way to the door, he suddenly stopped, turned around and said, "Coach, I won't let you down, I'll never let you down. Thank you."

Then he was gone. I looked out my door to see Alice's shoes two feet off the ground, her entire body covered by another bear hug from Zach. They had obviously made up from the first encounter a year earlier when Zach eluded her to sneak into my office.

Zach and Vince decided to room together again, sharing a dorm suite. They had developed a friendship that surprised a few people, mostly themselves. I counted three people who had entered Vince's circle this past year, all providing a new and positive experience. Tony met with Vince every couple weeks, showing him the inner workings of the administrative side of college sports. Zach kicked V in the ass when needed and took a few kicks himself, a give and take that good friends shared. Taylor was the surprise of the three, not recruited by me of course, yet she was good for Vince and to my delight, he for her. I kept my guard around these two for a while but finally realized it was in fact a sibling relationship after all.

My next step with Vince was the most important. I would introduce a fourth person into his inner circle this year, someone who had been patient, plotting the right entry point, the right time. I was ready and hoped Vince was too. After I jumped into the circle we would have Vince fully surrounded...protected. I just needed to find the right opportunity and hoped it would present itself during the season. But first it was time for some football.

First Game

Our first game was away at a smaller school. We were favored to win but only by seven points. No one, including me, had any real idea how well we would perform on the field. I tossed and turned the night prior to the game; in hindsight it should have been a restful sleep. I knew Mac would have the defense ready; he had some good talent and knew how to extract the last ounce of energy from the "ladies" on his side of the ball. The offense was a real crapshoot, our practices were uneven and Vince was unsure of himself in the pocket. He ran well with the ball and the team looked up to him, but his throws were all over the place. I could easily visualize three or more interceptions before half time. I tortured myself well past 2:00 a.m. until Amy had had enough. "Honey, he's ready."

"Huh, who's ready?"

"He's ready."

Now why did she say he's ready instead of saying they are ready? I asked and answered my own question, it was Ames after all and she knew what, or in this case who kept me away from the sleep I needed. "I don't know Ames, he seems ready some of the time, but other times he's so inconsistent. Maybe I am pushing him too hard."

"Bob, Vince does not strike me as someone who gets pushed that easily. He's ready."

I looked at Ames, and was jealous of her confidence, and her ability to sleep (except for her husband keeping her awake). "I bet you win by three tomorrow."

"Three points, we are favored by seven. Three would be bad Ames, real bad."

"Not three points, three touchdowns. Now start visualizing that in your head."

She turned over and went back to sleep. I took her advice and allowed my dreams to shift from interceptions to touchdowns, although I could not tell which team was scoring.

The rest of the evening and next morning flew by and I found myself standing in the visitors' locker room in front of the team. "Gather round men."

With those three simple words about one hundred people stopped what they were doing, took a knee, sat on a bench or stood at attention. If nothing else, my army knew how to take their cues from the general.

"We are supposed to win the game today, that's what

everyone tells me. If you look at things on paper, we should not even break a sweat. Maybe that's why I don't read the papers, because they don't know, they're selling a product and it's an easier sell when the stories are better. And today's story is an old one; the bigger school beats up on the little guy, takes their ball and goes home with a W.

"We are going to win today and it's not because of the team we are playing. I expect our opponent to be prepared and you should too. The reason we will win today is we have put in the work, during the spring, the summer, and every week leading up to the season. Each of you as an individual is prepared. You understand your roles and responsibilities. More importantly, we are prepared as a team; we have come together these past few months on both sides of the ball. And now it's payoff time. Not just because of the work, that's not enough and you know that. Your work, our work, has allowed us to gel as a team. I can feel it, taste it.

"Gentlemen, I have only one question for you. I will not ask if you are ready but I will ask you if we are ready. Men, are we ready for the game today?"

The kids let out a yell, much louder than I expected.

Damn, maybe these kids are actually ready. This could be some fun. I thought. I said to them, "Years ago, one of our country's leaders Benjamin Franklin summarized his feelings at the signing of Declaration of Independence. He was quoted as saying: 'We must all hang together, or assuredly we shall all hang separately.' "I can't put it better than that. Now, let's get out there and take the field."

Coach Mac and I walked through the tunnel together.

"What do you think Mac, are we going to enjoy ourselves today?"

"Coach, strap it on, we will win by three touchdowns and that's just the first half."

I looked at Mac and wondered if he and Amy were in cahoots, again. It turns out they were both wrong and not just a little wrong, they were dead wrong. At the half we were up by six touchdowns, not six points, a head turning 42-0 score. Everything came together, just in time for the season to begin. The defense was relentless ceding less than 50 yards and no first downs. And the offense scored on each possession with Vince throwing four TDs and running the other two in.

I stood in front of the team in the locker room, speechless. It was time to head back on the field for the second half and the only thing I could think to say was, "Men, let's have a repeat performance in the second half. But, we'll do it with the second unit, first team take a rest. You've earned it."

We ran the ball most of the second half and still put more points on the board, the final: a 56-10 blowout. I left the coaching to the coordinators the rest of the game so I could sit back and observe the team, those on the field and the starters on break. I especially wanted to see what V would do. The starters took seats on the rear benches, helmets off, a good days work completed. Our second team offense took the field after the kick-off and Vince left the bench. He set up camp on the sidelines and paced the rest of the game, up and down the field, yelling encouragement to the team, his team, and in particular Zach. V did the same for the defense, all game long.

I almost felt better about the second half than the first. Vince showed his leadership stripes on and off the field for all to see. He was hesitant to leave the first stringers on the bench, enjoying the celebration of our first half performance. Then he saw number 65 leading the second team offensive line onto the field. It was a trigger for Vince; he jumped off the bench to support his buddy. Z was in the game and V was his biggest fan, his cheerleader, and his friend. I don't believe Vince had many friends, not close ones anyway. But with Zach it was easy to see their closeness, how they watched out for each other, backed each other, defended each other.

The next four games followed the same script. We came out of the gates strong, our offense scoring through the air and on the ground while the defense allowed less than 15 points per game. We leaped up the rankings just outside the top 15, a first for our school in a very long time. Willy and I got together for a mid-season discussion.

"Bob, let's start with the alumni. They are all over me, asking for tickets and meetings with you. Some of them want access to the kids and the locker room before games. What do you want to do?"

"Willy, I've never had to handle this kind of attention, the best thing is to just keep everyone away from the team and me."

"Ok, Bob, I'll see what I can do, don't answer the phone unless you know who is calling." Then he asked, "What about Vince? You ready to put him in front of the press?"

"No. He stays out of the chaos, at least another few games. He's focused on football, let's not lose him to the glamour just as we get this train rolling."

"Bob, this ride is a real thrill, can you keep it going?"

"Yeah, I really believe in these kids. But we have not

been challenged yet, that's when we'll learn what we are made of. It's coming, I just don't know when. "

"Bob, I don't want to jinx this thing, but a top ten ranking, we are so close. You and the coaches are doing a bang up job, let me know if you need anything."

Hmm, top ten ranking, I was not used to hearing that. Interesting that Willy said top ten and not national championship. He dared not dream that big. Hell, neither did I, for now it was hard enough holding on for the ride we were on.

"I hear we are sold out of #12 jerseys, everyone wants V on their back. Let's order a few more and give Vince a cut of the profits."

I hurried out the door as Willy threw a book at me. He knew I was not joking, but this was not the time or place. I just enjoyed tweaking him every chance I got.

A few weeks later we had an 8-0 record and a top ten ranking when things came crashing down. We lost a nail biter to a bitter rival at home. We had control of the game, but fumbled twice on special teams in the last nine minutes, allowing a ten-point advantage to flitter away into a four-point loss. That was the first punch and it landed right in our gut, busting up a perfect season and making us wonder how good we would be at year's end.

The second punch took our breath and our hearts away. It was an off field error, a rookie mistake, a stupid thing and looking back on it I only blame myself. We were on cruise control, lapping up the adoration from fans, press, analysts, everyone who mattered. And then the story hit. It spread like wildfire; fueled by social media, the endless sports channels, and commentators. We tried to get our arms around the problem, tried to control it, but we were consumed, engulfed by the fire before we could swing a pick ax or grab a hose to put out the flames.

Willy and I sat in his office, our heads bowed low covered by our hands, both thinking of a plan, a step, any type of action we could take.

It was a moment of truth, a real test of the person I professed to be. Even though we lost a game, we were still in contention for a national championship with our 8-1 record. I could picture the trophy ceremony in my dreams. There was nothing more I wanted than public proof of my coaching abilities. But the accolades came with a price. We were a tarnished team, our reputation on the line, our character in question, all because of a letdown off the field.

Damn I wanted that trophy. I craved the recognition, the acceptance, the bright lights shining on our accomplishments. I wanted the crowning achievement of my career to be memorable, celebrated, recognized by the media, the analysts, my peers, and my buddies. After all these years, my buddies from school still meant everything to me. We did not see each other that much as the years passed and our lives went in different directions. But these were the guys who had helped shape the person I had become. They knew me, the real me, from those school years when souls and spirits are molded. We went to ball games together and shared bad whiskey from hidden flasks. We skipped classes together when happy hour was a higher priority, then pulled all-nighters in hopes we would pass final exams. We lived together, played together, and watched each other grow toward manhood. Most of all, we made memories together. They had put in the time with me when buddies were more important than anything else. Earning their trust, their respect, and their friendship mattered.

And I wanted to beat Seth. Hell, I wanted to humiliate the jerk, stomp on him while he was down and get a picture of my foot on his neck. Then I took the test. I asked myself the question I had been using for a number of years. The question I had learned from the meet-ups with my buddies. *What would Seth do?* And my decision was obvious. It was not easy, but it was clear and I wondered why it took me any time at all to consider a different option.

"We have to suspend him Willy. We need to act right away and get back in control of this thing before it destroys him and our program," I said.

"There has to be something short of suspension. Come on Bob, let's think on things over night'"

"Willy, it's on us. Everyone is waiting, watching, but who cares about that, the hell with all the critics. It's about doing the right thing, and suspending him is the right thing. Then we will launch a full investigation and we'll ask the NCAA for help. Let's reach out to them now before they come to us."

"But the season's not lost Bob, we still have a chance for a great bowl game."

"Willy, right now I'm trying to save next season, this one is over."

"Shit. I know you're right Bob, I just hate giving up."

"It's my fault Willy, all my fault. I did not see this coming and it happened on my watch, right in front of me."

"No one saw this coming, me included. It won't do any good blaming yourself, I won't allow you to do that. We need you to pull things back together after we clean up the mess."

I nodded my head knowing Willy was right, but I still planned on a long guilt trip that would involve kicking myself in the butt and a number of head slaps, for at least a few months. *Damn, how could this have happened?*

Willy brought me back from my guilt trip. "Is he here now?"

I got up and opened the door, looked outside and saw Vince sitting on the couch. "Come on in Vince, let's talk about our next steps together."

As we prepared for the upcoming press conference, I kept thinking about my buddies and how they and their firms handle crisis:

◆◆◆◆

When Harry was fired for fudging sales numbers, his company acted quickly and forcefully. Even though Harry could shift some of the blame to his boss, he felt the brunt of the punishment. Management would not tolerate lying or cheating and sent a clear message to their employees, and to Harry, although they did help with his job search, knowing he was not solely at fault. On the other hand, Seth's firm seemed to have a wide tolerance for shady behavior. Management preached values publicly but practiced deception privately, encouraging employees to take personal risk. The bottom line was achieving business results, period. Their knowing eyes saw it all, rewarding ill-gotten gains regardless of approach. Publicly they lauded innovative human resource policies, and received industry acclaim for things written on paper. Behind closed doors they rewarded a ruthless pursuit of higher revenues, lower costs, anything that increased the share price, rules and laws be damned, just don't get caught.

I began to understand more about Seth and his turmoil within. He was a product of his environment, he understood the unwritten norms that were expected and rewarded. He found a way to excel, to behave as management expected, to produce the desired results, knowing what to reveal and what to keep hidden. He understood the nods, the smiles, and the winks from senior leaders. Seth was no dummy, he just wanted to be part of the in crowd, part of the leadership team someday. He craved inclusion and would do whatever it took to get there. So what if he had to lie, just a little? No problem. So what if he had to squash some toes, throw innocent people off the boat? No matter. As long as he got the wink or the nod or, better yet, a smile from the general manager while reviewing the business results at month end. That's what really mattered. The winks, nods, and smiles were directly aligned with salary increases and stock bonuses. Seth's management knew how to pull the strings that controlled employees like Seth. It was easy, so damn easy.

For a long time I thought football was unlike other organizations like Harry or Seth's. They were in big corporations and we played a game, there was no comparison. But over time, as the game grew into a business and I became the CEO with a large budget, an ever increasing staff, and the trappings of new and gleaming facilities, I began to feel more corporate and less gridiron. My own behavior had evolved and I had achieved my personal goal of coaching with more passion and less spit. I had actually moved beyond that point this season, possibly due to the eight wins in a row and began coaching with polish and no spit. I was becoming corporate, a real executive, and the highest paid wonk on the school payroll. I was way out of balance and wondered if maybe Coach Mac had it right all along. I needed more spit and less polish in my life.

◆◆◆◆

We were sitting at the press conference, Big Willy, Vince, and yours truly, and all I could think of was *more spit and less polish…more spit, less polish.* That was my last thought, my last shot at preparation as the cameras rolled and the lights lit up.

"I'd like to thank everyone for coming today. Coach Bob will get things started with some remarks, then we will open up for questions."

Willy signaled to me, 'it's time.' The lights were bright; the room was packed, (no way another sardine could fit in the paced space). I looked out at the crowd: *More spit, less polish.*

I set my papers down, the ones with the prepared remarks Willy and I had agreed on. The messages we had written with the help of the press team at the U were cautious, careful, and a bit too formal. There was no spit anywhere and that's what bothered me. This was not the time for polish. I looked to my left. "Sorry Willy."

He could tell I was heading in a different direction than we had agreed and seemed resolved. "It's alright, just don't take any shit from the bastards."

I looked to my right at Vince and saw he had his game face on. I dared not wink nor smile at him, so I kicked him under the table then whispered. "Here we go V, it's game time."

I looked at the bright lights and the microphones. The vultures in the audience were getting restless but I didn't care. They were about to eat and eat well.

"Good afternoon. I was fortunate to have a great teacher when I first became a high school football coach. He taught me about football of course, more importantly he taught me about life and how to influence young men in a positive direction during their formative years. He taught me how to help kids become men and be better people. He taught me about outcomes that mattered, the scoreboard being the least significant. He instilled in me and showed me how to behave, not just as a man, also as a leader. He taught me that leaders show everyone else how to behave through their actions not just their words. Leaders establish the norms that are accepted and those that receive discipline."

I paused, not for effect but to catch my breath. My heart was racing, my blood flowing, and I was doing my damndest to keep the sweat off my brow, but had no idea how to really control that.

I looked in the far corner of the room and saw Coach Mac, standing erect and proud, ready to tackle any reporter who got out of line. Seeing my mentor, the person who taught me everything about football, and life, gave me the courage to get through the rest of my adlib speech. For those in the audience it was a fairly boring introduction but not for me. For me it was a confession. Now it was time to liven things up.

"If you measure the results of our football program by wins and losses, then you would likely say we are doing well. An 8-1 record when most of you expected no more than 3-4 wins the entire season is a laudable achievement. But if you measure results beyond the scoreboard, beyond the win-loss record then I will be the first to admit failure. I have allowed you, the press, the analysts, and all the critics to take down our quarterback. You attacked from the blind side and Vince never saw it coming. He never saw you coming because I was not there to block you."

This time I paused for effect.

"It's my job to protect our players, to teach them right from wrong, to behave like men, and to set an example for the community. It is partly my fault we are in this mess, not just Vince's. I share the blame and accept full responsibility."

I could feel Vince looking at me, but I did not acknowledge him. I could visualize the surprise on his face but had to keep going or would never finish.

"Today I am announcing two suspensions from the football program. Tom and I have decided to suspend Vince until a full investigation is complete that exonerates him or proves his participation in the actions we have been reading about these past three days. Vince's suspension is indefinite. He will not practice with the team, not utilize the athletic facilities, not be part of the program until further notice."

I hoped the vultures saw the directness with which

Willy and I decided to act. Perception is reality and there was enough evidence for the public to feel the kid was guilty, but not beyond a shadow. I still held out hope, but we had to take firm, immediate action.

I took a sip of water and thought of Ames and Taylor, and wondered how they would react to my next announcement, part two of today's program. I cleared my throat and looked at the cameras.

"The second suspension is my own."

I turned to look at Willy. "Tom, I am suspending myself under the same guidelines just discussed regarding Vince. If he is found guilty then you will have my resignation letter on your desk that day. On the other hand, if he is found innocent, which is my full expectation, we will both be back on the field ready to go, if you will have us."

That was my cue for Willy to take back control. It was time for Q&A and Vince and I were locked down, leaving Willy to address the crap coming over the wall of microphones. The rest of the press conference was a blur; I did not realize it had ended until Vince pulled me away from my chair. As we turned to leave the room, V went back to the table. He called an audible, a QB sneak. "Excuse me. I have one thing I'd like to say."

The entire room went still. The vultures were full but had room for dessert. It had been a good meal, a very good meal with a surprise suspension, the coach axing himself on live TV. How often does that occur? And now the star QB, the street punk that took down the program would make a statement. It could not get any better than this, or could it? I could see these thoughts on their faces, the damn bastards, as Willy liked to call them.

Neither Willy nor I tried to stop Vince or advise him. He was not on his own, we were right behind him, but we had no idea what he was about to say and I doubted we could influence him anyway. At these moments you learn the real meaning of trust.

"I will never let Coach Bob or his family down. Never."

Vince was not defiant or angry or even mildly upset. He still had the stone face on, his demeanor was all about winning and he knew this was a life moment, not just another game. To him, he simply stated a fact, and then moved on.

Vince turned and looked at me then took a slow step and another, coming closer and closer. He reached out and gave me a hug in front of the crowd; he let the moment last for a few seconds, then pivoted and left the room. Willy and I followed, our day was done and so was my season.

As I drove home to explain the news to Ames and Taylor, I kept going back to the first conversation I had with Vince when the story broke:

◆◆◆◆

"Vince, I have just one question. Is it true?"

Vince shook his head back and forth for at least a minute, it seemed like five. "Coach, there's doubt in that question. Why do you doubt me? Have I done anything, anything at all these past two years for you to doubt me?"

That was a fair point. Score one for Vince, and yes I had my doubts. Once a street kid, always a street kid, right?

No, I did not believe that, but it did cross my mind. "You're right Vince, there was doubt in my question and you have not shown any reason for me to doubt you. I apologize. Now, what's going on and what are we going to do about it?"

Vince accepted my about face or at least pretended to. "Coach, someone has set me up. I don't know who and I don't know why, but they set me up good. I know it looks bad, real bad. I will find out and deal with it and him, whoever it is."

There we go back to street kid. Now who's showing doubt? "Slow down V, let's start from the beginning. Let's focus on the facts we know and build a plan, one block at a time. Let's start with what we know."

The press had pictures, lots of pictures. Every paper, website, and blog that had anything to do with sports ran the pictures, all the time. V signing autographs on jerseys, footballs, body parts, anything and everything. Then the damaging part, V taking money, a wad of cash here, a wad there, rolls and rolls of money. The implication was clear; V was selling autographs for money, lots of it.

And then it got worse. Another story exposed a gambling room run by Vince and a third hinted at a prostitution ring, although those details were a bit shaky. Nonetheless, the three sordid stories came together into some powerful fiction and the possible demise of our program. The typical headline was something like: "Street Kid brings his game to the U."

I guess it didn't matter there were plenty of so-called street kids on our team, in our conference, hell across of all college football. There was just not that many street kids playing quarterback for an 8-1 team that was expected to be no better than a 500 club.

The whole thing reeked, it made Vince look bad, made me look bad, made Willy look bad, and made the U a laughing stock. But I didn't care about that, how I looked in the public was of limited concern to me, until they went after my family. The bastards had pictures of Vince and Taylor, innocent pictures they turned into dirt and slime. Some even insinuated Taylor was Vince's girlfriend and helped him manage the business behind the scenes. That's when Ames blew the roof off our house and I'm still looking for it to come down.

The combined story fed on itself and kept getting larger, growing by the day, by the hour, by the minute. Anyone with a pen or keyboard was trying to outdo his or her peers, spreading the story around the campfire until the truth did not matter any longer. It was all about the story, truth be damned. If any one of the stories was true, then it was THE story of the college football season, over shadowing Saturday games, more important and a lot more interesting than end of year bowls.

Willy and I talked about it for hours, dissecting each piece of the three stories, separating facts from half facts from bald face lies. The pictures of Vince taking money for autographs was the problem we had to face, the rest of it was make believe stuff.

"Willy, I hope no one talks to Mike. If they find out how we landed Vince in the courtroom just prior to being thrown in jail, we are toast."

"Yeah, I've been thinking about that and I called Mike. He's cool as a cucumber and we all know the whole thing was a set up to get Vince off the streets. You fell for it big time."

"A set-up, huh. Ok, I'll admit it took me a while to fig-ure it out. And I thought we were lucky."

Willy and I were not having much success coming up with a plan; we needed some help and needed it soon. The day prior to the press conference Vince shared some news with Willy and me. It began to put things in perspective so we could deal with things. Vince brought Tony with him to meet us, that was something I did not see coming.

Tony had been working closely with Vince and easily shifted into a mentorship role, as I had hoped. Tony was good for Vince and they had paved a two-way street between them. Tony invited Vince to help out with a charity focused on young children with disabilities. These kids were stars in To-ny's eyes, they would never become athletes as he had, but they had pure hearts and loved seeing Tony whenever he came by. Vince had never worked with a charity and was unsure what he could bring to the table, but he went along for the ride. It did not take long for Vince to fall for the kids just like his men-tor. After a few visits together with Tony, Vince started making solo trips. Each visit gave him joy, much to his surprise and delight.

Vince noticed the environment for the kids needed a lot of work. The playground had old equipment, not designed for children with disabilities and there were few ramps for wheel chairs to take an easy ride. Vince was never one to let things rest that he cared about.

"Coach, I signed all those autographs just like you saw in the pictures. The jerseys, footballs, anything that moved and some things that didn't. And I took money for doing it. More money than I thought possible."

Willy and I looked at each other and shared an 'oh shit' moment.

Then Vince took out some pictures of his own. They were photos of a playground with new equipment, new ramps for kids with wheel chairs, new beds and toys. Then he showed us pictures of the children playing, laughing, bouncing on Vince's knee or riding on his back. In each picture Vince was smiling or laughing, enjoying each moment with his new friends. Vince had expanded his circle without my help and in a way that he and I would never have imagined.

"And that is what the money paid for. Every dollar went to the charity to do something good." Vince emphasized the word good and I could not help but think Taylor had something to do with that.

Willy asked the question that would reveal whether we had a small problem or a larger one. "Vince, the pictures show you accepting the money, not someone from the charity. Did you keep any records of what you were paid and what you gave to the charity?"

That's when Vince knew he was in trouble. Not for taking money on behalf of a charity, for not being smart about it. And Vince was always smart. That was my failure, allowing Vince to get in a situation where someone could take advantage of him. Not the charity of course, whoever took and sold the pictures. Vince should have known not to handle money directly; he was out of the pocket in the open with no protection. The QB and the coach had lost control and someone with a grudge stepped in to make a few bucks.

"I put the money in my pockets, then emptied my pockets into a bag and once a week I took the bag to the charity. Every dollar."

We sat there taking it in, four heads thinking as hard as we could. Vince did a good thing, hell it was a courageous and loving thing he should be proud of and celebrated for, not reviled. This was really pissing me off the more I thought about it, so I stopped thinking and tried talking instead. "Vince, first off, I'm proud of you for working with the disabled children and caring that much. I can tell from your pictures the impact you were having on the kids."

I told myself to remain calm, still, yet felt my temperature rising, something was ready to explode. "What the hell were you thinking Vince! Taking money for signing autographs and putting it in your pocket right there in public. What the hell were you thinking?"

Vince tried to respond but I cut him off, and then Willy cut me off and took over.

"Now, we all know the issue here is that you took money directly rather than on behalf of a charity, at least in the public eye. The bag transfers can be backed up by the charity, but the exact dollar amount can't. The implication will be that you kept some of it, or at least that will be the perception of our critics."

"I believe we can find a way to deal with the autograph for money part of the story, but it will require some form of punishment. The NCAA rules are very clear on that, although I expect they might be lenient in this case. Let's set that aside for now and discuss the other accusations. What about the gam-

Yardstick

bling Vince? Where do you believe that claim comes from?"

"We played poker at the dorm, nickel and dime stuff for fun. It was just the guys on the team, except two or three times a few outsiders sat in."

Willy and I shook our heads and shrugged our shoulders.

"You guys ever played low stakes poker?"

Willy and I looked at each other, both of us biting our tongues to keep the smiles off our faces.

"Do you know the names of the non-football players? They must be the leak that fed the press a half-baked story."

"No, but I'll find out."

"Ok, find out but don't do anything V. Now what about the prostitution, where is that coming from?"

"Coach, I have no idea, it's made up. It's some kind of sick joke and, and, I'm so sorry Taylor got involved in the story about that."

"Vince, Amy and I both know you would never do anything to harm Taylor. There must be something else to the story Vince. Can you think of anything?"

"Coach, I've always had an easy time with the ladies. Some of the guys on the team haven't been so lucky, they don't know how to talk or act when girls come around. So, I set a few of them up on dates."

"Don't stop there Vince, keep going."

"Maybe one or two of the girls were expecting something from me after they went out with the guys. They might not have been very forgiving when I did not return their calls."

We had three separate, but now related stories; all balled into a tragic and false deception of Vince the street kid practicing his homegrown craft at the U. It was explainable, each individual story, but it would require some evidence, and some people to back Vince up, even the ladies who had been turned aside.

The night before the press conference I was restless. I kept thinking about leadership and the lessons I had learned from Harry and Seth's experience at their firms. The companies they worked for were large corporations with pristine reputations, built and steeled over decades, their brands protected and defended by the best lawyers money could buy. Externally their corporate identities were faceless, cold, and inanimate. Inside the companies, in the hallways, offices, shop floors and meeting rooms were a collection of people, real humans who craved genuine leadership. I kept wondering why Seth's firm and Harry's were so alike publicly, yet so different within. It became painfully evident to me an organizations' behavior and its values are shaped at the top, by just a few leaders and then cascaded down. The organization models itself after these few standouts, those who fall in line succeed and those who don't fail. It might take a few years, maybe even longer to figure out the norms and rules that really run the organization. A dedicated student of the game like Seth learns faster than most. He was guided by greed and hubris, traits easily stoked and rewarded by the management he so desperately wanted to please.

Willy and I had devised a good plan, but it wasn't a great plan. We would suspend Vince and launch an investigation. A two-step plan that felt so average to me, so predictable, and so unfair. Vince would get hit and hit hard and while he deserved punishment, it did not match up with the wrong he

committed. He had done so much right and I worried he might be too fragile to handle all this pain alone. Vince fragile? Yeah, he was fragile within, where it counted most. I was not there for Vince when he needed protection, friendly advice, and some leadership from his coach. I could not let V go down, not alone, he might not get
back up.

I finally found some sleep when I knew what I had to do, to make it a great plan. In order to clearly demonstrate the type of behaviors and values I wanted the team to follow, some self-sacrifice was in order. Self-sacrifice is not that difficult when you know it's the right thing.

◆◆◆◆

I drove my car into our driveway and saw Ames and Taylor waiting for me, arms folded, faces frowned. I was hoping this would be the easy part.

"Bob, what have you done?"

"Dad, do we have to sell our house?"

I opened my mouth to offer an explanation and before I could get a word out, both ladies in my life ran into my outspread arms.

"You were wonderful Pops."

"Yeah Pops, the kid is right, you were pretty good."

"How about Vince, Pops, can you believe he stole the show with just one line? He left them scratching their heads wondering what is really going on."

As usual I was the hero, but for just a short moment.

We finished the season a disappointing 9-3 record, going 1-3 our last four games. The coaches and players fought hard each game but I could tell their spirit had taken a hit, and who could blame them? The stories about Vince began to fall apart over the coming weeks. Tony took the lead to work with the charity to get the right messages and quotes out to the press. They had kept count of Vince's donations and presented him with a receipt for tax purposes, taking a great photo-op of V, the kids, and Tony. The papers and websites did not run the pictures very much; it only served to make them look like fools.

The gambling and prostitution claims were more easily solved. Vince tracked down the outsiders who had joined the low stakes poker games to recant the lies they had told. They were naïve kids trying to boost their personal reputations by telling a few white lies. One lie led to another and before long they could not keep track of the snowball running down the hill. They surrendered easily and willingly. The ladies held out a bit longer and Vince never shared the deal he made to get them on the record. They had never said prostitution, the press made their own leap to create that story. The players that had dates set up for them rallied behind their QB and put an end to it. They had never paid for a date and never expected to.

We had solved the lies, and taken our punishment and hoped Vince would soon be cleared. The one piece left open was the pictures of Vince taking the rolls of money. We did not track down the photographer. We looked and looked but could not find the person or people responsible. The press who ran the pictures did not have a named source, they claimed to receive the photos anonymously. We wondered if someone was still out there gunning for Vince, reason unknown.

We watched our team play in a December bowl game, which we lost. It was a dismal ending to a season of promise and Vince and I moped around the house looking for sympathy around every corner. Ames and Taylor had other ideas, sympathizers they were not. The ladies challenged us to a game of football; touch not tackle, in the backyard.

"Come on boys, are you afraid of a couple girls?"

"That's right Mom, these boys won't know what hit them."

They ran outside in the snow and tossed the ball around. I swear they were yelling "chicken."

Vince and I shrugged our shoulders at the same time, laced up some shoes and ran outdoors. Watching Ames and Taylor made me laugh and cry, usually together. Vince, the big coward was doing the same but he would hide his tears when they came. *He'll learn*, I thought.

The girls scored first and rubbed some snow in our faces. Now the game was on. We rolled around, the four of us, for an hour, maybe more. My cheeks hurt from laughing so much. Ames and Taylor gave us the relief we sorely needed and we ended the game without knowing the score. It did not matter.

Sophomore Year

Chapter 24

Junior Year Part One

The day after Vince was cleared we both showed up at Willy's house early in the morning. The sun was up, barely. We banged on the door and Willy opened up after a long ten minutes, dressed in pajamas, covered by a robe. I dared not laugh, although the picture of Willy in PJs would haunt me for years to come. The sneer on his face meant this would be a serious chat. "Coach, Vince what the hell is going on? Do you know the time?"

"Willy, we're on our way to the gym."

"Well, that's just great, why do you think I care about that?"

"Willy, we can't use the university facilities unless you agree."

Willy looked bigger than ever, and not just because he was standing two steps higher. He knew how to make a stern face when needed. His lawyering skills came in handy, I just

257

wished now was not the time.

"Bob, when did you last check your e-mail? I sent you my approval hours ago as soon as we heard word from the NCAA. Now get off my porch and let me get back to sleep."

We turned to leave Willy's, ready for a long overdue workout.

"One other thing gentlemen. Bob, Vince, I expect ten wins this season. Not nine or eight, a full double digit winning season."

Then he came down the steps, looked each of us in the eyes and shook our hands, a big grin on his face, a real genuine smile that told both of us everything would finally be ok. "Glad to have you boys' back. It's been a bit lonely and too quiet without you two fools hanging around my office."

Spring Press Conference

During spring drills we typically held one or two meetings with the press, I'd hardly call them press conferences. But this year, the start of our new season after "Vincegate," the football circus was back in town and the press came in droves to see the wild animals at play. Never one to duck a controversy, I paraded the three of us back in front of the damn bastards. We sat at the table in a stare down, waiting for the gun to start the race. Willy nodded to me it was time to begin. I cleared my throat, braced myself for the unknown and had just started my prepared remarks when Vince said, "Coach, if you will allow me."

"You sure Vince?"

"Yeah Coach, I got this one."

Willy leaned over and started to say something but

Vince interrupted.

"Yes, I know, don't let the damn bastards get me." Then he smiled at Willy and pivoted to face the vultures. They did not look as hungry as the last time we were all together.

Every head in the room turned toward V. Our quarterback was exposed again, at least this time he had reasonable odds at a fair outcome. And then Vince surprised me, and shocked everyone in the room. He stood up, grabbed the wall of microphones and turned them around, facing the vultures. "I believe the gentlemen and ladies of the press have something to say before we begin."

The room went silent, most heads bowed, the press stared at their shoes uncertain or too embarrassed to act. The cameras rolled and I wondered how long our standoff would last. So far it was the best experience I ever had at a meeting with the press. To me the silence was golden. The lack of courage and decency to respond to Vince's challenge spoke volumes. *Damn, I should have taped this press conference to watch it again later.* I thought.

Finally, a brave soul stood, a seasoned reporter from a local paper, not one of the big city boys down to see the circus. He was a high caliber reporter who was fair and often accurate. He cleared his throat, "I believe that I can speak for all, well most of the press, when I say the stories and pictures from last season went too far, way too far."

He sat back down in the first row. The three of us did not move, not a twitch nor muscle spasm of any kind. The silence returned and I enjoyed counting every second of it.

The same reporter got back up and went back to the

mikes. "I'd also like to acknowledge that we helped bring harm to the three of you and the U. We could have investigated the stories more than we did. I for one would like to get back to football and away from all the distractions. Welcome back Coach, Tom, and most of all Vince."

He stopped short of an apology, which may have been too much to expect. It was a good atonement and I could see most heads, though not all, nodding in agreement.

"Ok Vince, let's get our next season started," I said.

"Not yet, Coach, we need one more thing."

Vince signaled to Zach who was in the back of the room. He opened the door and in walked Taylor and Ames. The room turned around and saw my family, their pride and reputation fully intact. Amy and Taylor walked to the front of the room, a slow promenade, their heads held high, no smiles on their faces.

No one dared move nor speak. Again, the silence was music to my ears. All the pressure was on the vultures as they had the burden to act, to speak, or to walk out of the room, which would have been fine with me.

Finally, the same reporter stood for his third and last attempt. He was the one brave soul in a roomful of cowards. "Coach, on behalf of the press I'd like to offer an apology to your family, in particular your daughter. We should not.... There was no way we could have ... It was unfair how we...."

It was painful listening to the man. He could not complete his thoughts, he was stuck in a self made rut.

While we waited for him to find his place, I reflected back on last season, lost in my own thoughts.

++++

I had missed five weeks of the football season, five long hard weeks, the scariest episode of my career. There was a void in my life that was hard to describe. It was a black hole of some kind that I could not fill no matter what I did. I missed the game, the players, the coaches, the fans, and all the people who floated in and out of the team, even those who did not really matter, even the alumni. Hell, I missed the press, sort of. It was like a part of me had been ripped out and not replaced.

If I could get back to my job, to my team, I would have a better appreciation for all the things I took for granted, I realized. I promised that I would be a better coach, a better leader, and a better man. I vowed that I would even be kind to the press, those I had considered my enemies, the people who had spread lies about family. I concluded the reporters were not bad guys, not really. Like me, they were dealing with a perfect storm, three incredible stories that came together in some kind of tornado with little time to react. Publish or perish must have been their motto, the clock on the wall the real enemy of the press, facts be damned. It would have been easy for me to erect a wall between the team and the press, locking the bastards out, keeping the players, the team, and my family safe. But I knew that approach would not work, I would not accomplish anything positive, I would not teach the players anything at all. Instead, I took the opposite route; transparency would be my tool, my weapon of choice. The best way to get to the truth where facts mattered more than fiction was to be open, accessible, quotable, and kind.

++++

Finally he came up with one simple sentence that said it all. "Coach, we blew it."

He wanted to say more but did not have the words, unusual for a seasoned reporter. I guess apologies were not his strong suit; at least he had some fortitude to stand up for his profession.

Ames and Taylor seemed satisfied and walked back out of the room. Ames had finally found the roof that had been blown off our house a few months ago.

It was time to heal, someone had to take the first step, and that someone would be me. I turned the microphones back around, looked out at the audience without malice, put my best smile on, and said the words everyone wanted to hear, "Let's talk football."

I could sum up the spring press conference with two questions, each asked a hundred different times and a hundred different ways. Was last season a fluke? How will you handle all the distraction? The boys and girls in the press core were becoming very predictable, which made my job and life a lot easier. No, last season was not a fluke; we won eight games in a row and have much of our team back again this year. Distraction, what distraction? This year should be a breeze compared to last year.

Chapter 25

Vince

Vince and I had finally settled into a routine. Without saying much, we began to understand each other, respect each other, and dare I say, like each other. As a football player he commanded my attention, his talent and skill on the field was something special to see. As a person, he did not make it easy, not because he wanted it to be hard. He just didn't understand how to ease into a relationship, he had never learned how and besides he never needed anyone, certainly not the way he thought about it. This facet of his upbringing did not become apparent until I tried to answer Amy's question. *Where is Vince from?* Like the first peel of an onion, asking someone where they are from and getting a reply, allows the questioner to keep on going, peeling back all the layers until the core is revealed. The key thing is getting that first reply.

To get a response from V, I decided it was time for a road trip while we were serving our suspensions.

++++

Vince and I were brooding around town, unable to join the team, our hands tied, our stomachs in knots. We were forced to spend time with each other because everyone else in our lives was busy. They all had things going on, things to do, lists to manage; only the two of us had hit the pause button, not knowing when, or if, the reset button would be punched. It would be an adventure, I told myself. We might as well hit the road, go see the big city, visit Vince's hometown, see where he was raised, maybe run into some of his past.

"Vince, we're going on a road trip to the city. Get packed for a couple days, I'll pick you up tomorrow around 9:00 a.m."

I hung up the phone before the protest could be lobbied. The next morning Vince was on time for a change, though not an eager participant. It would still require some encouragement to get this show on the road.

"Coach, what are we doing?"

"Vince, we're heading to Chicago for two reasons. We need to get away from this place. It's killing us to be here unable to do anything.

"What's the second reason?"

"Vince, I want to better understand you. And the best way I know how to do that is to go see where you grew up, meet some of your past, get to know your family history."

There, I said it straight. No beating around the bush with V, he would smell a setup and escape from a trap. The best strategy with V was head on. I had my serious face on, the one that said don't mess with me, I hoped.

"Ok, Coach."

That was the reply I wanted, actually much better than expected. The first peel was done.

We drove in silence much the same as our first trip down to the U together, only this time we were headed into unchartered territory without much of a game plan, other than peeling an onion one layer at a time.

I vaguely remembered where Vince's uncle lived and pointed the car in that direction. After ten minutes driving in circles it was clear the car was lost due to driver ineptness, but the passenger was not in a helpful mood. I pulled to car to the curb and turned off the ignition. "Vince, does your uncle live nearby? Would you like to see him?"

Vince looked straight ahead and I tried to read his expression. There was a mixture of pain, confusion, and mostly sadness. I was not feeling good about the road trip, yet I was not ready to give up. There was bound to be some pain, it was the only way to get to the heart of things. I needed to peel another layer to get the ball rolling again. "Vince, Amy and I have enjoyed opening our family to you. I'd like to learn about yours now if you will let me."

Vince turned his head and looked at me, a tear ran down his cheek and his hands did not move to wipe it away. I had never seen Vince show this much emotion, well maybe the hug he shared with Taylor on Christmas Eve was on par with this moment, but that was it.

I nodded my head up and down, letting Vince know it

was ok; we would take our time, no need to peel the onion quickly.

"Coach, he's not my uncle. Not my blood relative, no relative of any kind. Mom had a number of uncles; they earned that distinction with the green they paid her. Not every customer was called "Uncle," only the best regulars."

I did my best to remain still, nodding to V that it was ok to keep talking. Inside I was dying a slow tortuous death. I felt as if my own son had gone through hell with no one by his side. I wanted to tell him it would be ok, everything would be just fine, but we had just started and Vince had a lot more to share. "Mom died when I was sixteen. She smoked the pipe and tried to get off the drugs but kept going back. It was her way to escape reality and the life we lived. She loved us kids and did what she had to do, to put food on the table after our father left. Just like the stories you have read, we did not have a traditional home, it crumbled around us when he hit the road and he never came back. Not while mom was alive and not after she died. To replace the father we did not have, mom called the nice ones "Uncle." There were two or three she favored more than the others, I think she hoped they would be there for us when she was gone. She knew she would not be around for long.

"After she died, there was nowhere to go, no father, no family, and no apartment. I hung around the streets and learned how to fight, when to run, where to hide, how to steal, and how to survive."

"Vince, you said us, what did you mean by us?"

Vince broke down, head in hands, crying out loud,

yelling a name. Serena, it sounded like Serena, a girl's name.

"Who is Serena, Vince?"

"Serena is my sister, my younger sister."

I had no idea Vince had family, a sister. That made all the sense in the world to me, and I understood what drew him to Taylor. We sat there a long time as Vince told me about his sister, Serena.

She was a year younger than Vince and a few years wiser as most girls are at that age. They hung together and protected each other as they watched their mom fade away. The apartment they shared had one bed and a couch that Vince and Serena shared. The bed was for business; the couch for sleep when business was done for the night. When the uncles stopped calling, everything fell apart. The rooms went cold, and the cupboards went bare. Vince and Serena did what they could to keep hunger and fear away, scraping and clawing, borrowing and stealing, hugging their mom in the morning and again at night. But it did not take long, their mom could not fight, could not beat death back, she was too weak to make a stand. Vince and Serena lost a mom in their early teen years, starved of a childhood and no one cared.

Serena, a younger sister, became a mother overnight. She encouraged Vince to stay in school and play ball. "Just focus on those two things so you can get smart and get out," she told him. When Vince would ask what kind of ball, Serena would say, "It doesn't matter. Just play ball, any kind of ball. Practice hard, use your talents, your skills, and show the coach how good you can be. Stay in school and play ball." Sometimes those were the only words Vince would hear from Serena for days. Serena and Vince stayed together as long as they could, disregarding one eviction notice after another.

A few days after the third eviction notice, one of the uncles showed up and offered a room at his place. Vince was thankful, but Serena was scared. He talked her into it, they had no other option and the apartment was warm in the evening. It didn't take long for the uncle to take advantage of Serena. She became the maid, the cook, and the errand girl, running all over town to deliver the uncle's "product," the same product he had supplied to their mother. Serena knew he would want more than that and one night he came for her after Vince had gone out.

Serena did not speak a word; she put food and warmth a bit higher than safety and comfort, anything for Vince. That's what she told herself, sacrifice for Vince, her brother was worth some pain.

But Vince knew. It was easy to see. Uncle showed his cards every time Serena walked by in her tight blue jeans. That chilly night Vince went out as usual, but turned back and stayed hidden just outside the front door. He peeked inside to see the uncle take Serena to the back room. Vince snuck back in the apartment and his gloved hand grabbed a baseball bat from the closet. He was determined to use the bat to get the uncle away from Serena so brother and sister could escape. Vince walked quietly into the back room and saw Uncle push Serena onto the bed. She stifled a scream, her eyes wild with fear as Vince stepped up to the plate. Uncle pulled back from the bed, a knife in his right hand. He laughed at the kid with the bat and challenged him to fight a real man. Uncle was quick and slashed with the knife, a move he had used many times before. Vince shifted back to escape the thrust, then pivoted forward and took a full swing at Uncle's left knee. Uncle went down to the floor with a loud yell, and then sat up, a tragic mistake as his head was in the strike zone. Uncle coiled for a second slash with the knife but Vince was quicker. He pulled the bat back for another whack and smashed the back of Uncle's head. Uncle sank down, his body limp, never to rise again. At age sixteen Vince had notched a kill.

Vince and Serena cleared out, taking with them all they owned which was not much more than the clothes on their back. They took separate paths, and vowed to meet up in three days to create a new plan. They would live together somewhere else, a place far away, and begin a new life. They had each other; they would always have each other. Serena suggested the time apart, it seemed a smart move at the time. They needed to put some space between themselves and their dead uncle. Vince reluctantly agreed and hugged his sister, then watched her go. It would only be three days. They could both handle three days apart. Vince waited at the meeting place on the third night and another nine nights after that, until he knew Serena would never show.

She could not keep secrets from her brother, her best friend, her only friend. She had to escape or he would see her belly grow and realize he had not protected her. Serena knew Vince could not take any more failure in his life; he was just a boy trying to be a man. No matter how tough he appeared on the outside, he was too weak where it counted. She would not show on the third night or any night, not until she had it all figured out.

On that tenth night Vince pulled a veil over his soul. He had lost everything, a mom who could not stay away from drugs, a father who did not want a family, and a sister who had to get away from a place that no longer felt like home. Vince and Serena both lost their innocence at an early age. He made a promise to himself that night to never feel again. That would be his escape; he would keep his emotions away, never allowing another to take anything from him. There was nothing left to take and Vince had turned to stone.

Vince lived on the streets for the next two years, going to school when he could and playing ball when he was allowed. He slept at another "uncle's" place, although they never established any real relationship, both knowing and not talking about the other uncle, the dead one. The police never questioned Vince, never looked for Serena, and never solved the baseball bat case, as it became known. There were just too many murders in the city for the police to handle and Uncle became another file that collected some dust. But the street knew, the street always knew. V had established a rep, he had built some cred with two swings of the bat and no one wanted to get in his way. The street did not care that Vince was playing defense that he did not intend to kill, that he reacted to the knife thrusts with protective instincts. All that mattered was that Vince had beaten a brutal man at his own game.

For Vince everything good in his life was gone, there was nobody in his corner, no one who really cared. There was only the street, and the dead body lying in the bedroom as he walked out the door and tossed the bat on the floor. There were no good memories of any kind, except the one thing, the only thing that had mattered his entire life, Serena. His sister had been the only good thing he knew, and he missed her. He realized Serena would never reenter his life if he stayed on the streets. She had escaped, must have escaped, and found a way to be good. He searched for some sign, anything that would show him a path to the good. Somehow he knew he had to help himself, he had to take an action to get off the streets, to get away from the bad, for good. He was alone and only he could turn his life around. He knew what gave him meaning, and the person that kept urging him on. Even though Serena was not around, she was always there, as a sister and a mom, quietly talking to Vince at night when he could not find sleep. Serena's voice would not go away, she kept encouraging Vince to be better. Serena told him it was ok to ask for help, to find someone willing to lend a hand, but only if he worked for it, earned it, and repaid it.

Vince knew the streets were where he belonged, but not where he wanted to be. The streets were the only life he knew, but there had to be something else, something more, and something good. Life expectancy was low, damn low for a punk kid who stole for a living. Vince had heard of Mike from other kids who had escaped and never came back to the streets. He would call Mike, ask for help, and see if there was someone out there who cared enough to make a difference.

I felt Vince's story, it seared my heart and burned a hole in my bones. It's hard to describe the hurt I felt when someone I cared about, someone who felt like a son, was in so much pain. My son was in pain and I wanted to make it go away. That's how I felt. The pieces of the puzzle were all put together now, and everything finally made sense. The escape from Cook County Court that Mike had arranged with the judge, the silent ride to the U, the raw talent that no one had tamed, the closeness V and Taylor had achieved. It all came together. I had finally peeled back all the layers and saw the fire burning in Vince's soul.

Vince was all talked out after sharing his story for the first but not the last time. I did not offer a solution to any problem, did not try to make sense of it all, and did not even try to speak. I offered the only thing that mattered, the love of a father for his son.

The minutes passed. After a while I decided our next move. "Vince we need to tell the authorities about Uncle and the baseball bat. I can give Mike a call and he can show us the right steps to take. You ok with that son?"

Vince did not speak, only nodded his agreement. He did not put up a fight, he was done fighting, tired of playing defense, tired of his past trying to catch up with him. The press stories, while not accurate, had hit too close to home, bringing V back to the streets, a place he longed to leave. The press had missed the real story, they had focused on gambling, prostitution, money for autographs, but they had missed the big one. They missed the killing of a brutal, bad man by a sixteen-year-old kid who was only defending himself and his sister. V, a street kid with no positive influence, no family, no mentors to guide him, had turned his life around by coming to the U. He crawled out of a deep hole and was paying it back. That's why he was so drawn to the disabled kids; they were his way to earn it.

While that was a genuine, heart-warming story, one that could be a positive influence on others, the challenge was actually getting the press to write a positive story about a kid from the streets. It was too easy to focus on the bad, and the belief that the bad sold papers. Maybe they should look at paper sales for the past 10 years. Bad was not selling very well.

We met with Mike the next day, he knew what to do, who to call, the legal processes to follow and the tactics to avoid. We stayed in Chicago the next week and Vince retold his story. The DA was fair and did not hold Vince in a cell; he believed Vince and wanted to clear an old case. We left Mike's office with renewed hope that Vince could finally put his past behind him. Rather than hiding from the truth, V was now out in the open, he laid it all on the table and put trust in someone else. Mike hired a detective to find the witness, the only witness who could back-up Vince. That was the deal we made with the District Attorney. We needed to find Serena so she could help her brother. We left the matter in Mike's capable hands and headed home.

On the drive back to the U, I thought of Jerrod and how his life was so different from Vince. All of us are shaped by our home, the schools we attended, the communities we grew up in, the friends we made, and the few buddies we keep for life. Jerrod had a strong loving family that valued education, discipline, and work ethic. Vince had a dead mother, a runaway father, and a sister he had not seen in years.
Jerrod had dreams and plans to make them come true. Vince had nightmares and did his best to escape them by closing himself to the world.

I tried to compare how and where Vince was raised to my own upbringing but quickly saw the futility. When will they learn? When will someone do something? These were the questions and reactions I always heard from neighbors, family, and anyone who lived in safe places. It's all too easy to put distance between them and us, that's how most people seem to think about it: them and us. It's just a statistic when another sad story is in the news. A short 24-hour cycle later, the story is gone and the news has moved on and then it repeats again, and again. That's what numbers do, they pile up and pile up some more, keeping the city calculators busy.

I did not have any immediate answers to the societal problems that Vince made me understand. The only thing I knew for certain was the statistics finally had meaning, now that it was personal for me. As I pulled into the driveway at home my last thought from the road trip was that Chicago would have been the big winner if Mayor Jerrod had arrived in town.

Chapter 26

Junior Year Part Two

I had never been more ready and better prepared for a football season than this year. I was well rested, our quarterback and leader had his head straight, our center showed others how to earn a starting role, our defensive coordinator had the energy of a man 20 years younger, and the press began writing positive stories about our team. The bad mojo from last year was behind us but not forgotten, lest we make the same mistakes all over again.

And something else fell into place for me, something more important than just about everything else. The road trip with Vince helped me think about how I measured success. I was still primarily motivated by helping "ladies become men," that was my inspiration, my motivation for getting up in the morning. That and the two million per year I squeezed out of Willy. The new insight I discovered was that I had role models for the players, real people with real lives and experiences who

I could point to as examples of how to build a positive path in life. My buddies, right there in front of me all this time had grown into the role models I could use to show the "ladies" how they could become men, real men.

The dots that were waiting for me to connect them, fell into place. I wanted the boys to take a lesson from Scott on how to help others build a sound financial plan for all the stages in their lives. I wanted them to look up to Kevin and learn how a corporate executive handles himself and makes decisions that affect people's lives. I wanted them to learn from Harry how to motivate their peers and rebound from trouble. The players could learn from Mike how to reach out to people in need and help them get back on the right road. They could look up to Willy and learn how to set a goal in life and go after it. My buddies were the examples for me to use with these kids.

I would also use Seth as an example of what not to do, although I did not want to tell Seth that. I called Kevin after figuring all this out; it was time for a favor and he was the perfect person. "Kevin, it's time for a favor."

"Hmm, a favor huh. Who's doing the favor and what do they get in return?"

"You're gonna love this one Kevin. This favor could be a great deal, with a lot of winners, including you."

I explained to Kevin what was needed and the role he would play. He would set up the alumni program to work with the players, while they were students and after they graduated. The program would include motivational speakers, mentorships, and a network to help with job hunts. Rather than doling out cash under the table as a few schools were doing, we would give career and life advice above board, out in the open and within NCAA guidelines. This would be a program about life after football, not consumed with the game on the field.

"What do you think Kevin, are you in?"

"Yeah, I'm in, definitely in. Give me a few weeks to get the program scoped, and recruit some volunteers. Then I'll be back and we can talk about a kick-off."

"Thanks Kevin, I think you will really enjoy running this thing. Before I forget, I have a player to set up with Scott and I'll get that connection made. Let's think of a good name for the program too, I'll leave that to your creative side. Now, what can I do for you in return?"

"Bob, the only thing I'd like is to watch the home games on the sidelines. I'll stay out of the way, hell I'll stay down near the end zone. It would be very cool to watch the games up close."

Football Season

All signs pointed towards a good season, perhaps a great season.

And then we lost our first two games.

We were favored to win the conference and began the year with a top ten rating. I never saw Willy smile so much; he kept repeating two words over and over: "Top Ten. Top Ten." Whenever I saw him coming I ducked down the hall, or hid behind a player, anything to escape Big Willy. We had enough pressure on our backs, I didn't want Willy's glowing smile to be a reminder of the lofty expectations everyone had for this team. Besides, Willy always made me laugh. And that was not a good thing, not when I wanted and needed to be in a serious mood.

It only took one game to remove the smile from Willy's face. Five turnovers will do that. We gave that first game away, a gift to an unranked, though talented opponent. They protected the ball and played a tough, conservative, time consuming running game, making it difficult for our offense to get on the field after we gave up the football. Vince threw three interceptions in the first half, each a fluke of some kind. The first a deflection that bounded off two players before being scooped up for a 75 yard pick six. The second went through a receiver's hands as he was crossing the goal line for a score into the defender's arms, and the third hit a lineman in the helmet, flew ten yards in the air and was caught by a linebacker for another touchdown return. We were down by seventeen after the first ten minutes! The other two turnovers were fumbles by our punt return team and broke our backs. Our defense kept making stops only to spend more time on the field as we fumbled the game away. Vince brought us back with four touchdowns in the second half, three by air and one by land but we could not recover the on-sides kick as time expired on the clock.

It would be difficult to rebound from losing the first game, but not impossible. There were plenty of teams that went on to win championship games with a loss on their record. But there were none I could find that lost their initial two games of the season. We had to win the second game; there was no scenario that worked if we didn't.

The second game was a nightmare that I will relive time and again. We played with no heart and no passion, as if the season was already over. Our opponent was a ranked team, a non-conference game that was scheduled years ago. We got outplayed, outcoached, and were run out of the stadium. The sad thing is we were a better team, a much better team, if we had only showed up to play. We lost by three points and missed a 50-yard field goal as time expired. The game was not that close and we all knew it. We got beat at all phases of the game and deserved the outcome, our second loss in two tries. On the plane ride home the team was quiet, deadly quiet. But their thoughts were easy to hear; everyone was thinking the exact same thing: "The season was over, a bust, a complete waste of an opportunity and we had no one to blame but ourselves." I never saw so many big strong men acting like such babies, heads hung low, shame in their faces, feeling sorry for their state in life.

The self-loathing lasted for half the plane ride home then shifted to finger pointing. The offense blamed the defense that blamed the special teams who held the offense at fault. Griping and name-calling soon replaced the deadly quiet. Threats were lobbied across the aisles, and emotions escalated as each player wanted to rid himself of blame and guilt. It only took two weeks for us to get kicked off our perch on top of the mountain and tumble down the hill to rock bottom. It's a damn ugly place to be. We were on the bottom on the outside with our 0-2 record, and we were on the bottom on the inside, each individual casting aspersions on another.

No one was more disappointed than me because I too had fallen for the lofty expectations and saw a champion when I looked in the mirror. I believed in the hype, what the press wrote, and what we thought about ourselves. What a fool I had been.

I walked to the front of the plane, stood in front of the team, and waited for silence. It did not take long for the griping and bickering to halt, the ladies knew when it was time for obedience and that time was now.

"Gentlemen, what can we do now to change the outcome of the game we just played? Anyone have a suggestion how we can put more points on the board and turn that sorry loss into a win?"

Silence.

"Will anyone give me an answer? Does anyone have the guts to answer the damn question? What the hell can we do right now to change the score of the game we just played?"

More silence.

"Look at yourselves, feeling sorry for your lot in life, feeling guilty for the block you missed, the tackle you did not make, the turnover you gave to our opponent. Is any of that self pity going to change the outcome of the game?" Huh, I want an answer!"

Vince rose from his seat. "Coach, we got beat tonight and we can't change the score. We beat ourselves since we didn't play the game we should have played."

It was real quiet.

"Anyone have another response? Anyone disagree with Vince? You're damn right we beat ourselves tonight. We got outplayed, outcoached, and kicked out of the stadium with our tails between our legs. We stunk and we lost."

Silence.

"But there's not a damn thing we can do about it now. It's over, done, in the rearview mirror. And it's not going to

Yardstick

change. The choice we have in front of us is what to do next. How will we prepare for the next game, the rest of the season? How will we behave? Will we act as cowards and blame the teammate or the coach to our right and our left? It's someone else's fault, not mine. Is that right?"

Silence.

"Well, let me be the first one to say, I screwed up. I blew it. I did not coach a good game tonight. But it's done and there's not one thing I can do about it now. Except learn from it, get better because of it, and win the next game."

I needed to end this rant but I was still upset, and wanted to hit something, anything. With everyone looking at me, I knew it was time to move forward. "A great man once said: 'We must learn to live together as brothers, or perish together as fools.' That was Martin Luther King, Jr. and we all know the journey he took in his short life, the pain he endured, the sorrow he saw, and the losses he experienced as they piled up one after another. But he kept going, held his head high, showed others how to behave and how to fight as a real man. He knew that others looked up to him and that one day, together they would win, but only if they kept trying, kept putting their best foot forward, never give up the fight, and most of all stay together.

"So tonight, I challenge you, each one of you, to not give up, to fight again next week, the week after, the entire season, and beyond that. I challenge you and I challenge myself to demonstrate the character we have as individuals, and the strength we have together as a team. "In other words, get over it and come to practice tomorrow ready to change our path, together."

The next day Willy asked for us to meet, usually we did not get together until half way through the season. "Bob, how is the team doing? Have you figured out what is going on?"

"Willy, I've been wracking my brain. I felt we were ready. Vince is back and in top form. Coach Mac has the defense rocking; they are even better than last year. I see two weak areas we need to address. First, our special teams play needs work; we are sloppy and making too many mistakes. Secondly, we underestimated the impact of last year on our psyche. We have not been in the game mentally and we need to snap out of it."

"What do you propose doing to get back on track?"

"I want to hire a new special teams coach, a guy named Tom Norman up in Michigan. He's a bit crazy, but there is no one better at special teams and getting kids fired up."

"Ok Bob, let's move on that as soon as you are ready. What about getting the team mentally ready. How will you snap them out of this trance they seem to be in?"

"Willy, we're going back to the fundamentals. In situations like this, I want to get the team focused on blocking, tackling, and hanging on to the ball. We are going to practice hard every day and eat a lot of turf, like Coach Mac taught us in high school. And, we're going silent in the media. No press conferences, no interviews, we need to look inward for a while and keep everything and everyone else out. You know how much I hate doing that, but it will only be temporary, until we get our act together."

"Ok Bob. You know I'm behind you. It's just so damn

disappointing to start the season with two losses and I know you feel that more than anyone."

"Damn shame Willy; it's a real damn shame. But don't count us out just yet, we still owe you ten wins this year and we're going to get it done."

I left his office before he could respond.

Chapter 27

Junior Year Part Three

We spit up turf for the next six days. Even the coaches were doing drills and they were not very happy about it, but no one dared to complain. Coach Mac and I drilled everyone, it was a week of spit; there was no polish anywhere to be found. We got back to basics and beat the hell out of each other.

"Run it again."

The offense was working on pass protection and a new set of plays I installed for Vince to take advantage of his ability to throw on the run, out of the pocket.

"Again. Run it again."

After three days of hard practice and no motivational speeches, the offense was in a real good groove. Players ran out of the huddle to the ball, eager to dole out punishment to the second team defense.

"Run it."

I could do this all night. Mac was drilling the defense

on the other end of the field and I could tell he was back in his element. Turf never tasted so good. It was getting late but I was not done, not even close. I blew the whistle and Mac and the defense came over and the players knelt down, waiting for the closeout speech to end practice. *Not a chance ladies, we've got more work to do.* "First on first. Let's find out how ready we really are for the next game."

I did not hear any groans, no hesitation, the players rose quickly into their huddles. First team offense against first team defense was never something to take lightly. Mac huddled with his team and the offensive coordinator and I huddled with the offense.

Vince took his red jersey off as he stepped in to call the play. He wanted a real game without the protection of the red. That's what I liked about V; he always wanted to put everything out in the open.

I blew my whistle. "Vince put the red back on. I may be crazy, but I'm not stupid."

We went hard for thirty minutes, real hard. Both sides claimed victory, although I called it a draw. I saved the next thirty for special teams and Coach Tom who joined us two days earlier. I could not wait to see him perform on the sidelines on game day.

Saturday came quickly and we were ready, we were finally ready. The hard practices had broken everyone down and pushed out any and all thoughts about last year and our first two games this year. All spit and no polish may have removed our shine, but it gave us an inner strength, a toughness, a meanness, and we wanted to take it out on someone else.

"Gather round men."

It was finally time to take the field for our third game and I wanted the players to go out there and release all their bottled up frustration on our opponent.

"Ok men, we begin conference play today. One of our top goals this year is to be conference champs and we get to set our path starting right now. We had a hard week of practice, full of fights, blood, bruises and a lot of ice. I'm pretty sure we broke the damn ice machine and if we did, I'll buy a new one because we are going to use a lot more the rest of this year. This week made us tougher, it made us better, and it made us ready."

I had an edge to my speech; the players knew I was still mad. Hell I was damn angry about our start to the year and I knew they felt the same.

"There is a quote from a United States General that should be useful for us today. 'The object of war is not to die for your country, but to make the other bastard die for his'."

The players laughed at that, but just a little. They were not ready to shift from anger to laughter until after they earned it on the field.

"That was General George S. Patton, and that quote sure sounds like the man I have read about. Men, you have been eating turf all week and I know you're damn tired of it. How about we make our opponent eat the turf today and take a lesson from old George? "Let's get out there and get a win!"

The players stormed out. I hoped they retained some energy for the game and did not leave it all on the practice field and in the locker room. I could see the walls were bashed in, that was going to cost me some money too.

Mac and I walked out the tunnel together as we always did. I usually initiated our conversations, but not this time. I was all stone, rigid, and uptight.

"Coach, our opponent is going to see some hell today."

"Mac, we're going to play our game today. About time, about damn time."

Our opponent won the coin toss and elected to receive the ball. Coach Tom got his kick-off team together on the sidelines and I saw a lot of head slapping, and players hitting each other to get ready. The kids were excited, I was excited, the whole stadium was screaming with anticipation.

And then I heard it. I heard the growling. Coach Tom was growling like he did when we were in Michigan together. He was running up and down the sidelines, yelling at his players, and growling up a storm.

Our kicker lined up and placed the ball on the tee. My memory banks flashed a warning light, which traveled quickly to my brain, and I realized Tom was growling and his kick-off team was on the field. I looked down the sidelines at Tom and he gave me a grin, a big beaming grin.

Oh shit.

The kicker raced to the ball and dribbled a high bouncer forward about eleven yards. Our opponent did not anticipate the on-sides surprise and we recovered on the forty-six line. The crowd went wild and I saw Tom leap into the air, surrounded by the kick-off team. In one play our special teams had recaptured its pride and sent a signal to the entire team, it was time to play some damn football.

The offense took the field and went right to the ball. We skipped the huddle, and would seldom use one the entire day. Zach and the line got in their stance ready for the first play. That's when Zach saw the tape. Every defensive player had tape on their left wrist and written on it the numbers '0-3.' The numbers were printed backwards so our offense could read the intended insult. The middle linebacker snickered his disrespect.

"That's right boys, you're going down. Oh and three baby. No wins and three losses after today, you can bet the house on it!"

Zach rose from his stance and pointed to the linebacker. "He's mine, all mine."

Vince audibled at the line and changed the first play from a pass to a run. He wanted the offensive line moving forward into the defense, not back pedaling. He would give Zach a chance to put the LB down on the game's first play.

A bead of sweat dripped from Zach's forehead onto his facemask and sat there for three seconds before it fell to the ground. Zach wondered if blood and tears would join the sweat before the days end. He put his right hand around the ball, feeling the laces across his thumb. Z liked knowing he would be the only person to touch the football on every offensive play. He looked up and saw the middle linebacker shift forward, then backward, trying to get Zach or some other lineman to jump off sides. The cocky kid was yelling again, singing his favorite tune: "Oh and three...Oh and three."

Zach snapped the ball and charged ahead. He stayed low, kept his head up as he was taught, and searched out his target. The LB was coming toward Z. It would be a collision on the first play of the game. They smashed into each other; Z was lower and had the leverage. He drove his right shoulder and helmet into the LB, grinding with his legs.

Grind. Grind. Grind.

The whistle blew.

Grind. Grind. Grind.

Zach pushed the LB back two yards, five yards, ten yards. He heard the whistle but did not stop, not yet.

Grind. Grind. Grind.

He heard the whistle again, now two whistles were blaring in unison. He began to lift up.

Grind and lift. Grind and lift.

He felt the LB moving up into the air, his feet off the ground. Just another inch or two and Z would have the angle.

Grind and Lift. Lift. Lift.

Z had him. Now force him down. Down toward the ground, then drive the shoulder through, jamming the LB hard into the turf.

The LB felt himself going up in the air and tried to shake the block. The LB turned his body to the right, trying to struggle free, but to no avail.

Grind. Down. Grind. Down.

Zach drove the LB into the ground, hard. The LB was in a poor position because he had twisted himself around as Z had set him up for the fall. The LB's facemask hit the ground first, his chinstrap broke and the helmet popped loose and flew up in the air.

Grind. Grind. Grind.

Now the LB had no head protection, his cheek was on the turf, then his mouth. Z kept pushing, hard. The LB yelled for the ref, for his coach, for his mom.

Z landed on top of the LB and gave one last push, a hard hit with his shoulder. Then Zach reached out and grabbed the LB's wrist, the one with the tape. Z ripped hard and the tape came off.

Z had his scalp. He tucked the scalp into his pants then rose, and turned back toward his team. Z did not speak, he did not taunt, and he did not celebrate. He simply turned around and headed back to his team to set up the huddle for the next play.

Z heard the laughter and saw the finger points. His mates were laughing, pointing and telling Zach to turn around. Z turned around and saw the LB. He was on hands and knees, his head down, hacking, coughing, and making gurgling sounds.

The LB was spitting up turf.

Z set the huddle up another 15 yards back. He did not look for the yellow flags; he knew they had been thrown. Z put the LB in his place and set the tone for the day. The fifteen yards was a small penalty to pay.

Vince got ready to call the next play and noticed the tape hanging from Zach's pants. Vince knew to savor a moment, and use it to motivate the team. As everyone waited for the play, V went in a different direction.

"Z, I just want to know one thing. Did you get the tape off that damn LB?"

Zach pulled the tape from his pants and held it out for everyone to see.

"Ok boys, one down and ten to go. I want to see eleven by the end of the game."

Then Vince went to work and scored our first touchdown in just five plays and we were up by seven after two minutes. V ran right for eighteen yards, passed left for twelve, ran a QB draw up the middle for fifteen, threw a screen for six, and threw an eighteen yard TD to our tight end for our first score of the day.

There was nothing our opponent could do to stop the madness as we went up by six touchdowns at the half. Our offense scored four, the defense ran back a fumble recovery, and the punt return team even scored a touchdown. It did not matter whom we played this day, we released a year's worth of rage and achieved the outcome we expected, unlike our first two games.

Zach shook ten hands that day, all of them starters from the opposing D. Not a single defender had any tape remaining on their wrists and there was no mention of the "oh and three" rants that began our game. Zach would have shook eleven but the LB was nowhere to be seen.

We won the next eight games all by a wide margin and were gunning for the conference championship. The press turned back in our favor and we were ranked in the top 25 again. And then I got the call.

"Coach, it's Mike on the phone."

"Put him through Alice, thanks."

"Hey Mike, how goes it?"

"We found her Bob."

Serena. Mike must have found her. My gut clenched

and I hoped for the best.

"Is she ok?"

"Bob, she's fine. We found her up in Milwaukee, she's a secretary at a small manufacturing company and she goes to night school. Serena has her act together."

"God, that's great Mike. I was so worried, we were all so worried."

"Bob, she wants to see Vince. She won't call him on the phone, says it has to be in person and she wants it to be a surprise. She'll take the train down from Chicago tomorrow. And Bob, she's not coming alone."

"Not alone?"

"She's bringing Vince's nephew with her. Serena is married and has a two year old boy and they seem a very happy family together."

I asked Taylor to meet Serena at the train since she arrived during our practice. Taylor drove Serena to the field and they sat in the stands. The guys were accustomed to seeing Taylor at practice and thought nothing of her being at this one.

Vince called out the play at the line. He scanned the defensive scheme and saw the coverage he wanted. He shouted the audible to the left then to the right. Z hiked the ball back to V in the pocket as the wide receiver flew down the sidelines. V threw to the back shoulder as the receiver turned toward the ball, a solid forty-yard strike.

Taylor sat quiet in the stands, not her usual mode.

Zach formed the huddle and the offense moved into a circle. As Vince came to the huddle he noticed Taylor in the stands, took a closer look and saw she was not alone. Vince stepped toward the huddle ready to call the next play, and then froze. He pulled back, away from the team, and turned toward the stands for a closer look and then whispered the name he longed to say, "Serena."

Vince tossed his helmet to the ground and ran to the stands. His whisper turned into a yell, "Serena!"

She came running down the steps into Vince's arms. Brother and sister were together again after a long eight years apart. Everyone on the field stopped to watch the reunion, few of them knowing the story. Most guessed V had a girlfriend, which was a shock, as he preferred to play the open field. After the long embrace, Vince looked at the two ladies in front of him.

Finally Vince noticed the young boy.

"Vince, this is Ramon, your nephew."

"My nephew?"

"Yes, Vince. Our family has grown."

Chapter 28

Senior Year

The next season started the day after our bowl win, a January game against a top ten team. We got Willy his ten wins and I kept my job for another year. We were playing way above our normal place and I knew it couldn't last forever. Most were betting we had one more year before we hit the skids. What they really meant was before Vince graduated and went to the pros. I did not argue against that line of thinking when cornered at parties, bars, and restaurants, anywhere I went in town. I just nodded my head, all the while thinking V had one more year, and we were lucky he decided to stay.

Willy and I got together for our annual review.

"Bob, once again you were the highest paid employee at the U. At least you got the ten wins you promised or we would be having a different kind of discussion today." Willy tried to keep a straight face but he had to duck his head to hide the smile. He was not very good at hiding emotions, which is why he seldom won at poker anymore.

"You know Willy, those two losses should not have happened. We just weren't ready to start the year, but the boys rebounded and I'm damn proud of them."

"Ok Coach, let's look ahead, any big changes planned this year?"

"We might lose our offensive coordinator, he's on a lot of lists for head coaching spots and he's ready."

"How about Vince? Is he good to go for his senior year?"

"Yeah, we are damn lucky he's still around Willy. I just don't think he was prepared to leave the U just yet. This place has become home for him, replacing what he never had as a kid."

Football Season

Where the hell are Zach and Vince?

Practice had started twenty minutes earlier and these two fools were nowhere to be seen. Our first game was in two weeks and I did not know whether to be worried or angry. Each minute that went by made me more upset. Our starting QB and center were not on the field with the rest of their team. We had two gaping holes and both were leaders who the rest looked to for direction. It was out of character for these guys to be late for practice and I hoped for their sake there was a good reason, a damn good reason.

◆◆◆◆

Vince received a text as he and Zach had walked from their

apartment to our practice facility. It was a single word message from Taylor, and it was all in caps.

HELP

Vince stopped, grabbed Zach and showed him the text then quickly replied.

WHERE

The next thirty seconds lasted a long time as they waited for a reply.

SCHOOL HURRY

They ran to the car they shared in the nearby parking lot. Z got behind the wheel as V sent his response.

ON WAY

◆◆◆◆

As Z drove to the school, V thought back to the day when Serena re-entered his life. They were the kind of siblings who could complete each other's sentences. Vince was determined to keep his sister this time and not let her get away, not let anything bad happen to her again. Taylor and Serena quickly became friends, one the older sis the other the younger. Taylor was surprised when Vince introduced her as his adopted sister. The next time they were alone, she toyed with Vince as only a sister could. "So, now I'm your sister. When the heck did that happen Vince, tell me just when I agreed to that."

"Come on Tay, it was an emotional moment for me."

"What, did you mean it or not Vince?"

Vince flashed his famous grin and Taylor knew she had been had. V had turned the tables and had her guessing as only a brother could. Then he turned serious. "I did not plan on introducing you as my sister, it just happened. It was an honest thing and it seemed natural. How about it, you in for the ride? You think you can handle me as a brother?"

"Oh yeah, I can handle you. But we will see if you got the goods to take care of your little sis. You can never let me down. You must always love me and protect me. Got it?"

"I got it Tay, that's a sweet heart deal if I ever heard one."

Vince had nearly lost one sister because he had not done his job. He felt he had not protected Serena as a big brother should. It did not matter he was only sixteen and not a real man at the time. He was the man. It was his responsibility and felt he had let her down.

He was not about to fail this time with Taylor.

"Drive faster Z. Drive faster!"

✦✦✦✦

We finished warm-ups and it was time for the first team offense to run plays. I was getting edgy, nervous about Z and V not being at practice, fear began to replace my anger. I called both on their cell phones, only to get kicked to voice mail. *Damn, where the hell are these guys?*

✦✦✦✦

Z and V arrived at the high school, unsure what kind of the help Taylor needed. Z went to the front and V covered the rear.

WHERE R U?

BOYS GYM

SAFE?

OK COME IN

V and Z went to the gym and found Taylor sitting with a boy in the stands. Nothing looked out of place; there were no danger signs, until they got closer. That's when they saw the gun.

"Vince, Zach, this is John."

V and Z nodded their hellos and stood ready to grab Taylor and run for the hills.

"John is in trouble and I told him you could help."

John waved the gun, establishing his control of the situation.

"What kind of trouble?" Zach asked.

"It's his sister. She's in the hospital, in critical condition."

V relaxed, but just a little. The gun still worried him, but now he could guess why Taylor had texted him.

✦✦✦

We were halfway through practice and were still missing our starting QB and center. Their cell phones kept going to voice mail and no one knew where they were. It was hard to concentrate on practice but that's what we had to do.

✦✦✦

Vince and John went for a walk. They stayed silent for a long while until the kid was ready to share. John was the driver, his younger sister in front by his side. She did not like seat belts and he let her take that risk, having told himself it was a short ride to school. He never saw the truck; it ran a red into the right side of the car. His little sister took the hit; big brother did not have a scrape. Now she had tubes down her throat, the life clock was ticking and John blamed himself.

◆◆◆◆

We ended practice with an elephant on the field. I asked the team to pray for V and Z, making a bet they needed some help.

◆◆◆◆

V shared his own story and John realized he was not alone, not the only big brother to let a little sister down.

"John, you ready to hand over that gun?"

Vince saw the debate raging inside John's head. Give up the gun or take a life.

The GUN or a LIFE.

Then Vince wondered, whose life? That's when he realized it was Taylor's life at risk and probably John's as well.

"John, you need to know something else. Taylor is my little sister, you might say we adopted each other and I promised to take care of her and never let anything harm her. No harm. Ever.

John stared straight ahead, his feet frozen to the ground.

"You hearing me John?"

Zach and Taylor heard the bang, a loud shot that

shrieked across the courtyard nearby. They looked at each other both thinking the same thing. Is Vince hurt? They ran toward the noise afraid of what they would find but not too frightened to run away.

Another shot rang out and Zach hit another gear, his stride at full speed as he burst through the doorway into the open yard. He saw a prone body behind a large oak tree...or was it two bodies? Taylor arrived at Zach's side and they both moved cautiously toward the tree, hands clasped tightly together, hoping for some good news.

"Vince are you ok? V you ok man?

Neither body moved, both lay still as Zach and Taylor edged closer. The pool of blood trickled downhill bringing the bad news they feared. At least one body was in poor shape, although the red blood did not give away which. As they moved closer, Taylor began to cry. "Vince, please no."

Taylor knelt down and gently caressed Vince's arm, edging closer to his wrist hoping to feel a pulse. She closed her eyes and prayed for a beat.

Zach moved toward John's body and kicked his heel then braced himself for a response. As he waited the long seconds for a reply he traced the river of blood to John's head. He knew then there would not be any movement, not ever again.

Taylor sighed with relief as she felt a beat then another and another. Vince was out but his pulse was strong, damn strong.

"He's alive Zach."

The ambulance arrived minutes later to find Vince sitting up against the tree, his head hurt more than the bleeder on his left arm. The bullet grazed Vince as he twisted away from the shot causing him to fall hard to the ground, head first. Vince was out when John made his move.

Vince stared at Taylor and Z as the medics wrapped his head and bandaged the arm. They were his family now as much as anyone was family. He shed a tear that was long overdue. "That was me a couple years back, alone and afraid I had lost everything."

The three of them left it at that, together in the silence, nothing more needed to be said.

+++++

I walked into my office and kicked the desk. *Where the hell are those guys and what the heck are they doing?*

Then my cell phone rang.

"Hi Pops."

First Game

We began the year in the top ten and Willy wore a big smile everywhere he went. I didn't even try avoiding him, the smile was contagious and I was determined to be in a good mood all season long. This was my fourth and final year with V and Z, and possibly Coach Mac who was eyeing some property on a beach. I knew these four years were an important phase in my life, and all of our lives. I wanted to slow the clock down so we would have more time to savor this last season together as players and coaches, brothers and sisters, mothers and daughters, fathers and sons. Whether we took the marbles home or not was less important than the time we spent and the memories we made. But I wanted the marbles, all of them.

Our practices were hard, efficient, often brutal; the players released stored up energy anyway they could. Even our meeting time was productive with players actually paying attention rather than dreaming or napping as they often did. Everyone could feel the tension about the season and this year in particular. It was not stress or pressure, it was more like a sling shot, stretched to its full length then held, and held some more. We were pent up and ready to be set free, ready for the release.

Our first game began and our kick-off team readied themselves for action. I envied those guys. I wanted to be on that field, soaking in those few seconds before the whistle blew. I wanted to share that moment, when the players lineup, stare down their lanes, ready to takeoff and run at full speed downfield. Then the whistle blows and the kickoff team launches themselves forward, legs pumping, always pumping, their eyes seeking out an opponent, anyone with a different color jersey, ready to throw their body into another human, pads crunching pads and feeling the full impact of that first hit. Then the release comes and along with it an awakening that you caused and survived a collision. And if your aim is good, and your legs fast, there's a man down with a ball right in front or you. The first tackle of the game is yours.

Man, that was the feeling of football and I missed it. I was as close as you could get, right there on the sidelines, right next to many of the collisions, so close to the impact and the release it gave that I could hear every impact, every grunt, groan, and exhale of air.

We did not surprise anyone on the field that first game. We simply ran them over, again and again. I tried to keep the score down and was embarrassed at the handshake at game's end. The ten touchdowns and 70-0 score on the scoreboard said it all. Willy smiled even more broadly, if that was possible. "Great game Coach, great game."

As I made my way to the camera and TV reporter, I took a moment and asked Willy a favor before taking the first question. "Willy, can you get that scoreboard turned off? There's no need to have that score up in lights any longer."

Willy understood and got it done, calming the celebration and removing the yells so our opponent could finally have some peace.

We easily won our next two games and entered conference play rated fifth in the country. Winning was a cure-all for just about everything. We walked downhill wherever we went, sliding and gliding our way through practices and opponents. We worried more about beating ourselves than the competition and won our next three games without breaking much of a sweat.

Undefeated at 6-0 looked good, damn good, and felt even better. The stress and pressure of retaining our number three ranking did not faze the team nor me and we improved to 12 and 0 after beating our archrival in our closest game of the year, a win by seventeen points.

We were riding high, maybe too high and would come down sometime, somewhere, but we had no idea when or where that would be. In the meantime, I let the kids have their fun. Vince loved to kick the football, booming punts during practice, most hung in the air longer and gained more distance than our starting punter's effort. He pleaded with me to kick one in a real game, but that was not a risk I was willing to take. As the season progressed and our wins mounted, I had a weak moment, and relented during a blowout win. "One punt Vince and then you stop harassing me. That's the deal, got it."

"Got it Coach, one punt. It will be a thing of beauty."

We were far ahead of the opposing team and I would soon pull Vince for the second string QB. Vince handed off the ball for three short runs the next series and I gave him the nod to punt his one and only punt. Vince lined up about 15 yards deep and took the long snap from center. I never saw a ball kicked that far, high in the air, a perfect spiral. Only one problem with the kick, the ball went straight up, no 90-degree angle, straight in the air and then began its descent, heading right toward Vince. I had never seen V unsure what to do on the field. He looked right, left, and then straight up. Fortunately he caught the ball in the air, downing the punt for a seven-yard loss. The team did not know whether to laugh or cry, the announcer unsure the call to make.

Coach Mac made his observation. "Damn, you ever see such a thing coach?"

"Yeah, saw it once before. You remember Coach; our high school tight end was also our punter. We called him "Stone Hands"; he never could catch the ball. He downed a punt once, claimed it went about five yards beyond the line.

"Yep, remember that one. Damn Stone Hands, he argued for days it was a forward punt. Didn't matter, he caught hell for years."

Vince and the team trotted off the field, his head bowed low, teammates ribbing the captain for his folly.

"We all done with the punting thing now V?"

"Yeah coach, we done. Bet you never saw that before, huh?"

Coach Mac and I grinned at each other as V walked away.

Chapter 29

Pre Bowl Game

Seth called me the week of the bowl game, asking for a favor. He wanted me to meet him and his corporate pals for a drink. It was not my highest priority, although I had always wondered what some of his colleagues were like at the big firm. I did not owe Seth a damn thing but guilt and curiosity got the better of me. Besides, Seth seemed unsteady, something was clearly bothering him. "Seth, I'll meet with you and your pals from the office for a quick drink, on one condition: You gotta' tell me what's eating at you."

"Bob, I'm in trouble, big trouble. I took over a new business at the firm, it was an acquisition, my brainchild and it's not going well."

I could tell he was only part way through the story so I let things hang in the air, waiting for him to continue.

"The former CEO was getting in my way so I had him fired and took the thing over. I let my big mouth run, bragging

307

about the results that would come, but they never came."

He was finally getting to the meat. I glanced at my watch and silently urged Seth to complete his confession so we could get on to his penance.

"So, I lied, I cooked the books, made up better results than we achieved. And I got caught. And before you remind me about Harry's lesson, this is way worse than that. I can't tell if they are mad because I lied or because I did not achieve the expected results."

Almost done, let's go for one last round Seth old buddy. I thought.

"I'm a bit concerned they will dump me, hell they should have fired my ass long ago, all the crap I have pulled. They're fine as long as the numbers are good, but mine aren't."

Go figure, I thought. *Seth is about to get fired, not for lying but for missing his numbers.* As far as I was concerned Seth was getting his due and he did not like it one damn bit. He was supposed to be the one who stepped on everyone else and had no idea how to respond to his own demise.

As much as I wanted to gloat, Seth needed help; he needed a friend. *Damn, why me.* I asked myself as Seth awaited my reply. *What would Seth do?* That was easy, he would pretend an important call was on the other line or some similar lame excuse and leave his buddy hanging in the wind. Seth would not lose a wink, he would get his eight hours and rest easy, buddy be damned.

But I was not Seth. After all these years and all the crap Seth dished out, I still felt responsible for helping him out. *Was I the bigger man?* I wondered. *Was I the better man? Had I fi-*

nally won the competition with Seth? None of that really mattered, not when a buddy asks for help. "Seth, do you think a drink with me will help any?"

"Bob, it can't hurt, and I already promised you would."

How much more confession would there be? I decided instead of thinking of him as my old friend, I would counsel him as if he were a member of my squad. "Seth, did it occur to you the former CEO who you fired, could have been a great teacher and mentor for you? Perhaps he could've shown you how to run the business, or a new business approach? He must have been doing something right for you to buy his company."

Seth had no reply, so I let the truth sink in a bit further, hoping it hurt enough to create a lasting memory. I knew Seth only had a few more chances to get his act together. "Ok Seth, let's have a drink, but just one drink."

"Thanks Bob, I owe you one."

"Just buy the drinks Seth. And do yourself a favor, call that ex CEO and apologize. It won't be easy, humility is not your strong suit."

I ended the call with Seth, another head shaker. I wondered if he would indeed get fired and what the reason would be for his termination. My guess, liars were tolerated at the big firm so long as they delivered the numbers. Perhaps Seth would be hired back as a contractor at a cheaper rate. Finally Seth might feel the sharp end of the stick he had carried for so long.

My plate was full with game prep and numerous bowl responsibilities, including an upcoming press conference. Making matters worse, I let my offensive coordinator go, reluctantly right before the big game. He had crossed a line, foolishly and unintentionally, putting a turd in my lap. The press turned the story into an ugly firing of a jealous coach who wanted my job; suggesting he would be the head coach of a conference rival instead. That last part was true; his new head-coaching job would be announced soon, along with my full endorsement. It was not supposed to be public knowledge until after the bowl game; he let it slip to a female reporter in the sack one evening. She chose the story over him, but did not know which school he was going to.

I expected some difficult questions ahead, and my game duties had doubled, leaving me without a play caller. I made my way downstairs to the bar with a lot on my mind.

Seth introduced me to Arnie, Mark, and Bill his pals from New York. They were on their third round of drinks since I was running late. After quick intros they hit me head-on, asking about the firing.

Arnie started it. "Coach, what's the inside scoop on your offensive coordinator? He must have done something awful to get fired before the big game."

"There's really not much of a story, he's a good man who made an honest mistake. I expect he'll recover quickly, and I wish him all the best."

Mark chimed in, "Was it a performance problem Coach? Or, did he violate a human resource policy, chasing female trainers around the locker room after practice?"

The four of them laughed a bit too hard at Mark's poor joke. I kicked Seth in the leg, planning to change the subject. Instead I went for the other side of the coin.

"Tell me how do you guys handle firings at the big firm. You must have a lot of practice with all those worldwide employees."

Arnie, Mark, Bill and Seth all grinned, more like a smirk really.

Mark took control. "Our focus at the firm is to lop off the bottom ten percent each year, improving our hand with new talent through acquisitions and selective hiring."

This guy was smooth, certainly had the corporate speak down, I observed.

"What's your approach, how do you determine the bottom 10%?"

Arnie sat up straight and responded as if he were being interviewed. "Each year we have a formal review process called, 'Team Decision Making.' The managers from each business unit meet together to rank each of the employees on a four-point scale. They discuss all the employees, and rank them based on criteria, which includes business performance, teamwork, attitude, and a couple of other benchmarks. The managers all need to agree to the rankings, contributing their point of view on each employee."

Arnie seemed proud of his corporate speak, although he looked more like Napoleon, trying to sit taller in the chair then his frame would allow. "Do the employees understand the process? Do they realize all the managers have a say in their ranking, this 'team based approach,' as you call it?"

Mark answered, "Yes, they are definitely aware of the process. There is a great deal of jockeying and positioning throughout the year, each employee trying to get ahead of their competition."

Did he really say that? Employees view each other as the competition?

Arnie leaned forward intimating his next statement was for "our ears only." He was eager to make the next point. "It's a corporate sport for us executives. We get to watch how the employees and the managers get ahead of their peers, pushing themselves to look better than the others in their peer group. There are a lot of games played, as you can probably imagine, we reward the best players, and let go of the losers."

"Let me get this right. In my world, if we used your process, the assistant coaches would get together and discuss all the players. The defensive back coach would have input on the quarterbacks, the offensive line coach would have input on the linebackers, etc. Each of the coaches would have the same weight on the rankings to keep things fair. Is that right?"

Seth tried to make things positive. "That's right, Coach, good analogy."

"The players know the rules of the game ahead of time, and position themselves to beat their 'competition' throughout the year, hoping to get into the top ten percent, avoiding the bottom ten percent. Is that right?"

Arnie replied, "That's right, Coach. Sometimes the smallest things can differentiate someone from the bottom ten percent and the next group up. Each employee knows to work the system, to influence as many managers as possible to look better than their peers."

"So, the defensive back coach and the linebacker coach could gang up together on the quarterback, forcing him down the rankings even though the QB coach felt he was the best player on the team? Is that right? Could that happen in your 'team based' decision process?"

Mark smiled. "Sure, that's more than possible. If two managers have a strong view of an employee, their opinions can have a lot of weight on the outcome."

Arnie winked and said, "All it really takes is one negative executive in the room to drive someone to the bottom of the rankings."

"Ok, I think I got it. Tell me, how does your process instill the right values into your workforce? For example, how does the jockeying for ranking position enhance teamwork?"

Arnie turned his head to the side as if it had been slapped. "Teamwork is one of our criteria, that's not a problem for us."

"Well, let me use another football analogy. An offensive guard might miss a block to make the running back look a step slow. It's hard to know what happens in the scrum of the line sometimes, so the guard gets away with it and the running back drops in the rankings. Or, the safety intentionally blows coverage and the cornerback gets blamed for a long completion. How does this behavior improve teamwork?"

Mark leaned forward. "We don't have that kind of discipline problem with our employees. They know the stakes and realize teamwork is important. The executives preach the value of teamwork to the employees; it's part of our culture."

Arnie and Mark were getting irritated, their smirks had changed to frowns and another round of drinks were ordered. Bill just seemed lost, unsure how to react.

"I get it. In football, we ingrain teamwork into our players too. Fortunately, we have a culture that self corrects itself. If a guard is missing blocks, his teammates will figure it out and deal with him fiercely, well before the coaches get there." I let that sink in and then continued, "Both of you mentioned the competition. Do employees really view each other as competitors at the firm?"

Arnie jumped in quickly, "They most certainly do. That's how they get ahead."

"What do you think Bill?" I asked. "You've been pretty quiet."

"Oh, I agree with Arnie and Mark."

This Bill guy didn't have much on the ball. It seemed Mark and Arnie kept him around to have someone who would agree with their opinions and help carry out their schemes. I did notice he did not include Seth's name, only Arnie and Mark. *This can't bode well for Seth.* I tucked that thought away for later.

"I have a lot to learn about how things work in the corporate world. We tend to keep things simple on the football team. We have very clear lines regarding the competition; it's the opposing team. And we have a culture that is dependent on good teamwork. The eleven men on the field can't get their jobs done, can't look good, unless each one of them is performing at a high level, together as teammates, supported by the coaching staff"

The conversation lagged for a moment, the only sounds coming from ice cubes rattling in Mark's glass. The cubes were taking a pounding, two of them rimming out onto the floor.

"I'm curious, what is more important to an employee, getting in the top ten percent or helping the business unit meet its goals?" I asked.

There was another long pause, Arnie and Mark chose not to answer my question while Seth fiddled his fingers and Bill looked for some sign or direction from Mark on how he should behave. The room had quieted, the corporate execs at the table looked at each other and then down at their drinks. I felt bad for Seth. I started to realize the world he had been living in the past twenty years. He had been influenced, shaped, and molded by these corporate processes, by these men sitting with us at the table.

"Is it possible employees spend more time scheming to get a high performance review, which detracts them from doing their real job and helping the team win together?"

I should have moved on and called this game over, but something in me could not resist one more comparison. "One of the principles we establish each year as a new season begins is something we call 'positive intent.' We ask the players to assume their teammate means well, that he has positive intent in his actions. We have found over time that team morale can be fragile and easily broken if players adopt the opposite view, namely that their teammates have negative intent. For example, let's say a tight end drops a pass, making the QB look bad. Or the lead back misses a block and the runner gets creamed. You can see how things could unravel quickly if teammates assume the worst of each other."

Seth looked at me with a plea in his eyes, but I was too

far down this road.

"As I mentioned, I have a lot to learn about corporations. But, it seems as if your firm is somewhat based on negative intent. If I were an employee, I'd be looking over my shoulder, wondering the true intentions of my peers: the competition. And I would be scheming how to get the managers to speak on my behalf. I might also be more focused on personal accomplishments than team goals, based on the process your company uses to rate and rank my performance for the year."

I could tell the guys had had enough. Their blank expressions led me to believe that they considered this football coach clueless on how to run an organization. It was time to make an exit. "Gentlemen, I need to wrap this up. Meeting with you this evening has been very educational for me."

I shook hands with each person, wondering if our conversation had any meaning for them. As I turned toward the exit, something did not feel right, there was a gaping hole that had to be filled. I turned back. "The scoreboard on Saturday will tell you if we meet our team goal this year. Good day gents."

The meeting with Seth and his pals helped prepare me for the next day's press conference. The corporate boys reminded me how important it was to treat people with respect.

Chapter 30

Press Conference

Before my butt hit the chair hands were raised, and questions and jabs were ready to be fired by the gents and ladies of the media. I dispensed with opening remarks so we could get on with the show.

"Coach, why did you fire your offensive coordinator?"

That didn't take long, I observed. *Skip the prelims about the game and the players, and go right for the negative story. Hell, aren't we playing in a championship game? Why is the press so predictable, so very predictable?*

I took a sip of water, looked right at the reporter who asked the question and responded, "Next question."

"Coach, there's a rumor he's going to State, your biggest rival. Is that true? Is that why you won't talk about it?"

I shook my head and smiled. "Next question."

"Coach, who will be calling the plays today?

Now, that was a good question. Normally our offensive

coordinator had that role but not this time, not this game. "I will be calling the plays today."

That one got them all riled up and more hands shot in the air. The rest of the press conference droned on, and on until it was time for me to go. I allocated a set amount of time for these things and indicated the clock had run out.

And then I signaled for the encore. "If the press will remain for a few minutes, we have a few people who will join us for an impromptu announcement."

Got 'em. I surprised the press, came up from their blind side and nailed them with a jolt, a crushing blow and it felt so sweet. I dare not say it; the grin on my face spoke enough volumes about my real feelings.

Willy and his peer from State appeared on stage and sat next to me along with Brian, my former offensive coordinator. The four of us sat together on stage in front of the national media; two fierce rivals that wanted to beat the tar out of each other were smiling and acting like friends.

Not a hand was raised. They knew to wait this time. A few of the senior reporters nodded in my direction and gave a tip of the cap, a sign of respect I graciously returned. They knew what was going on.

Willy made opening remarks and his peer made the announcement about Brian taking the head coach role at our biggest rival.

Then it was my turn. "I just have one thing to say about the announcement. We all make mistakes in life, all of us. I stopped counting mine long ago, although you folks in the media do a fine job of keeping the tally for me. I only say this because the media has focused way too much on one mistake that Brian made and you missed so much of what he accomplished here at the U. We're going miss him terribly, and I sure wish he were heading west or east and not back to State."

Now the hands were up and the questions were lobbed from all parts of the room, except those senior reporters. They just donned their caps again, and exited the room, a good enough signal for me to do the same.

Chapter 31

Bowl Game

"**O**k, gather round men."

We were about to take the field to begin the game. I had one last chance to shape the emotional spirits of the team prior to kick-off. I looked at the kids and coaches and held my breath for a few seconds, and took a snapshot in my head. This was a moment to treasure, to remember, and most of all to not screw up.

"A great coach once said to his team at a moment similar to this one: 'Perfection is not attainable, but if we chase it we will achieve excellence.' That was Vince Lombardi, coach of the Green Bay Packers."

I breathed in deeply. "Now, most of you know it's very difficult for me to cite anything positive from Green Bay, but I have to give Mr. Lombardi credit."

The team laughed, it was good to keep them loose before the game began.

"Men, we have been chasing perfection all year, and as a team we have a perfect Win-Loss record. I am damn proud of that record, and the effort each of you put into making that happen individually and together as a team."

I paused to collect myself and looked out at the players and coaches. They stared back awaiting instruction, motivation, inspiration, something they would remember from Coach before the big game.

"Ok men, I highly doubt many of us; any of us, will experience another season like the one we have had this year. Undefeated and top ranked with one last game, one last opponent, sixty minutes of playing time to go. For many of you these will be the last sixty minutes of your football career.

"There's one last thought I want to leave with you before we take the field, and yes it will include one last citation, since I know how much you boys enjoy them. A great man, one of the greatest men of all time was quoted as saying: 'In the end, it's not the years in your life that count. It's the life in the years.'"

I let that settle in for a bit and repeated the last sentence, "The life in your years."

The locker room was silent.

"Men, make this day count, make these sixty minutes count, 'cause you will remember them the rest of your lives."

I expected the team to get up and take the field but they all sat there. Finally, Zach stood and said, "Coach, you gotta' tell us the source. Who is the great man?"

Maybe these boys had paid some attention to my sermons and citations. I realized. Hell, what did it matter, I liked them and it was the only shtick I had going. "That was Abe Lincoln boys, now let's get out there and make this game ours!"

Chapter 32

25-Year Meet-up

As you may have guessed I had hosting duties for our 25-year meet-up, and chose the bowl game as our meeting place. It was not a hard decision; I knew the guys would enjoy the experience, although I was a bit concerned about the distraction during the week.

The day after the big game we played golf then gathered for dinner and our benchmark discussions. Many of us sensed this would be our last meet-up, it was getting too hard to coordinate schedules and there was waning interest in sharing our souls with each other. We had learned from each other over the years, and the benchmarks brought a level of honesty and transparency that is usually hard to reach for most men. Our days of baring souls was coming to an end, we were spent. It was time to move on and I wanted this last meet-up to be somewhat special.

I offered the guys a choice of seats, the 50-yard line or

a private suite, unsure which they would choose. It heartened me when most of them asked to sit with Amy, helping her get through the game. I am fairly certain Harry wanted to be closer to the cheerleaders. *Why not give the man a small pleasure?* I thought. I could not look at my buddies in the stands during the game, it would have broken my focus, and I was simply too busy trying to stay calm in front of the team and the crowd. I stole my only glance at Amy and the group just before the last play. By then I had done all I could to win, it was out of my hands at that point and I was relieved.

The golf day started strong and only got better. All the carts stayed upright for the full 18 holes, an accomplishment we were determined to achieve, and celebrated at the end of our round. Mike still refused to ride with Harry so I took his place, saving the shotgun seat for Skirt. I had no problem riding with any of my buddies, but letting Harry drive a golf cart was not a smart risk. I had not hit the white ball in quite a while; some of the guys were in top form, whining about client outings they had to attend. *Right.*

After golf, I invited a guest to join us for dinner and drinks, knowing the guys would want a firsthand account of the game, from someone besides me. They wanted the inside story from someone who would also talk about the coach. The guys wanted their cheap thrill and I fully intended to give them one.

As we sat for dinner, I looked across the table at that grin, nodded my appreciation to Vince for making the dinner and putting up with my buddies. Vince barely had time to finish a few bites of his meal, deftly handling the barrage of questions from the guys. I tried to intercede on more than one occasion, but my buddies threw the yellow flag and kept me at bay. Besides, Vince did not need much help; he was quite the entertainer.

Mike asked, "Vince, tell us about the last play. How did you know what play to call with the game on the line? What options did you and Coach discuss?"

Vince grinned, and winked at me. "It was a pretty short discussion; actually we did not talk about the play very much. We had practiced one play all week long from that distance. One play, with three options: passes to the wide out at the post or the tight end at the flag or run it in. When I got to the sidelines, we both knew what the play would be. "

Harry was curious. "What were you thinking after the defense called time out? Did you two consider a different play then?"

"Well, that was a bit funny. We had no intention of changing the play, but Coach told me to go to the left, a more difficult throw for a right-hander."

The guys were confused. Vince had not thrown a ball on the last play; he did not even fake a throw. The play we called, the perfect play we practiced all week, would not have worked.

I could not let it go any further, the truth had to be told. "Ahem, Vincent."

The guys looked at me and then back at Vince, wondering about my little outburst. Vince smiled and retold his story. "I called an audible at the line. We had the perfect play and then the defense shifted into a formation we had not seen all game and not on film. They knew we would head to one of the sidelines, we all knew. That left the middle wide open, but it was a long ten yards to the goal line. I felt good that Z, our center, would clear a path for the winning score and hoped that Coach would trust me to make the call."

V and I shared a smile, both knowing he ran the play I had made fun of during the time out. He gave me a wink as drinks were poured and high fives given all around. Vince knew it was time for him to leave; he stood and began to say good-bye.

Kevin asked for one more question, "Vince, what did Coach say to the players at halftime? You guys came storming back in the third quarter after that slow start."

Vince looked at me for a brief moment, not for help, more so for acknowledgement, as he was about to reveal a truth from our sanctuary.

I gave him the go ahead with a nod and a smile

"Coach reminded us how we got to this point, the hard work we put in all year, and how we came together as a team. He usually cites an important person or episode in history to inspire us, but instead this time he told us a story, a personal story that had inspired him for 25 years."

The room went quiet as Vince took a drink, necessary sustenance to continue his speech.

"Coach told us a simple story, as he put it, about six guys who were buddies from school and how they met-up every five years and bared their souls to each other, benchmarking their successes and failures in life. He talked about how much he had learned from the meet-ups and how these six guys had always been his team. Coach had stressed the value of team to us, but we thought it had boundaries, limited to the field and the locker room. He explained that some teams in life have no boundaries, no limits. He asked us to not look at the scoreboard the rest of the game, not worry about our opponent, and instead look to each other and imagine spending the next 25 years with this team outside of football.

I stared at my drink as Vince talked, then looked up to see my buddies looking at me. It was not an awkward silence; it was more of a relief to have a deep truth told about how much your buddies mean to you.

Scott moved us forward. "Vince, what happened next? How did you guys react to that story?"

"It was quiet for a while and we noticed Coach was choked up, but he was not done. Coach said he was lucky to be part of three teams, his family, his buddies, and the guys in the locker room. Then he told us about the success story he planned to share with his buddies at the upcoming 25-year meet-up. How a group of young men rallied together at half time, and, together as a team, recovered from a 21 point deficit and kicked ass all over the field in the second half."

My buddies were quiet, taking it all in, knowing this would be our last meet-up, the final success story relayed by Vince. The yardsticks we used to assess ourselves had changed over time, most for the better. I could see my buddies taking one last measure, one last accounting before we ended this last chapter. The silence we shared in that moment probably lasted less than ten seconds, yet I would remember it the rest of my life.

Vince said his good-byes leaving the six of us at the bar, a fitting last stand on familiar ground.

Harry stood tall and raised a toast. "Bob, you done good."

Leave it to Harry to have the last word.

Epilogue

I sat on my stool and sipped a brew and marveled how Graham's had survived these past thirty years. One of the owners pulled up a seat, patted me on the back, and we reminisced about days long gone. Jimmy had been buying my beer for more than three decades, a debt I could never repay. I finished another free one then went for a walk and found myself at a familiar place, a large three story red brick house with four tall white columns in front. The Fraternity on First Street struck a unique pose, both inviting and fearsome at the same time. It seemed steeped in memories and winked at me as I walked by. If those columns could tell stories, some men would weep and some men would hide, but most men would roar with laughter and order another round.

Another five years passed by and it would have been Seth's turn to host the meet-up, but nothing was on the books. A lot has happened since our last get together; many lives continued on their course, some changed for good, others for bad.

Seth was fired a few months after the bowl game. The insider-trading rumor was more fact than fiction and the Feds stung Seth at the office on a dark Monday afternoon. Seth had bragged once too often, holding court to impress his pals and his girls, sharing secrets for favors that he should have kept. His colleagues at work stepped gingerly for months as they envisioned Seth making his deal. Faced with prison and fines, Seth would finally turn to the truth, the last remaining play he could make. There were no more lies to tell, no more cheats to make, no one left on his boat to push into the sea. Seth gave up his corporate badge and his photo with the dark suit, red tie and golden smile. A picture with stripes and bars replaced it; everything had turned to black and white.

Scott hired a super salesman who was just as good with the old ladies as he had been decades ago. Zach honed his new craft from a true investment pro; it was all part of the plan that Scott and I had created.

Vince played on Sundays, and Mondays, and sometimes Thursdays as the NFL took more and more of our time. But I didn't mind and watched V roam the field and marshal his team every chance I could.

Coach Mac called it a day and found his paradise on a beach, a small town in the Carolinas. I received a postcard from Mom a few months after Mac moved away. It was mailed from somewhere in South Carolina. *Coach and Mom?*
Go figure.

Kevin found his old guitar and penned beautiful tunes in his spare time, usually on long plane rides as he bounced from one acquisition to the next, saving more jobs with each assignment.

Mike soldiered on in the criminal court system and continued to send me recruits, many street kids like Vince who found relief at the U. I had not him seen lately, but heard his baseline shot still blew wind through the nets.

Willy signed on at the U for another five years. He and Tony were a formidable team and found some way and some money to get the new stadium built, then put the pressure back on me to field more winning teams. On occasion, Willy would host a back room game, just nickel and dime, and a quarter or two, until Mike showed up and everything went green.

Taylor was a senior at the U and graduation was only a few weeks away. Ames and I would soon lose our only daughter to the big city and her job with some social media thing I did not really understand. She would ride El trains to work and probably meet some boy who never played ball. Better be a guy with a plan, if you know what I mean.

Harry got some advice from Amy one evening that changed his life.

"Harry, have you taken inventory lately?"

"Huh, inventory, what do you mean?"

"Harry, honey, don't you realize what you are good at? Actually exceptional at?"

"The only thing I have excelled at lately is failure. I keep going from one job to the next. Failure and booze go hand and hand with me."

"Harry, you big fool. It's going to take a woman to tell you what you should already know. Look at me Harry 'cause I'm only going to tell you this once. Harry, you are good with women. Maybe the best I have ever seen."

Harry smiled; he couldn't help it. "Yeah, I've been lucky in that department. But so what, how does that help me. Besides, I'm married."

"Harry, have you ever thought about selling to women? Think about it. I bet you could sell to women all day long."

Harry shrugged his shoulders as his cheeks reddened. He started to respond but Amy put her hand around his mouth.

"Now, do you know where women make most of the

decisions? The home Harry…in the home. You should get into real estate and sell houses to women. You'd clean up Harry!"

Amy shared some of her experiences as an agent and also some of her stories. And she had some crazy stories. Harry took Amy's advice and another "lady" found a path to becoming a man.

After thirty years in the show, I had a new itch that I ignored and ignored some more. But the itch kept coming back, again and again. "The Mayor" was stuck in my head and he was pushing hard.

Finally one evening I let Ames know my plan. "Ames, do you think a lot of people in the state know my name?"

"They sure do honey."

"Ames, do you think people in this state have a positive image of me and what I have accomplished?"

Ames put her book down. "Yes honey, they respect you."

She left the book on the bed and waited, and waited some more. It was clearly my turn to speak.

"Ames, I'm thinking about running for office. You know how mad I get at politics and lifelong politicians. It's time I put my own butt on the line and do something about it. I really think I can make a difference in people's lives."

Ames was stunned.

"What do you think Ames? Will I make a good governor?"

Ames opened her mouth, but nothing came out.

Now that was truly a first.

The End

Acknowledgements

A buddy has a genuine smile, a firm handshake and knowing eyes that flashback to memories made. You might not see a buddy for years, yet you both feel at ease.

Bob, thank you for the idea and encouragement to write a story. Thank you Scott for always being there. Thanks to Mike and Tom for playing ball and cards, games that taught us life lessons. To Harry, the sweep around end was a favorite play. Amy, thanks for being a pal.

Kevin, your music inspires, keep on playing. Lori, I thank you too. Tom and Michelle, hope to see you in Austin soon. To all my D Chi bros, thank you for the many laughs.

Thanks to my mentor Per, for your counsel and friendship and Lillian, for never holding back. To Ed and Ingrid, our dear friends.

Thanks to the many work colleagues around the world who helped me understand the value of hard work and good teaming.

Thank you coaches who invested time in semi-skilled players like me. You taught and instilled character, strength, and discipline.

Thank you Mindy and Danielle at the Authors' Assistant for guiding me through this first one.

Wade, Jeff, and Beth, we make a fine team with all the spouses and kids. Mom and Dad would enjoy it all. Merete, thanks for taking me in all those years ago.

To my dearest Kati and Sara, you make me proud and happy, there is nothing more a father could want.

Most of all, to my wife Kim, you make everything possible.